THE LAST BATTLE OF ATLANTIS

SECOND CHRONICLE
THE STORY OF ATLANDREOUS

THOMAS D. TURNER

authorHOUSE®

AuthorHouse™
1663 Liberty Drive
Bloomington, IN 47403
www.authorhouse.com
Phone: 1-800-839-8640

Published by AuthorHouse 12/19/2012

ISBN: 978-1-4772-9346-1 (sc)
ISBN: 978-1-4772-9347-8 (hc)
ISBN: 978-1-4772-9348-5 (e)

Library of Congress Control Number: 2012922187

The book is dedicated to my grandfather
Albert Clark Turner

To the person who taught me to work hard and dedicate myself.

Thomas D. Turner

CONTENTS

FOREWORD/AUTHOR'S NOTE

If you have a chance today, look at the people that surround your life. In any society, there are people that feed off others. Because of being afraid to fail, they let others take the burden of everyday events, but there are leaders that excel and make things happen for the greater good of their peers.

In difficult situations, there are very few people that want to take on hard and strenuous tasks. The ones that take the chance in taking the assignments and excel are considered heroes. Most people push themselves to do well. Sometimes they do not know why, but they keep going forward to better themselves, or for their colleagues. The true leaders put emotion to the side and go forward to make things happen.

In history books, there are a few people that take on the unattainable. The ones we know are the ones we learned about in school. The historical heroes never wanted the challenge. They just did it. The responsibility became an obsession to make it through the event at hand. Because the assignment was very hard to conquer, the person became larger than life to that society.

With new discoveries in science and archeology, man is finding new ideas about what really happened to mankind's past. Because some stories took place so long ago, it is hard to find concrete evidence of exactly what happened. There are so many stories and theories, but mankind is never satisfied with the results. People hear what they want to hear.

In every society and nation, there are heroes which make their populace proud of who they are. Before written history, there had to be someone that man has forgotten until now.

CHAPTER 1
THE ULTIMATE DISCOVERY
{PRESENT DAY}

"Yes! Where do we go now?" Duncan says in his sleep as he twists and turns.

Kyle, who is Duncan's assistant, goes into his tent and says, "Wake up Duncan. Wake up. You're having one of your dreams again. You told me to wake you up so you could remember what you were dreaming about."

Duncan comes back to a conscious state and says, "I'm having dreams again of the ancient city we've found. When I was in a coma last year, I dreamed and saw what this civilization went through. I am still living these ancient people's lives in my dreams. I can't believe I'm having these thoughts. Before the discovery of this ancient society, I never was in this frame of mind. The visions in my sleep must be my subconscious telling my conscious mind what I want to see."

Kyle sits on a chair and replies, "What you saw in your coma is what we are discovering right now. Your unconscious visions are correlating with our new discoveries. It can't be by chance that you are having these supernatural dreams. There has to be a reason. There are some things that just can't be explained, but, I believe you."

Duncan gets up from his cot and says, "I can't believe what is going on. I must be going mad. No one else is having these visions except me. I don't even want these dreams. I feel I have no privacy in my own mind. It is not a good feeling. Every time I close my eyes to sleep, I feel as if someone or something is hovering over my soul and putting things in my mind."

Kyle looks confused and asks, "What did you see this time?"

Duncan replies, "I saw an ancient city far from this land going through changes. There is something lost or forgotten every time I see this civilization. I feel as if a puzzle piece is missing. In our discovered ancient city here, we are going to have to decipher these ancient writings to fully understand this antediluvian society. It's destroying me. At this point, we are not even sure if this is a part of the Atlantean Empire or some other ancient civilization that no man knows about."

That same morning, the archeologists go to the ancient city inside the mountains of Spain. The teams of excavators have uncovered unbelievable treasures. The archeological find is breathtaking. It seemed a large empire placed all their treasures inside this mountain. The size of the city could not come up with this kind of wealth on its own. With the city being close to twelve thousand years old, the archeologists did not think gold and silver was worth anything to people during that particular time period.

Rachael is looking over some ancient writing inside the city and is still trying to decipher the text on the walls. She has fifty binders which she is using to relate back and forth. The excavators have been trying to understand the ancient writing for over a year. For Rachael, it has become an obsession. She does not want to let Duncan or herself down.

In one part of the city, there is a carving of a man standing with four cities surrounding him on a wall. To the archeologists, it seems to be a person which brought the civilization together. It is the only thing that makes sense to them. In the background of the picture, they find a bull's head. It seems to be the coat of arms of their civilization. A year ago, they found a silver plated breastplate with the same coat of arms. Time has almost erased all of the carved writing on the walls. To Duncan, this is something Plato wrote about in the Atlantean story. But a bull is a strong figure, and any society might have used it for their insignia.

As Kyle kneels down at the text writing, he points at an almost erased inscription.

Kyle says, "What if there are other cities like this one all around Europe."

Duncan replies, "If that's true, the undiscovered cities can explain what happened to this society. These texts may lead us to it. This methodical inscription and drawing can be a map. What about the writings in the religion hall? There is the same man there with a similar picture, but at a different point of the drawing. The picture could be the Straits of Gibraltar. If we can find the third point and use the point of this city, we may find another city which has not been discovered yet."

Kyle says, "In the main ancient library of this city, there is a picture of six mountains. There also seems to be a drawing of a large lake in the same illustration. It can be connected to what we might be looking for."

Duncan, Kyle, and Rachael go to the ancient library and look right at the picture on the wall. They see the image of six mountains and a large body of water near what seems to be a mountain range. In the picture, three mountains are together as brothers in the clouds. In the background, they can barely detect of a man's face. Right in the middle, there is a little dot which can be erosion or something the ancient people put there on the mountain. It is unclear to the archeologists.

They go up to Duncan's tent to use the internet to look up the sixth largest mountain in the world. The archeologists search all of Europe, but know it is not what they are looking for.

Duncan looks at the computer and says, "Rachael, look up the sixth largest mountain in Africa and see if there is a lake near it."

Rachael punches in the keys and a picture comes up. All of the archeologists get very excited. But at the same time, they know it may not be what they are looking for. It is still a long shot.

Kyle looks at the computer and says, "Look at Mount Stanley. The largest lake is Lake Victoria. This can't be right. Why there? I don't understand. This is where we should go next. It is something we should look into."

Duncan replies, "It is a very rich area. I am going to ask Callaway to see if he has any connections in Uganda."

The next couple of days, Duncan and his team look at the pictures on the ancient walls. They all come to the same conclusion that it is something to investigate. They know they have no choice but to go to Uganda. They have found the discovery of the century with the ancient city inside the mountain. In their little collective group, they call their ancient city in Spain, Naissance. With what they have found, it may lead them to another new site and discovery.

Mr. Callaway calls Duncan and tells him he knows the president of Uganda. He tells the archeologist they can go to the mountains of Rwenzori to find whatever they can. In the year two thousand ten, Mr. Callaway helped in the relief fund which exceeded a half billion dollars from the United States to Uganda. The president of Uganda cannot say no. With all the publicity from Naissance, Duncan has become a very well respected archeologist, and the president of the African country is elated he is coming.

In the years past in Uganda, it was not safe for anyone to explore the region. Now, the nation is becoming a little more stable. The United States has given a great deal of aid to the country. Now, Westerners are able to enter the nation.

Two days later the archeologists are on a jet to an airport near the Rwenzori Mountains. When they arrived, they were welcomed by the Ugandan President. Duncan, Rachael, and Kyle get off the jet and shake the Ugandan President's hand. The archeologists are known as heroes of the world.

The Ugandan President says, "Thank you for coming to our country. I hope you find what you're looking for. I could have had my own people look for your discovery, but, I don't know where to start. If you find treasure, you will receive ten percent of the find. I hope we can put Uganda on the map and in good standings with the Western World."

Duncan replies, "This is just a hunch. I will do what I can. I will need guides and men for this expedition."

The Ugandan President says, "You will get whatever you need. Take your time. I will also send an armed escort with you to protect you. They will be at your disposal. Even though they are a part of our military, they will do as you say. The Democratic Republic of Congo is on the border where you are looking, but they are not as stable of a nation. It can be dangerous for you and your coworkers."

The next couple of days, the archeologists receive the supplies they need for a two month journey. Callaway is backing this expedition as well. The tycoon has sent some of his own men to help. It is summer in Africa, but at high altitude it still gets cold at night. The archeologists will not be carrying light on this expedition.

The Rwenzori Mountains are large and Duncan's teams are not accustomed to the harsh environment. The mountains are at high altitude and very cold.

After traveling as far as they can by jeep, they start to hike up the trails through the Rwenzori Mountains. After a couple of days, the altitude is affecting the explorers and it is becomes harder to breathe. The archeologists have to take more breaks during their journey.

After they reach their destination, they start to explore the rocky area. Because the air is thin, the teams cannot work for long periods of time. If something is here, there is a one in a million chance of finding anything. Duncan wonders if this is a wild gooses chase or if there is something underneath the snow which can never be found without decades of searching. It is a shot in the dark, but, the explorers are hoping to find something. The only good news about the region is that no one has looked in this area like this before. The only advantage for the explorers is that the earth is warming up and the snow and ice are subsiding. Yes, people have climbed the mountain region, but no one has gone on an archeological exploration to find anything from the past.

Duncan has over two hundred people to help him explore the mountains. Everyone goes in teams of five. They comb the mountain range searching for something unnatural. The teams have no earthly idea where to start. There is great deal of area to cover for two hundred people.

On the third day of the excavation, it is looking grim. The teams find only rocks. Because of this, it is easy to overlook something that can be important. On the fourth day, Duncan looks at Kyle as they look at the mountain peaks around their location. On this day, it is sunny, but cold at the same time. It is a beautiful landscape.

Duncan says, "If this is what heaven looks like, I will love the afterlife. We haven't found anything. It is a stunning view, but we are getting nowhere."

Kyle replies, "There is something here; I know it. The mountain range is spectacular. Over the last twelve thousand years, someone had to put something here for us to find."

Duncan says, "I am still having dreams of the civilization we found back in Spain. Arriving here, the dreams became more real and unusual. The ancient civilization to me seems as a school boy's dream with its opulence in culture. Imagine pure discipline, architecture, and striving to make mankind better as its main goals in life. It is not what we see today. Compared with today's society, mankind is totally selfish in its own gratification. In my dream culture, the society I see is totally superior to ours. The visions in my sleep are becoming more vivid. If Naissance is the beginning of the end, there has to be a true beginning. I feel we are near a real discovery, even more so than in what we found in the Mountains of Spain."

Days go by and nothing is uncovered. Nature is the enemy to the archeologists. Rachael goes to a base of a cliff on the mountain and looks at every stone formation. There is still nothing. The archeologists feel as if they have lost valuable time. Looking back at Naissance, they still have not broken the code of the ancient writing. They feel as if they should not have left Spain.

Two weeks into the expedition Kyle looks at the mountains around Stanley. His team sees Stanley and Speke and marvel of what nature has done. Over the fog, they know the Bujuku Valley is right below, full of life and vegetation.

From two different parts of the mountain side, Duncan looks at Kyle over the valley and talks on a walkie-talkie and says, "The snow from these mountains feeds into the Nile River. This is the beginning of life for the Egyptians. The civilization of the ancient Egyptians would have never happened if these mountains were not here. It is incredible what these mountains have done for mankind. Maybe they can give something else to man. It can show what there was before our written history."

Kyle pushes speak on the walkie-talkie and replies, "A city can't be inside these mountains. We are looking for something else other than a city."

Duncan is climbing a slope and pushes talk. "We may be looking for something these people wanted to keep from the rest of the world."

Rachael, talking on her walkie-talkie, says, "Duncan, you need to come over here quickly!"

Remembering where she is located, Duncan starts to climb the mountain side of Mount Stanley. It is not really steep, but yet is getting harder to climb. She is only about half a mile away, but it will take almost an hour to get to her position. There are jagged rocks, and she is on a steeper slope.

Kyle says to his team, "Here we go again. I know that certain tone of her voice. She found what we are looking for."

Kyle runs and climbs where Rachael is excavating. Kyle really hates his climb in the cold, but it is a discovery that he knows he cannot miss. He has to be there to see what she sees. In all, she has the gift of finding what most people overlook. Duncan can see Kyle from a distance, and they race each other to Rachael's location.

When they get there, only about ten people can safely stay on the edge of the mountain without falling off the cliff where Rachael is exploring. It is a ledge which has been carved out by man. It looks as if nature built it, but level. At the same time, there are clues man made an effort to chip away the mountain for construction of something, and it leads to a large rock formation. The carved stone is about six feet long and four feet wide. The stone has been there so long that dirt and dust has filled its cracks. A stone door totally fits the curvature of the mountain. Even from ten feet away, it is almost impossible to see it is man-made. The archeologists know they are going to have a difficult time removing the structure from the mountain. They do not know how far the stone goes into the man-made structure.

Duncan looks at the doorway and says, "Whoever did this took a great deal of effort to hide something. This is a remote area. With hundreds of men, it would have taken years of construction. Rachael, you've done it again. You have the gift that most of us don't have. I don't have this talent. There are no carvings on the rock. It is here to hide whatever is inside from the rest of the world. Even though I think this is linked to city of Naissance, the society made this very carefully to hide something. There is nothing here to show man even ventured into this area. If it was after the Ice Age, the people who built this here made sure it looked natural. It is something man thought impossible for the time period. There are details here which are not what we would have expected from any society twelve thousand years ago."

For the next couple of hours, the strongest people get on the ledge to try to force open the doorway. Duncan removes the dirt around the edges. It looks only two inches thick. Because the doorway is so perfectly made, the archeologists do not want to destroy it. They use ropes and pulleys to pry the door. After three hours, Duncan's teams are able to remove the structure to the right. They move the stone so only one person can go in one at a time. Moving the door anymore would make it go over the edge of the cliff.

Duncan looks at the doorway and says, "Rachael you have found what we couldn't. You should be the first to go in."

Rachael replies, "It is your expedition. I would not be here right now if it wasn't for you. You have taken me under your wing, and I can't do that because of the respect I have for you. It is yours to take."

Kyle looks at Rachael and says, "I agree with Duncan. Go in."

Rachael goes in the opening of the mountain. She is totally swept away with emotion. The hallway is completely carved in straight lines. Rachael cannot detect any chisel marks as she shines her flashlight. The hallway is seven feet high and eight feet wide. At the end there is another doorway twelve feet from the entrance, Duncan's teams go in one by one, and they take their equipment with them. The archeologists shine their flashlights on the second door and take their lanterns inside. On the stone walls inside, there are pictures of what is similar in Naissance. To the archeologists, the two sites are totally connected to one another.

The second door has been cracked by age, and is barely stable. Duncan gives the okay to pull it down. The doorway is three feet wide and six feet high. The archeologists can tell the door is only an inch and a half thick. They take their crowbars and shove it into the cracked door which is four and half feet from the ground. In one motion, the top of the door falls to the ground without injury to the excavators. Duncan shines his light into the cavity.

Duncan excitedly says, "This isn't another city. It is a tomb."

Kyle asks, "What do you see inside?"

Duncan replies, "Good things, Kyle, good things."

Duncan asks his men to push him over the doorway into the chamber. After doing so, he goes head first to the floor, using his arms and hands to break the fall. He stands up and takes his flashlight to look and shines his light on every wall which is full of texts. In the center are two stone caskets. Duncan sees there are little or no artifacts inside the tomb. He knows it is a mausoleum and has not been looted. The burial chamber is simple, but elaborate at the same time. It seems that the people who built this burial chamber went out of their way to accommodate the person's wishes after their death. He can sense the person was a very important person to this civilization. It takes Duncan's eye because of its simplicity.

The rest of the crew comes in. They shine their lights all over the walls. It is very cramped for the archeologists, but they have to be the first to enter the tomb. To them, this does not make sense. When they found the city inside the mountain in Spain, they thought they would find something of the same size. This burial chamber is isolated from the rest of the world. The writing on the wall shows nothing else the archeologists can use to the next step of finding answers to what happened to this society. To Duncan, there is no reason for this place to be here.

Kyle uses his flashlight to see the back of the tomb and says, "Duncan look over here. Is this something I am imagining or is this really here?"

On the far right of the wall inside, there is a picture of a man, and he is pointing at a bright star with others behind him. To the archeologist, it shows a person bringing people together. On the bottom of the wall, there is a picture of only one deity over the masses with a bright star.

Rachael says, "Can this be God?"

Kyle replies, "It seems there was something which brought these people together during a difficult time, and religion was a major factor. Back in Spain, their civilization also believed in one god."

Duncan says, "I agree. Religion, legends and history go side by side. I don't understand this myself. When something in history happens, it is translated to become bigger and better later in legends. Maybe these people had a star explode during something important in their saga. The belief in one God is unmistakable in these carvings."

Rachael replies, "I believe this has something to do with Christianity."

Duncan says, "It could be the beginning of the word of God."

Kyle shakes his head and says, "This find can take the word of God and turn it upside down."

Duncan replies, "No, I don't think so, God started somewhere. It could be that God made man what he is today through the faith of this civilization. It could have taken thousands of years before mankind could think of such power as God. Mankind might not have been ready to understand His word. These people had an understanding of Him. It could have taken man thousands of years to except it."

The archeologists open the burial casket to the left of the chamber. In the middle, they find a skeleton and a sword made of gold. It has different writings than the city they found in Spain. They know this tomb is linked to Naissance, but they know this place is older than the civilization they found a year ago.

The archeologists open the second casket and know right away it is a female because of the hips of the skeleton. There is nothing except skeletal remains. The grave site is basic and bare of treasures. Except for a sword, there is nothing else of value. The excavators can tell there was a great deal of time spent in preparing the interior of the tomb. Duncan is assuming the two were married in some form or fashion. To the archeologists, it seems they were equals. In past societies, women were considered second class citizens. This was an advanced society compared to others from the past. Both caskets are the same size and equal in the chamber.

That night, the archeologists looked at their digital-cameras to find out what was in the shadows of the tomb. The excavators took countless pictures. Duncan, Rachael, and Kyle looked the images of the man and the star from the camera.

Duncan says, "Do you remember Sodom and Gomorrah in the Bible?"

Kyle replies, "Yes, Lot's wife, Edith, turned into a pillar of salt. I remember reading it as a kid."

Duncan says, "In two thousand eight, a cuneiform clay tablet was studied and somewhat deciphered. Archeologists think a Sumerian astronomer wrote about an asteroid hitting the earth in three thousand twenty-three B.C. The asteroid hit a mountain and exploded and created a landslide in Austria. Well, the explosion created a mushroom cloud that fell back on the Mediterranean near the Dead Sea. People think that was where Sodom and Gomorrah were located, and the mushroom cloud brought fire and destruction to the two cities. What happened to Lot's wife could have been explained by Lot seeing her as a pillar of salt in the distance. Another theory was that Lot's family was shielded from the blasts by mountains and they saw Edith disengaged by the heat from the asteroid entering the atmosphere."

Kyle replies, "There is little writing about Sodom and Gomorrah except in the Bible. I agree with you that science and Biblical history can be as one. There are things the people during that time didn't understand, and saw it as God's will. We don't understand this place at all."

Duncan quickly says, "I am not saying that God didn't send the asteroid to destroy the two cities, but what man knows now is much different than what man knew back then. A thousand years from now, man will see what we see as a miracle as something simple. My thought process of the picture in the tomb is that this society wrote about this man bringing the word of their god. Who is to say God didn't create advanced societies thousands of years before the Sumerians or Egyptians, and He destroyed most of them so mankind could be reborn? It happened with Noah in the Bible. Maybe a star exploded during the time of this ancient society's important outcome. Another star exploded and brought forth the rebirth of Christianity. God works in mysterious ways. I will never doubt Him or question His existence."

Rachael says, "There are so many ways a person can look at this wall. With the way people are so set into their religions all over the world, I think we should omit this one. We will be questioned the rest of our lives about religion and what we think."

Duncan replies, "No, man changes in time. I think it is time for mankind to see things differently. It may not be the city of Naissance which is so important. It may be this tomb. I believe God led us here to show mankind that God is more than what they know from the Bible. If you stick to the Bible only, Man will stay in the dark ages. Mankind must evolve in time with God. Maybe He has other thoughts of man's existence, and this place here can be the beginning. Finding this tomb and its contents can make mankind better. I will not let this be overlooked because of what some will think. God isn't a coward, and neither am I."

That night, Duncan goes to sleep. The dreams of the civilization he had seen a year ago still preoccupy his visions. He does not talk much about it because he does not want to be seen as a freak or someone who is looking for attention. The archeologist knows history, and it could be a manifestation of his conscious entering his subconscious dreams.

The next morning, Duncan wakes up and remembers some

parts of his visions in his sleep. He saw people living and making new discoveries.

Kyle comes towards his tent as if he is defeated.

Kyle enters Duncan's tent and says, "This is it. There is nothing we can see to lead us towards another place or where these people came from."

As he gets up, Duncan replies, "No, it isn't true. This man here was someone who was important and didn't want to be significant. He was someone who didn't have a big ego. He just wanted to lie here in peace. The civilization of Naissance saw this person as a very important figure. I think this was the first person that jump-started their civilization. The Naissance Religious Hall and the library are high indications of this man who made these people who they were. There is little we can do here. I say this person was the reason for such a society and coming here was not in vain. We will leave tomorrow."

The archeologists go through the tomb again. From the burial cloth, they will find out how old this place is. They found a sword made of gold, but they found it of little of value compared to Naissance. They will give the sword to the Ugandan President and look at it in more detail later. Duncan and his team feel they need to break the writing in Mountains in Spain to go forward in this mystery.

The archeologists put the door back into place to keep it out of sight from other people. This is a burial site, and the people who lie in the tomb will be laid to rest again. With so simple of a tomb, most people will not want to venture into the burial chamber. It is also not an easy site to go to.

That evening, Duncan receives a call on his global phone. Mr. Callaway has been watching the weather, which can affect the archeologists' efforts of going back to Spain. During the excavation, the weather seemed ideal, but things are changing toward the possibility of a bad storm which can last for a couple of days. The crews of Callaway and Duncan are ordered to stay put. Because the teams brought gear for bad weather, they will ride this one out. Helicopters cannot fly to reach Duncan without the chance of crashing. There is strong wind in the area because of the front. Each of the archeologists go to their tents and waits for better weather to descend to the valleys below in Uganda. Because of fog and strong winds, it is not safe to go down the mountain range.

Duncan goes to his tent and waits. On the first day, it is cold, and with the snow and continuing strong winds it is hard to see even three feet. The archeologists yell at one another from a short distance and laugh, knowing they are so close but cannot see one another. Duncan and Kyle start to go to their tents and look at the images from the tomb.

Duncan looks at Kyle. "The way we see God and science just changed. It will be hard for man to accept it. I fear one day I will be walking down the street and some person will shoot me because they think they are preserving God's word. In my standpoint, I think it is time to go towards the next step of evolution of faith. The dark ages kept mankind from advancing towards the future. I think not putting science and God together will destroy both sides to the equations. God and science is math. Manmade math has helped humanity understand His domain. God made math and the answers are in the numbers of the universe. This tomb is a number to what He is all about."

Kyle replies, "I see what you're saying, but a great deal of people will never open their eyes. If you bring this out, you might as well wear a bullet proof vest the rest of your life."

Duncan says, "I agree, but I will not let fear bring me to failure. I will bring this to mankind. Something failed with this civilization. I will not let it happen to ours. It may be God wants us to see this to preserve the next step for man. It can be that God is ready for us to go towards the next step of human evolution through science and religion."

Duncan and Kyle go to their tents to sleep for the night. They both do not know how long this weather will last. With the winds starting to pick up even higher, it could be days before they can go back to Uganda.

Duncan goes to sleep and continues the visions of the civilization he has dreamed of for the last year. It is a light sleep and he knows he is about to go towards the next realm of slumber. He starts to dream of what he just found. He knows he can wake up, but he wants to know what his subconscious sees. In his thoughts, it is a dream to fill a void. Duncan sees giant elk, giant sloths, mammoths, and wooly rhinos, which humans were able to tame. In his dreams before, he could only see mammoths. He wonders what changed from now and the dreams he had before. What is making him think and see things differently? Duncan can hear the winds in the background, but very softly. He feels very relaxed. The archeologist feels as if tiny ants are crawling all over his body. But he knows it is only a feeling that he felt when he went under the first time when he was back at Naissance. The winds from the outside seem to tell the tales of these people. Even the archeologist is reluctant to go onward; the winds tell him to go forward and see what he wants to see.

CHAPTER II
THE DERIVATION

"It's not bad. I can make it through this competition. This cut is not as bad as it looks," Atlandreous says to his father after he just won against an opponent during the largest sparring match of the year in his kingdom.

Thanos, father of Atlandreous, replies, "Look—if you keep fighting, you will probably win the next match, but you will lose to the last opponent because of your injury. In the next twenty minutes you'll lose enough blood to either fall right on your face or die. I can't lose my son because of a sparring match."

Atlandreous, who is in good physical shape, with brown eyes, and brown hair, looks into his father's eyes while he holds his arm and says, "This is not my ego or being stubborn. I will not fail here no matter what the cost can be. You told me, Father, a person has only a few times in his life to make a difference. I only have to defeat two more opponents to win this competition. I am going to make the difference right here and right now even if it kills me. I will wonder for the rest of my life if I could have won here today. If I don't do this, it will destroy me into my old age."

Thanos, who is forty-five years old, with olive skin, and dark hair, looks at his son and replies, "I understand. You are becoming a true leader. If you don't go forward, you will be dead inside anyway for the rest of your life. Either which way, I am taking a chance right here of losing you in different ways. Fight because it is in you, and I will accept your decision. If you die, I will see you in the next life."

Atlandreous is in a sparring match in the Kingdom of Alnilam. The stadium is the second largest arena on the byland. The only amphitheater superior in size is in Alnitak, which can hold up to seventy thousand spectators. In Alnilam, where Atlandreous is sparring, the stadium is over capacity and half the enthusiasts are standing up. The Alnilam stadium is full of beautiful statues and stone artwork from all over the kingdom. The façade of the arena is over one hundred feet tall, and the sports ground is oval shaped. Every year, the inhabitants of the kingdom make the arena more elaborate. Every year to show pride for their sport, there is always something added to the stadium.

The spectators at the sports arena have been waiting for this game for months. The energy at the sparring competition is ecstatic. After each match the crowd gets more boisterous. It is a day for the Alnilam people to remember for the rest of their lives. The competition is more aggressive than any prior year.

Atlandreous lives on a peninsula with five city-states. Each city-state is ruled by different kings. The cities on the byland trade with one another, but there have been religious conflicts between the societies. Each city believes in different gods. Even though the religions are all similar, there are many extremists, who keep the cities from becoming one empire, but there is a movement to one religion which is starting to spread. Some of the city-states inhabitants are going to one god. It is revolutionary for the time to believe in one deity.

Atlandreous gets up to fight the next contender. Thanos covers his young son's wound, but the young Atlandreous is still bleeding badly. The fifteen year old, Atlandreous, is sparring against older and more experienced competitors. He is the youngest person ever to get to this level of competition. Over thirty thousand people are at the stadium watching the contest.

Each of the contestants wear leather armor, which has very good protection from the dulled swords, but Atlandreous' injury, was one in a million. His own thrust from over extending his arm caused the accident. Because of the discipline of the contenders, there was no blame towards Atlandreous' adversary. In the stadium competition, the contenders use real swords and shields, but to score, a person has to hit the breastplate which is made of thick leather and bronze. Atlandreous missed a block, and his opponent cut his arm right to the bone. Because the thrust did not hit Atlandreous' breast plate, his competitor did not win the competition. Using his wounded arm is almost impossible, but young Atlandreous is not giving up.

As the match begins, the young injured combatant looks at his opponent and lets him have the first move. Atlandreous is conserving his energy for a quick blow to wait for a potential victory. The swords fly and Thanos' son sees an opportunity thirty seconds into the match. Atlandreous blocks with his sword. After the block, he jumps and knees his opponent in the chest, knocking him off balance. In a split second, he hammers his adversary on the top of his skull with his elbow. With such a shocking blow, it renders the rival unconscious. Atlandreous' antagonist falls to the ground, and the crowd goes wild. No one has ever done a maneuver like this one before. Atlandreous wins and goes to the next match.

Thirty minutes go by. Atlandreous has to fight his last challenger. His wound is getting worse. Every time the young boy moves his arm, it opens the wound even more. He is still bleeding and getting weaker. Atlandreous' wound is well concealed where his opponent cannot tell how bad it really is. But Thanos knows his son is about to run out of steam. The young teenager is starting to feel the pain. The young boy goes into his own psyche. Atlandreous disciplines his mind to take on this last challenger in attempting to win the tournament.

The two contenders start to fight. Atlandreous' opponent goes on a very aggressive offensive. Atlandreous' opponent knows he is hurt. The young teenager counters and goes on his own offensive for a couple of blows, but he is too weak to keep the momentum. Atlandreous knows he only has enough strength for a couple of counter moves, and hopefully has an opportunity for a lucky strike to win. The young teenager wants to faint because the wound is opening up even more. But Atlandreous concentrates to the point that he is seeing everything in tunnel vision. Every blow Atlandreous' opponent is throwing is in slow motion in Thanos son's mind. In a split second, the fifteen year old takes his last bit of strength to counter his opponent. With Atlandreous' challenger over extending his blow with his sword, the youngest contender of the games sees a weakness in his foe and capitalizes on it. It is done; Atlandreous wins the sparring match. After the match, he knows if he takes one more step, he will fall to the ground. The young teenager just stands in the middle of the stadium. The crowd goes wild for over four minutes while Atlandreous looks into the stands. Thanos, who is very strong for his age, rushes to his son to hold him up and takes him off the sparring field. The crowd cheers as he his led out of the stadium by his father.

After the match, Atlandreous is stretched over a large cot in Thanos' tent outside the arena. Thanos' son is already starting to get an infection from his cut. After he gets his son settled down, Thanos stitches his son's gash the best way he can. This is the most pain the young teenager has felt in his entire life.

On the first day, Atlandreous starts to go into a sweat, trying to fight off the infection. Thanos starts to think his son will not make it. Atlandreous' father starts to regret his decision of letting his son fight the last two opponents in the competition.

For days, Thanos does not leave his son's side. Spectators come by Thanos' tent to see the young boy. Everyone is amazed with the determination of such a young man. Generals from Alnilam's military even come by to see if the young boy is going to make it. If Atlandreous does make it, Thanos knows his son can make something of himself in the Alnilam Kingdom.

After the fourth day, Atlandreous starts to break his fever and starts to recover. Because he is young, his body is able to fight off the infection. Thanos is so thankful he did not have to take his son back to his mother to be buried. By mid-afternoon of the fourth day, the fifteen year old boy still fades in and out of consciousness, but Atlandreous can understand and comprehends what his father is saying from time to time.

At sunset, Thanos sits at his son's side and says, "I am a lucky person to know my son won the match and survived. I don't see you as a young boy anymore, but a very distinguished young man."

Atlandreous wakes up, smiles, and replies, "I thought I was going to die. I didn't want to let you down. You are the best thing that has ever happened to me. You have always been there by my side. Thank you for letting me to take on those last two opponents. I know it was hard for you. If the circumstances were reversed, I don't know if I would have had the courage to let my son take the same chance."

Thanos says, "In a couple of days, you'll be able to get around. The King of Alnilam wants to speak with you in three days. He saw your talents at the stadium, and I think he wants you to help with our kingdom's army. At the age of fifteen, you're becoming extremely popular with our nobles."

On the third day after the young teenager's fever broke, Atlandreous and Thanos ride through the city of Alnilam. The two ride on their giant elk. The giant elk are over seven feet tall, and their antlers are twelve feet across. It is a little challenging to get through some parts of the populated streets, but people have adapted to such creatures. The pedestrians walk under the antlers like they are not even there. Very few people have such animals because it is difficult to obtain and tame the giant elk. In the past, people have hunted these creatures to almost extinction. Now, the giant elk population is coming around again, but at a slow rate. Mankind has figured out how to use nature rather than eat and destroy it.

Atlandreous is feeling better and is able to ride through his capital. The young boy looks around the metropolitan area and sees construction being done everywhere. In the last seventy years his people have discovered cement. Because of the new discovery, buildings are stronger and more grandeur. The city has changed considerably since Atlandreous was in Alnilam three years prior.

Other than the inhabitants on the peninsula, people see cement as evil. Because it is seen as a liquid first and than becoming stone, people see it as unnatural. On the mainland, everyone lives in wooden and stone dwellings. Every building outside the byland is no more than one story tall. The inhabitants of the peninsula are the only ones seeking the technology and architecture to make spectacular buildings.

On the peninsula, architects have developed better mathematics in constructing more elaborate structures. Some of the public edifices are four stories tall with giant round columns for support. Alnilam's main streets are made of brick and there are sewer systems which were constructed discreetly underneath the roads. Aqueducts are made from the same cement, and water is transported to all major cities from as far away as fifty miles.

In the middle of Alnilam there is a central market place where items are traded with other city-states. With transportation getting better from sea and land, Alnilam is getting more goods from far away societies, which are traded with other cities. People are coming from all around the peninsula to Alnilam to find exquisite items. The inhabitants of Alnilam are starting to strive because of their sea trade. However, using ships comes at a high price. It is cheaper and more efficient to get trade by land, but, the more elaborate items are coming from far away, and ships are the only way to obtain these items.

Alnilam has a natural harbor which houses their ships. The ships are small, and have to be in sight of land to navigate around the seas, but they venture out far from the peninsula to find new trading products. The largest Alnilam ship constructed is close to two hundred feet long and forty feet wide. The capital is building larger ships for trade, but they have different styles of ships. Each ship is constructed differently for different tasks. Alnilam is starting to use mathematics to travel beyond the coast. Because of this, they are finding more diverse goods to trade with other kingdoms.

The cities on the peninsula trade with one another, but there is a great deal of greed with the wealthy politicians of each city. In doing so, each city-state uses religion to make the masses believe in the politicians' favor. The trade is making people rich, but greed is hindering their progress.

Alnitak is the largest kingdom of the city-states on the peninsula, and closest to the entrance of the main continent. The city has the best logistical spot in the known world. With trade prosperous in the byland and the continent making good trade, sixty percent of all goods goes through Alnitak. The city is flourishing. The best salesmen are in Alnitak, and are very wealthy. It is the land of opportunity.

Alnilam is building ships to take out the middlemen in Alnitak. In turn, it has made some of the other city-states concerned of their own trading ability. Masaba is closest to the other outlet to the main continent. Outside the peninsula the majority of the human population lives on the east side of the giant land mass. Between the east and west passages out of the peninsula there is a mountain range going straight north, blocking trade which can go through Masaba.

Because of such politics and greed, Alnilam needs a good military. The city-state of Alnilam is having trouble with their organization of their army. In the sparring games, the Alnilam King looks for good warriors and leaders to make his soldiers better. Atlandreous knows the King of Alnilam will ask him to be a part of his army. Even though Atlandreous won at the largest sparring match of the year, he really just wants to go back home to Mintaka and help with his family's business. Mintaka is his comfort zone. Now, since the young man has reached this point, he is having second thoughts. Atlandreous will have to conform to new ideas. Before, in Mintaka, he was doing all the teaching.

Because of Atlandreous' personality, people listen to what he says. Back home, the young man is already a leader and respected. He has helped others meet their potential, and they are grateful for his support and friendship.

Atlandreous' techniques in fighting and people skills come naturally to him. There is no one like him in the world. The thought he may have to start all over again to rise to the top is making him reconsider taking the responsibility of being an officer.

In the Alnilam society, the only way to get anywhere is through their military channels. Everything revolves around the armed forces. Many resources are given to the army, and it is depleting the Alnilam society. With the loose alliance with Halotropolis, Alnitak, and Masaba, the Alnilam people know the treaties could collapse at any time. In the last ten years, the cities have had skirmishes between each other, and new treaties had to be made, but it is inevitable for another war to break out. No city-state knows which kingdom they might have to fight, or what will start a conflict. The kings of the city-states know when it is time for war; it will be backed with greed and religion. Bad politics will start a chain-reaction with bloodshed.

CHAPTER III
THE NEXT STEP

Atlandreous and his father reach the King's palace of Alnilam. A messenger of the king tells Atlandreous and his father to meet the ruler at his garden inside the palace. Servants are there to take care of their giant elks, and bring food to the guest.

When Atlandreous and Thanos get to the garden, they are astonished. The garden has lavish waterfalls and lush green plants. Most of the plants are from different parts of the world. The architecture of the garden is full of statues and ponds which hold exotic fish.

Atlandreous has to wait for some time. He goes into a trance looking at the fish as they swim around the pond. The young man is wondering what King Icaras really wants from him. Atlandreous just wants to know what to do next in his life, but the King is very busy in politics and logistical problems with water and food for the kingdom. The king is running behind schedule.

King Icaras finally shows up with open arms towards Atlandreous. He is wearing his white political toga. He is tall and a little out of shape for being thirty-seven years old.

Icaras says, "Thank you for coming."

As he bows to his king, Atlandreous says, "Thank you sir."

Icaras replies, "I made time to talk with you. There are a hundred things needing my attention every moment of everyday, but I want to talk with you one on one."

Atlandreous looks humbly at his king and says, "Sir, I don't understand. I might have won a sparring match. But there is nothing so important here to take your time from our people. What can I do for you?"

Icaras replies directly, "I was there at the games, and I saw what you did. It has nothing to do with winning or losing, but what you did in the match which makes you a leader. You were cut, and you should have given up. You didn't. Furthermore, you pushed your soul until you won the match. No one at your age has that kind of discipline anywhere in our realm."

Atlandreous says, "I just wanted to see if I had what it took to win the match."

Icaras replies, "I need that kind of leadership in my military. I understand your age and who you are. What I hear about you from your village is unbelievable. Everyone I have spoken with has told me about your gift in the art of the sword, but there is another side of you. People really respect who you are. Looking at your trade, you and your father help irrigate water to farmers. If it were not for people like you, our population would starve. Yes, you have an important trade, but I need your gift with the sword, and social skills to protect our kingdom. I am asking for your help. I need you to bring four people you spar with to Alnilam. I need you to train your friends for the next generation of Alnilam's army. In doing so, I will reward you and your friends for the rest of your lives."

Atlandreous says, "I do have friends which want to improve themselves. I spar with them every single day, and we do help each other to better ourselves. I do know the people you're looking for, but you do understand I will be giving up everything I know for our kingdom. My youth stops here."

Icaras replies, "In doing this, I will grant you the title of Captain in our military. There will be only ten people above you in rank, and you will be one of my generals one day."

Atlandreous asks, "Can I go home to speak with my friends? I will return to you with what you ask. Sir, my life is about to change. I hope I am as good as you want me to be."

Icaras says, "You have three weeks to complete your assignment. Because I need this done quickly, I have to give you this time frame. Our kingdom thanks you for being who you are, so let us start the beginning of a new military right here."

The meeting is over. Atlandreous and Thanos go home as fast as they can on their giant elk. The elk can travel vast distances without tiring. It will not take them long to get home. It will take Atlandreous three days to get to Mintaka.

On the way home, Thanos thinks about the future of his son. He knows he is about to lose his teenage son to the Alnilam's military. Atlandreous is becoming a man. A father can never be as proud as Thanos is at this moment. Atlandreous' father has brought his son up to make decisions on his own. The fifteen year old boy has a great deal of discipline for his age, but he is also very humble to his father and the people around him. Atlandreous understands the art of war in the degree that it is nothing but instinct to the young boy. At the same time, the fifteen year old is somewhat a maverick in his confidence and skills. What Atlandreous knows is hard to teach. He will have a hard time explaining his frame of mind to others. Life and death in combat is only seconds from one move to a counter move. The way he thinks is faster in countering opponents for most to comprehend. Atlandreous can see battles in his head and make the right decision for victory before most know they are even in trouble.

The long journey is over; Atlandreous and Thanos arrive home in Mintaka. They are welcomed by their village. The village is starting to become a small city. Huts are turning into grander houses. The roads are becoming stoned and maintained by their small community. There are stoned buildings for public events and a small stadium for the games. Thanos was one of the first to have a stone dwelling. Atlandreous' father is a noble of his community. Even though he has no say in Alnilam politics, it is a matter of time before Mintaka becomes a known city and recognized by the Senate of Alnilam. Because it is on the outskirts of the Alnilam Kingdom, it is too far to really govern, without depleting the resources of Alnilam's treasury. At this point, Mintaka is not worth the resources of Alnilam's interests.

Other people from nearby rural communities are there to welcome the young warrior. People cheer for Atlandreous and his father. It has been told to everyone Thanos trained his son in the arts. Atlandreous' father did not want this kind of attention when his son arrived back from the games in Alnilam.

In front of his dwelling, Atlandreous gets off his giant elk and hugs his mother and sister. He walks towards one of his cousins and embraces him as family. Everyone is giving praise to Thanos' son.

Atlandreous goes to Erasmus who is a close friend and dedicated sparring partner. Erasmus is a couple years older than Atlandreous.

He is six feet tall, with blue eyes, and very fit. He has worked hard in the art of war and has taught Atlandreous a couple of things in sword fighting. Erasmus practices two hours a day on combat skills. He enjoys learning and figuring out battle techniques with his sword.

Atlandreous walks straight to Erasmus as he is feeding his horse near Thanos' home. The fifteen year old cannot wait to tell his friend. Even though Erasmus could not wait to see his friend, he backed off out of respect of Atlandreous' family.

Atlandreous walks straight to Erasmus and says, "I have won at the stadium. I have gone to Icaras. He told me to bring four friends worthy of protecting our kingdom back to Alnilam. The Alnilam King wants a change in his military. I want you to be a part of the transformation."

Erasmus stops what he is doing and replies, "You are my best friend. I am on your side. If I can help, I will be there."

Atlandreous says, "You are excellent with the bow and sword. You have talents that most people will never have. I need you there with me. I know you're only seventeen, but it is time to go towards your next step in life. I hope to the gods this helps you in becoming more. I need you tomorrow with me to talk with Tarasios. I am a little reluctant to get him involved. Tarasios is a little eccentric even though he has the talent. I need all my friends in Alnilam. This is an overwhelming responsibility for anyone."

That night, Atlandreous goes with Erasmus to talk with Tarasios. The village is eighty-five miles from Alnilam going northwest towards Masaba. No one from Mintaka has ever been in this kind of spotlight from their capital. Atlandreous has put his village on the map. Even though most people from Alnilam do not even know where Mintaka is located, the village is becoming an overexcited whisper in Icaras' city-state.

Atlandreous knows Tarasios will be very unenthusiastic to go to the capital. His name is very well known in his community. Tarasios' father has molded him to take his place in making aqueducts after he passes to the next life. Because cement has just been invented in the last seventy years, there are not many people with the know-how to build such structures. In the realm of Alnilam, construction of aqueducts is past down from father to son, and there are very few generations to pass the art down to.

With the population exploding inside the five major city-states, irrigation and aqueducts are the only way to keep people fed. Because the five city-states are on a peninsula with mountains and hard terrain, it is very difficult to get food from outside their kingdoms. The people from the continent are not as developed in producing enough food for the byland. The only way to feed the city-states is through irrigation inside the peninsula.

Atlandreous and Erasmus go toward their friend. Atlandreous and Tarasios hug as brothers. With enough short talk, Atlandreous sits Tarasios down.

Atlandreous says, "You know why I'm here. I need you to come with me to Alnilam to help with our army. I will be a captain, and I need you to help me bring a new way of fighting to our realm. This can save our kingdom in the future. I know we can make something happen for all of our futures. Even though Mintaka is not recognized by the Alnilam Senate, our community will receive recognition with me going to our capital. The people here will have a predominate future."

Tarasios replies, "I can't. I have my father's ambitions to tend with here. My father is from Masaba. If I have to choose down the road, I will have to go there. I want to help, but I will not be happy going to Alnilam knowing my father has the full burden of our trade. You knew my loyalties would be with Masaba when we were younger. My family is respected in Masaba. I hope you understand. I will continue with our art of fighting here. I will teach the younger generation how to defend our small district, but I must continue my father's trade. Generations of our city-states and my family's future depend on what I do here."

Atlandreous replies, "I totally understand, but when there is no alternative, I want you on my side in battle. I know you will have to go to Masaba, but I will not fight you if our two cities have to wage war against each other. The politicians will have to fight each other to get what they need. They will have to fight sword to sword. Wouldn't that be a sight?"

Tarasios says, "We are eighty-five miles from Alnilam and forty-five miles from Masaba. I will stay here and train our people here. I will also visit Alnilam and get refreshed with new battle techniques. Alnilam needs to know how to defend itself in case of war. Being here will only help your cause and our kingdoms in the future.

There has not been any conflict with Alnilam or Masaba for eighty years. The chances are grim of fighting one another."

Atlandreous asks, "What do you think of Nieander and Hamon? What do you think they will do?"

Tarasios says, "They want to leave Mintaka. They need a new beginning. My main priority is helping my family right now. Their families are more loyal to Alnilam than Masaba. They will go."

Atlandreous replies, "I respect your thoughts. I will leave in two days. I see you as a true friend, and I will never forget that."

Talking with Nieander and Hamon, they agree to go to Alnilam. Atlandreous will leave in two days. Thanos' son needs one more to take with him. He thinks he knows who to approach next. He knows he has to ask Orion. Orion has sparred with the three, but he just got back from working in Vasic.

The next morning, Atlandreous goes where his friend may be. Orion, who is the maverick of the young sparring partners, is at the village market getting things for the family. Atlandreous knows it would be a good possibility to find his friend there. Orion, who is five feet eleven, inches tall, with dark hair, is not as strong in leadership as Tarasios. Nevertheless, he can be very loyal to Atlandreous. He looks for Orion for a while and cannot find his friend. While searching for Orion, Atlandreous starts to talk with some acquaintances about the sparring match, and what he will be doing in Alnilam. While he is talking to a group, he looks around for his friend.

Atlandreous sees Orion at a distance and yells, "Orion!!!"

Atlandreous rushes to Orion. Orion stops what he is doing and draws his sword.

Atlandreous asks, "What are you doing?"

Orion says, "For the rest of my life I will be drawing my sword for you. I just wanted to draw it for myself one last time. I want to remember this. I know why you're here. It is all over the village. I will go."

All four friends go with Atlandreous to Alnilam earlier than expected. The fifteen year old wanted to show his king he is ambitious and ready to go. Atlandreous' friends hope they made the right decision. Their district is small and Atlandreous' friends are ready for a change. Erasmus, Nieander, Hamon, and Orion never thought they would be given this honor to become something important to Alnilam. Because they are so far from their city-state, they experimented with different techniques which are different in sword fighting than the Alnilam Army.

Atlandreous and his friends are ordered to the Alnilam Military College. In some ways it will help them in training, but in other ways, they will be known as nonconformists. Since Atlandreous won at the games, the five will go in the school as radical thinkers.

The warriors from Mintaka go and learn at the military academy in the middle of the city. The military institution has just been built and is one of the most lavish buildings in the capital. Atlandreous only has ten people ahead of him in ranks in the Alnilam Army and he is treated well at the military school. This kind of stature is unprecedented for their age and Atlandreous is humble, but confident, to his new acquaintances. Erasmus is a lieutenant under Atlandreous' command. Nieander, Hamon, and Orion are considered second lieutenants. They are to teach the rest of the army how to fight differently. The army of Alnilam accepts the decision of the king, but they are not completely acknowledging the idea. The warriors from Mintaka are being rebels in the norm of fighting skills. In sparring matches, the people from Mintaka win a large number of tournaments with their techniques. It is making things harder for the five to fit in the Alnilam military because of the victories at the sparring matches. The Alnilam military students are not taking it well that they are losing so many matches. Even at their age, Atlandreous' friends work through the rough treatment with each other's friendship. They talk with one another to help with their everyday politics. They are a team, and friendship is the bases of that team.

In a week, Atlandreous is making headway in teaching the new way of sword fighting. Atlandreous and Erasmus have a good friendship and work well together in the arts. The two have taught each other moves and counter-moves to be the best in the world, and now they are teaching warriors of Alnilam. After their schooling, they spar for two hours a day just thinking of new ways to beat a competitor.

During the first couple of weeks, Atlandreous goes against some of the military teachers in battle tactics at the school. Scenarios are thrown in fictitious battles, and Atlandreous does not go with the main flow of what his military teachers want to hear. The thought in the scenarios does not make Atlandreous rebellious, but it makes him different. None of the military teachers can say yes or no to Atlandreous' tactics. During one of the sessions, Atlandreous is asked to speak in front of his peers. Everyone at the school has to come up and say what they think in regards of making their military better. It is Atlandreous' turn.

Atlandreous stands in front of his peers. He waits for a minute until everyone is completely silent.

Atlandreous says, "We are all young except for our military teachers. If you are a teacher, try to remember when you were our age. War is like courting a beautiful girl. If you both don't want war or courting, there will be no war or love. If the man and woman want to be with the opposite sex, they will totally disagree with each other even though it is sometimes on purpose. I know everyone here can relate." The whole crowd goes silent after laughing. Atlandreous continues with more intensity, "Kingdoms and empires have the same process as courting. In our profession, militaries do little until there is no choice but to use force. It is the self-interest which makes conflicts. We need to know our potential enemy's self-interest. We have to understand our enemy before we fight. If we don't know our enemy, we will eventually lose. You have to know your enemy in every aspect. Every time I think of a scenario and tell my military teacher, I think of other city-states and nations which we can be fighting against. I think of their religion, background, and what I know of their military. In my thoughts, they are all diverse and every battle will be different. I understand what we are being taught here, but I think we should know our potential enemies abroad. Women are the same way. Even though we cannot understand them, we have to understand their main motive in doing anything, or we will be the ones who sleep outside. Or maybe another man will take our soul-mate. There is no one in Alnilam looking at our potential enemy's strengths or weaknesses in complete detail. Military and politics are one. I think we should plant a seed in every city-state to see what is going on with our friends and potential foes. I think we should call these people planters, and they should report back to our military school. Our other city-states may be doing the same thing, and we might not know they are here. The person right beside you may be really from Masaba or Halotropolis. Tactics are great, but knowledge is the key to winning battles. Understanding outside politics can prevent bloodshed. I do have other things that may be useful, but I think I have already over extended my thoughts in our group."

Atlandreous sits down, and Erasmus looks at his friends.

Erasmus says, "You don't waste time, do you?"

Atlandreous replies, "Either they're going to hate or love us. I can always ask for forgiveness later from our teachers."

Icaras gets wind of the speech. Atlandreous is asked to go to the king's chamber right away. The fifteen year old has astounded the military teachers, and they are looking at Atlandreous differently. He looks at war and his surroundings as one. He can make his peers understand. Atlandreous is a prodigy in war tactics and people skills.

Atlandreous goes to Icaras and bows to him.

Icaras says, "What you said back there in the military hall is nothing I expected. The military teachers don't know what to do with you. They want to take you out of the school, and I agree. I want you by my side to make our military the best in the world. One day we will have no choice but to fight our neighbors of Masaba, Alnitak, and Halotropolis. When this happens, I want to be prepared. You have the gift no one has in the world, and you will save our culture and heritage. You will be head of council in our military."

Atlandreous asks, "What about the people I brought from Mintaka?"

Icaras says, "That is up to you. They are under your command. You are the commander of Alnilam's Army now. On the battlefield my generals will be in control, but you will help me direct them to win battles."

Atlandreous says, "If I do this, you have to trust me. I think completely different than what you have been taught from your father and the fathers before them. There will be changes."

Icaras says, "Agreed."

Atlandreous goes out the door knowing he has so much on his shoulders. He wants it, but at the same time, he wishes he was in Mintaka. The only thing he can do is to have patience. Even though he is in charge, the military of his capital will not be comfortable with sudden changes. He knows he will have to change their order of discipline to make things happen more quickly. It is almost overwhelming for the fifteen year old. But he knows in his heart, he can make it happen. He knows changing people will not be easy. Atlandreous knows it will be a long time before he can do what he knows he has to do to make Alnilam's military the best in the world.

CHAPTER IV
THE VIBRANT CITY OF ALNITAK

Two months after Atlandreous wins his sparring match in Alnilam, another city is going through politics like any other city. People do what they have to do in everyday life. The children play in the streets like any other child does in the world, and the people work hard in their city to make their lives better.

In Alnitak, it is mid-afternoon, and all of the council and military advisors from and around their kingdom are ordered to go to their capital. All high officials know it is a routine meeting. The city is having problems like any other kingdom, but resources and expansion is the main forum of today's talks.

Colligitar, the Alnitak King, is going to speak to his advisors in the Alnitak Hall. The Council Hall is spectacular for its day. The building spreads over twenty-five thousand square feet in the middle of the city. Each archway of the building is over twenty feet in stature. To support the weight of the building, the structure has over two hundred columns. The whole building is painted in bright blue, red and tan. There are over two hundred and fifty statues in and around the building. It is the first grand building on the peninsula which was built a hundred and ten years prior by another king. There is no building like it in the world. The Alnitak Hall is where all the buildings on the byland get their inspiration to build grand structures in their own cities.

All over Alnitak, older buildings are getting demolished for the next public project. In the last fifteen years, buildings inside Colligitar's city have been getting more grandeur in size and appearance. Mathematics and cement is becoming pivotal in building opulence in the metropolitan society of Alnitak.

On the peninsula, Alnitak is larger than Halotropolis, Alnilam, Vasic, and Masaba combined. The city has no fear of the other four cities-states. Because there is so much diversity in the societies on the byland, Alnitak knows the other city-states on the peninsula cannot become a formidable threat even if they all came together to fight the great city.

For Colligitar's city to strive, he needs the outer continent and the peninsula's cities. Because Alnitak is right inside the mountain range on the byland, it is the middleman between the city-states and the world.

The largest metropolitan city on the byland is not getting the resources they need for their ever growing population. The only way they can change their situation is through war and taking land away from less structured civilizations outside their peninsula.

Colligitar is thirty-eight years old. He has blond hair, blue eyes, and is very lean. The women of his kingdom adore him. He does not want to attack the peninsula's cities. Because Halotropolis, Masaba, Vasic, and Alnilam have powerful militaries, it can strip the military of Alnitak and leave it vulnerable to the rest of the kingdoms on the main continent. Being in the middle of the known world has its disadvantages. Colligitar has to watch out from both sides of his borders.

Florick, who has jet black hair, medium height, and dark olive skin, is the Supreme General of the Alnitak military. Anyone who has stood against him in battle has lost. The General has a great number of good military officers which are very loyal to him. The Supreme General has very disciplined warriors, and they will die to protect the ideas of their land. Kassandra, Florick's wife, is also a very strong leader in her society. The two are very important to the Alnitak's social structure of the city.

Kentor is the strongest man in Colligitar's city, and he is second in command to Florick. He is the tallest of all Alnitak generals. In battle, he has never stood behind enemy lines. Kentor leads his men in battle. His men admire his courage. Kentor's tactics are very aggressive, but effective. It is all or nothing on the battlefields. The second in command has killed over a hundred and fifty men in hand to hand combat without a scratch.

In the last decade, Colligitar's military has taken in more land on the main continent. Right now, Alnitak needs to take more resources to their North in the Girulic region on the main continent. Alnitak has put satellite bases outside the peninsula to protect their annexed lands. The outside cities are protected with Colligitar's armies. Because of resistance, Colligitar gets reports of his warriors being killed, but they are acceptable losses for the resources needed for the expansion of Alnitak.

Florick goes to Kentor to talk over logistics and supplies needed to take on more land outside their kingdom. Kentor is wrapping things up with his officers to take Girulic. To Kentor, it has been difficult to get the resources needed but the quest is obtainable. It is very taxing to the second in command.

Florick walks in and asks to speak to Kentor alone.

When the Alnitak officers and councilmen leave, Florick says, "What do you think this time my friend?"

Kentor laughs and replies, "I understand taking in more land for expansion, but our armies are spreading thin."

Florick says, "I totally agree. I don't like our men spreading out like they are right now. A strong resistance can disrupt our occupied lands."

Kentor replies, "If we take on more land beyond Girulic in the near future, it may start a war. We are pushing too hard and too fast. We have to stop and regroup our resources in manpower before we try to take any more. We have to stop for at least three years to build up our military before another conquest."

Florick says, "I agree. Now, let's go to the meeting and see what politics has in store for us today. Every time I go to these meetings, I feel it is the one that may destroy us, but kingdoms and empires that are not aggressive will never grow and make it. Every society has to grow; it is in human nature."

North of Alnitak on the main continent, there is a northern empire called Tarentum. The Northern Empire borders are over a hundred miles from Colligitar's realm, which is also taking in ungoverned territories. The Tarentum Empire is totally different in culture and religion than the people on the peninsula. The people of the Northern Empire believe in totalitarianism and different gods.

Both Tarentum and Alnitak are starting to want the same lands between their borders. Baylonis, Tarentum's emperor, is becoming more powerful in his part of expanding borders. Baylonis and

Colligitar's realms are superpowers of the world. The leaders of Alnitak and Tarentum need each other for economic growth. Both superpowers' nobles make very good trade with one another. Every six months the two superpowers come together and speak of lands and trade between them.

With borders becoming ever so close together, the two imperialistic societies watch their next move so as not to start a war. Because the cultures are so different, they make borders miles away from each other.

At the hall, King Colligitar stands up and looks at his council. He is very confident the talks will go in his favor. Everyone is focused on the Alnitak King.

Colligitar says, "The talks with Tarentum and our people will happen in two weeks. We need more resources to our north to grow. The trade between our realms has made each of us stronger. But most of the population of the world is in and around Tarentum. We can fight each other in battle, and I know we will both lose. Baylonis knows this as well."

Florick says, "We can't take Tarentum even if all the city-states on the peninsula want to become allies. There is a great deal of distance between us and them for a surprise attack, and their cavalry is six times stronger than our own. Our new defensive walls are the only thing keeping Tarentum from attacking our city. We must regroup our military and not be so spread out."

Protemous, head of the Alnitak council, says, "The territory of Girulic is the solution to our resource problem. Even though the territory is ninety-five miles northeast of here, it almost overextends our military, but the resources we need for our kingdom are there. At the same time, Baylonis' empire is about to take it. He is going from tribe to tribe trying to take it under with diplomacy. If we take it by force, we must take it quickly. About half the population in Girulic wants our protection, and the other half want Baylonis' rule. In the near future, the territory will become an issue between our two civilizations."

Florick replies, "Starting a war with our kingdom will only deplete Tarentum. If there is any interruption to their economy, they will not be able to recover. Baylonis will avoid a war with us at any cost, and we will do the same."

Colligitar says, "One thing I know is to be completely

independent. Don't count on anyone except yourself and the people you rule. We cannot rely on the other city-states on our peninsula."

Scratching his head, Protemous replies, "Hurrasium can be an answer to our problem. To the East, we have harbors which will have little economic impact to our city if we give it up. Yes, we build ships there, but the resources in Girulic outweigh what we need in our harbor. We can trade our land there for Girulic."

Colligitar says, "That is what we will go with. Baylonis will accept the deal. We are still strong enough to inflict major damage to his empire. We are like two teenage bullies in a village. One of us is about to get bigger than the other. If we are a bully, we better slap the other across the face before he gets overconfident and he tries to do the same. I will talk about the territory of Girulic in our next summit."

Florick stands up and says, "I will go to the border of Girulic. Baylonis will not send his troops in. He knows it will bring war between our people. We have to play the right politics and have the military force to back it."

Colligitar says, "War is not an option right now. Get your military battle ready just in case. I will get the Senate ready for war so we can do it on a moments notice. The chance of a war with Baylonis is becoming more inevitable. We have to prepare our government for the possibility of war."

Two weeks later, the summit starts. Baylonis, who is thirty-four years old, six feet tall, with long red hair, wearing his military attire, is less talkative than before. The two are both careful of not talking about the Girulic territory. The two leaders are in a tent without council or generals to listen. They both sit at a table across from one another. They sip on wine, and there is silence between them.

In a calm voice, Baylonis says, "I see that we both want the same thing. My military and your military are on both sides of Girulic. Both sides can take it with ease. It will be taxing to me with supplies and manpower to keep the whole territory under my rule. Help me out. Why do you need it so badly?"

Colligitar replies in a humble voice, "I need the natural resources. I knew this was going to be part of our discussion today. I am so glad our councils are not in here right now. If you do, let me take it under my rule. I will give you our harbors in Hurrasium. It is far from my kingdom, but the territory has what you may need to build ships. Hurrasium will help you in transporting goods to your eastern rule. It took my people decades to make the harbor what it is today. But I need the resources in Girulic more than what I need in Hurrasium."

Baylonis says, "I have personally gone to Girulic and have spoken to their leaders. I have worked hard to get these people to become a part of my empire. I have most of them agreeing. Let us split the territory, and let the people of Girulic decide where they reside on the new map. We must compromise. Tell me where your natural resources are located, and you will have it. I only need the farmland to feed my people, and the whole region has fertile soil."

Colligitar replies, "If we do this, we will get the lower half and you'll get the northern part of Girulic. Where do you think we should draw the lines?"

Baylonis replies, "I will give you the first choice in drawing the new map. I will take the second choice. We need each other for economic stability. I'm not going to make this assembly into a thought of war. I know each summit is getting harder to compromise. Your people and my countrymen are asking more from these gatherings. I respect your kingdom, but the people I rule are a different story; they are getting greedier. Greed from my empire and your kingdom will only start a war. I have to keep them in check."

Both leaders need the resources from the same area. Baylonis thinks the harbor would have been a good deal, but the farming resource from Girulic is more important to his people. The Tarentum Emperor has more to worry about in his empire than to be anxious about the talks of land issues with Colligitar.

The next day it starts to rain. Baylonis and Colligitar are in a tent setting up new borders. The two leaders can hear the rain hitting the tent. It is a tranquil sound. With so much riding on the new borders, nature's rain has set the tone to help the compromise.

After the talks, the new map is made. The two superpowers will be bordering one another for the first time. Because the Girulic is so important to both societies, there are no buffers. Before, Alnitak and Tarentum had at least a ten mile safeguard from the two different cultures. Now, there will be stones placed for boundaries. Because the two civilizations are totally different in religion and culture, both leaders think it is best to keep the diverse societies from colliding with one another except in trade.

Each of the societies gets half of what they truly need. Because they are both superpowers, the people of the territories cannot do anything about it. In the last couple of years, it has been a rat race to take territories. Alnitak and Tarentum are growing at a mad rate. If they do not continue to grow, their populations will become stagnate and an uprising can start in their governments. The economics on both sides depend on expansion. At the same time, they cannot attack each other because it will knock out the balance in their trade and political stability.

In the tent, Colligitar studies the new map for a while, and the king and emperor say nothing to each other. The Alnitak King looks at Baylonis.

Colligitar says, "In the next couple of years, all of our borders will be connected. The world will be either yours or mine. In the near future can I count on the next generation of the Tarentum people for peace?"

Baylonis replies, "Are you saying we will start fighting each other in the near future? No, I think the economics and trade of our two societies will grow. We will become more dependent on one another. Are you asking if I'm greedy enough to attack your kingdom? No, your people are very important to my civilization's future."

They both go back to their lands. Colligitar and Baylonis are not completely satisfied with the results of the summit. Each of the two leaders does exactly what they said they would do in the conference. The inhabitants of Girulic go to the side they want to go to reside in. The greedy politicians from both sides are satisfied for the moment. The majority of the people of Girulic rejoice in the superpowers take over. To them, it will bring more economic growth and a better standard of living.

Colligitar goes to Florick outside Girulic. The Alnitak Supreme General is preparing to send the second wave of men into their new annexed territory. Florick is speaking to some of his officers when he sees the Alnitak King. Florick goes to his king and kneels.

Colligitar looks at Florick and says, "Everyone leave us. What do you think of all of this?"

Everyone around clears out quickly.

Florick replies, "It is not as good as we think. We might have borrowed a little more time, but in the next decade, we will have to go to war with Tarentum. I have another concern; we will have to keep a quarter of our military around Girulic for stability. In doing so, our other territories will suffer without enough soldiers."

Colligitar says, "We must make our military and our defenses stronger here. We must concentrate our resources so we can protect this region. I will get the men you need."

In the years to follow, Colligitar and Baylonis' territories grow. The leaders negotiate territories and taking in more land outside their borders. Florick, at the same time, starts to make his army larger and greater. Because a great deal of the revenue is coming from the new territories and trade with the peninsula cities, it is not an economic strain on the Alnitak economy. Florick is getting more funds to make his military stronger. He knows there will be a conflict with the Tarentum people. It is just matter of time. Colligitar is working really hard to keep the world from having a war, but the Alnitak King knows too well that greed and preservation of his culture will clash with the Tarentum Empire.

CHAPTER V
FINDING NEW DISCOVERIES

At the age of twenty-one, Atlandreous is still working hard on Alnilam's military. Before he took over leadership, The Alnilam Army was not well organized. It was strong and comparable to the other city-states on the peninsula, but no different.

Consistency, training, and discipline are Atlandreous keys to success. The Supreme Commander goes by those guidelines every day with his men. Even though he has a great deal on his mind towards the next step to make his army better, he reminds himself of those three basic words.

Before Atlandreous, the Alnilam Army was comprised of four divisions, and each of them was disciplined and taught differently. Each division leader had different numbers in archers, infantry, artillery, and cavalry. Atlandreous changed all of that to a more standardized number for each division. Now, Icaras' army can utilize their diversity to fight as one. If a general of a division is killed or cannot continue on the battlefield, another officer from another division can take his place and know exactly how to use his men in battle.

The old Alnilam military was hurting the economy of Colligitar's city. The Supreme Commander had to think of ways to keep his military strong and economical. In the last six years, the population of Alnilam has not changed much. There are over two hundred seventy thousand people under Icaras' rule. In the past, there were over twenty thousand soldiers on Alnilam's military budget. Now, Atlandreous has cut it down to two divisions of five thousand men and made two more divisions in reserve. The Alnilam's reserves are the veterans of the realm which have fought in past wars. Each of them meets up twice a year for a week of drills and reconditioning. The reserve military are civilians fifty weeks out of the year. They are compensated for the two weeks of service, but most of the veterans' revenue comes from trade. The veterans use their leadership in commerce, and most are doing well. In doing so, the society of Alnilam is starting to have a better structured economy. Because of military cuts, more manpower and resources are used for science and exploration to the seas and oceans. In the science aspect, medicines and new weapons are coming from Alnilam's scientists. The new medicines are making some people rich in Icaras' realm. Everyone on the peninsula seeks the new medicines.

During the last five years of Atlandreous' military rule, Icaras has taken his navy further than anyone on the continent or peninsula. The King has discovered a new world. His captains and admirals have kept their discoveries from the rest of the world. In their new insights to the globe, they have found new and unusual giant beasts. In the past, the Alnilam's military has used horses, elephants, and mammoths in their armory against their enemy, but Alnilam's threats also have the same beasts in their cavalry. The giant animals have been used to destroy infantry and fortifications.

Atlandreous has been asked to accompany Icaras at a remote location outside the walls of Alnilam. The twenty-one year old rides his giant elk, goes inside the compound, and wonders what the king has to say.

Atlandreous is inside the compound and sees a large animal with giant claws, similar to the size of an elephant. The twenty-one year old is in shock and awe. Icaras is only twenty feet from the creature. The king has no fear of the animal. Atlandreous stops and looks at the beast and than looks straight at Icaras.

Icaras says, "What do you think Atlandreous? Can we use this beast in battle?" As the beast jumps upon a tall tree and takes its large claws to hold on to the tree, the giant animal starts to eat the leaves from the tallest branch. The beast pays no mind to the two men around it.

Atlandreous replies, "What is it?"

Icaras says, "It is what we know as a giant sloth. It is slow, but do you see its claws. We can get more. We brought back three. With our ships able to go thousands of miles, what we can find is endless. Masaba and Alnitak have a superior cavalry to ours. I am looking for anything that can give us the advantage on a battlefield in case we go to battle with our brothers."

Atlandreous replies, "We can find its strengths and use it in battle. If this animal can be trained, it can be useful in destroying our enemies. This creature is slow. I know it cannot be used offensively, but I think it can be used for defensive purposes. I will talk to Erasmus about this animal tomorrow."

The next day Atlandreous takes Erasmus to look at the creature. As they look at the animal, it seems to be a pet rather than a creature of death. The two friends look at the beast. It is a tamed animal. With a swipe from its claws, it can kill a mammoth. Because of the giant sloths, Atlandreous decides to put his military mind to work. He wants to go to the next step in his military reorganization.

Erasmus looks at the creature as Atlandreous did the day before and cannot even speak.

Atlandreous asks, "What do you think Erasmus?"

Erasmus replies, "This world never surprises me."

Atlandreous says, "I am leaving it up to you to use our resources to get more of these creatures. You're in charge of the next generation of our infantry. This beast will give you the advantage you need on the battlefield."

Erasmus asks, "Why me?"

Atlandreous answers, "As of right now you are the Field Marshal of our infantry. With our reserves and military, you will be required to organize our generals to act and react in battles. This creature can't be used with our cavalry. It is too slow, but it can protect against an opposing cavalry."

Shocked, Erasmus looks at Atlandreous and asks, "Help me understand, what are you asking of me? And why am I the Field Marshal of Alnilam's infantry?"

Atlandreous smiles and says, "You have the talents and willpower to make our infantry great. I believe in you. What do you think about the beast?"

Erasmus replies, "We will have to make these creatures hate other cavalries and love ours. Look at the animal; I think it would rather give you a hug than kill something."

Atlandreous says, "I agree. If we use these creatures inside our infantry for defense, we can use the full strength of our cavalry anywhere on the battlefield. They are slow animals, but any animal will protect itself. Make these beasts work towards our advantage."

Icaras has ordered all ships to the new world. Because his ships are small, they can only carry two giant sloths on each ship. It takes a great deal of time and manpower to bring these new beasts to Alnilam.

After the talk with Erasmus, Atlandreous takes Nieander to Alnilam's cavalry grounds. Atlandreous knows the strengths and weaknesses of Nieander and knows how to talk to him.

Atlandreous and Nieander ride in Alnilam's giant stable. Mammoths, horses, giant elk, and giant rhinos are being ridden by the Alnilam's military inside the compound. Some are in cages and others are conducting military drills. Everyone salutes the two when they enter deeper inside the compound.

Atlandreous says, "This is your assignment. You are going to make our cavalry more powerful. I need you to concentrate on our cavalry and find new tools to make our cavalry the most powerful of any military."

Nieander replies, "There are more qualified people than me to do this."

Atlandreous says, "It is good that you are humble. This is new to me as well, but all of us see eye to eye. On the battlefield, we can anticipate each others next move. That is the most valuable component on any battlefield. Let us say there are some more qualified than me on the battlefield. Would you want me there or someone more qualified?"

Nieander replies, "You sir, I trust you to make the right decision."

Atlandreous says, "We can see each other's moves and make our own moves to destroy our enemy. I have confidence in you. Make it happen."

Nieander replies, "I understand, and I will follow you to the end."

The idea that Atlandreous envisioned is coming together. The next couple of weeks, Atlandreous works with Erasmus and Nieander on their assignments. Orion and Hamon wonder when their time will come to make the difference. Two weeks into the new plan, Orion watches Nieander and Atlandreous working on new infantry and cavalry battle techniques. They work together with Alnilam's military to work as one. Before Orion goes to Atlandreous, he sees a different military than before. It is becoming a killing machine.

Orion goes to Atlandreous and waits until the right time. They talk when the infantry and cavalry goes into formation as if they are going into battle.

During some small talk, Atlandreous pauses and says, "Are you wondering what role you will play in this?"

Orion asks, "What is going on? You and I are brothers. We have worked together and learned a great deal from one another. I am wondering what you have planned for me?"

Atlandreous says, "You will have one of the most important tasks of all. I need you to take our archers and make them the protectors of our infantry. On any notice, you will have to make the difference on the battlefield. Work with our archers and make them better."

With the new assignment, Orion goes and finds the best archers in Alnilam and works on his assignment. Everyone is working on the new ideas for Alnilam. Because of good politics with the other city-states, Atlandreous knows the chance of war is very minimal.

Knowing that Hamon will follow suit, Atlandreous decides to go to him first before he thinks he is outside the loop. The twenty-one year old goes to Hamon's home.

Atlandreous says, "I have a project for you. Hamon, you will have the most difficult task in making our military the most technological on the battlefield. We have catapults and crossbows. We have to have better weapons than our enemy. We have to use our artillery to destroy as many men on the battlefield before they can attack us. You have to make more and better weapons. You will have to bring fear into our enemy. We have the same weapons as our potential antagonists. You have to think. How can we be more unapproachable, and what hell on earth can you bring to our enemy when they try to attack?"

Hamon replies, "Our schools are teaching us the basics. I will make monster machines to terrify our enemy."

Everyone starts to think outside the box. The ways the Alnilam's military has been taught in the past is starting to change. Atlandreous' four friends are starting to do their job. There is trial and error, but in months Alnilam's military is changing towards the better. The four meet up once a week with Atlandreous to work up plans to combine the four military components to make the best killing machine in the world.

Inside the last two years, Atlandreous has totally reconfigured Alnilam's military. Every general has been replaced with Atlandreous' friends from Mintaka. Because it has been eight years since Atlandreous resided inside the capital, the military of Alnilam has accepted his leadership. It has been hard, but he has complete loyalty from Alnilam's military. He changed ideas slowly to keep people from rebelling. Atlandreous has the gift to get what needs to be done with little resistance. He works with his men and treats them as family. His father works with Atlandreous in public affairs. Because Thanos can see the details of high officials' emotion and desires, Atlandreous is able to work on other things. Thanos works hand and hand with politicians to get what Atlandreous needs to make Alnilam's military better.

CHAPTER VI
COMMITTED TO RESPONSIBILITIES

At the age of twenty-three, Atlandreous is still perfecting his military. The other city-states are taking notice and looking at Alnilam as leader on the peninsula. Icaras' city is nothing like the power house of Alnitak, but his city is making leaps and bounds in new developments. With economic reform and new items to be traded, Alnilam is becoming a very prosperous kingdom. Atlandreous' military leadership has started the economic boom for Icaras' city.

Meanwhile, the King of Halotropolis knows his city-state is changing. There is a religion revolution inside their realm's borders. Because of the changes in religion, Halotropolis cannot go forward in policies or growth. About sixty percent of Halotropolis believe in the gods, including the Senate and high officials. Everyone else is starting to believe in one god. The new religion is sweeping the realm. The movement to one god is coming from the younger generations of the kingdom.

In the last two years, there have been accounts of religious uprisings inside Halotropolis. Numerous riots between the two religions are tearing the kingdom apart. Cetrono, King of Halotropolis, is asking for a meeting between the city-states. With Cetrono's city in disarray, Alnilam can take Halotropolis with their war machine, but Atlandreous knows there will be high causalities. Masaba or Vasic has enough resources after the conflict to destroy Icaras' city and take it under their rule.

The King of Halotropolis does not know what to do at this point. Cetrono is asking Icaras for help. With Halotropolis and Alnilam being the big boys on the peninsula, the Alnilam King agrees to the meeting. They meet in a neutral city of Vasic. On the byland, the other kings, except for Alnitak, are there to see how this assembly can affect their kingdom. The Alnitak people are not really worried about the other city-state's drama. They have enough problems outside the peninsula.

The meeting starts. The best architectural building in Vasic is where the meeting is taking place. The masterpiece of engineering is about four thousand square feet in size and two stories tall. The outside walls of the building are made of black granite. It took over three years to complete with over tens of thousands of workers. The best builders from across the peninsula built the structure. With Vasic wanting to be put on the map with the other city-states, the construction of the building almost destroyed the city economically.

Cetrono, Icaras, and kings from the other city-states sit with other political councilmen inside the building. The people in the assembly sit and talk about trade and religion.

In the middle of the meeting, Cetrono stands up and asks to speak to the crowd.

Cetrono says firmly, "My people and military are starting to stray from our forefathers' foundation. All of my councilmen agree. It is God which is destroying my kingdom. Where this came from, I don't know, but it has to stop."

Icaras replies, "In my kingdom, God is starting to have an influence in my land as well. I believe in my gods like most people here. But every month, I see more of my people going towards one God. Shrines are being built in my kingdom. I can stop the temples from rising, but it will only start a rebellion. After the temples were built, there are some followers. Inside three months, the places of worship are over flowing with new people."

Richcampous, King of Masaba, wants to say something but waits until there is a silence.

Richcampous says, "I also have the same following to one God. God—is taking over. Ten years ago, God was a whisper in my kingdom. Now, He is screaming to my people to go to Him. I don't know what to do. It is the younger generation that is starting this. Like Cetrono's city, the religion revolution will influence my kingdom inside two years. The whisper of God is getting louder.

I don't want it escalating to the point where Halotropolis is right now."

Cetrono says, "To keep our values grounded, our governments will have to see eye to eye. I need stability, and I need Alnilam's military to keep control of my people. My military is torn between God and gods. Yours on the other hand is still with the gods. Icaras, everyone on the byland is seeing your success. I can't see any other way to stop this religious movement. Your military will have to help keep my government together. In a year, my government will be completely wiped out of existence. The trade with our kingdoms will decrease dramatically if we don't act fast."

Icaras replies, "If we do this, Alnitak will think we are coming together. In doing so, it will bring other concerns of war with the largest military power on the peninsula. The four city-states can't take on Alnitak, even if we came together as one."

Cetrono says, "I am about to lose my government because of this religion. Icaras, I need your alliance. I also need a high political figure to marry my daughter, Tess. In doing so, it will slow down this movement where it can be under more control. In the high scheme of this, we will not say we are coming together, but let what is unsaid in the marriage carry the weight of my burdens. In the back of this religious faction, the marriage can calm this down to a more manageable level."

Icaras replies, "I will help as long as everyone inside this room understands what we are trying to accomplish here. I don't know who can be influential enough to slow down this movement. Wait a minute—I have a thought."

Icaras goes out of the building and yells at one of his servants to get Atlandreous. Every high official looks at each other and wonders what Icaras is doing. The Alnilam King knows Cetrono can be a very powerful ally to his kingdom. It makes sense, but it is up to Atlandreous to do the task.

Three minutes go by and Atlandreous is at Vasic Council Hall asking for permission to enter the room where the assembly is taking place.

Icaras says, "Come in Atlandreous."

Everyone in the room is gazing at Atlandreous as he stands in the middle of the assembly.

Atlandreous says, "What can I do for you, My Lord."

Atlandreous looks at the King of Halotropolis and says, "Cetrono, it is a pleasure to be in your presence."

Icaras replies, "I need you now like I've never needed anyone before. We need to stop the religious civil war in Halotropolis before it destroys our economy. You and I have worked hard to be where we are right now. I need your help."

Atlandreous asks, "What do you ask of me?"

Cetrono knows what Icaras is doing. The King of Halotropolis is getting the idea. Cetrono sees this and wants to implement this immediately.

Cetrono replies, "I totally agree about what we have to do. Good idea Icaras."

Atlandreous looks around the room while the councilmen and officials whisper to one another. The twenty-three year old knows he is in trouble, but has no earthly idea how to combat this scenario.

Atlandreous laughs as if something is a joke and says quickly, "I don't understand."

Icaras looks straight at the twenty-three year old and says, "I need you to play hard core politics for our people and Halotropolis."

Atlandreous says with puzzlement, "I can fight battles for you, but I don't know how to fight in this arena of politicians. Tell me what you ask of me."

Icaras, in an almost joking way says, "To play the right politics, you are going to marry Cetrono's daughter, Tess."

Cetrono and Icaras look intently at Atlandreous. The whole room goes silent. Atlandreous just starts looking at the ground. He does not know what to say. This took him completely by surprise.

After seconds of silence, Atlandreous looks face to face at both kings of Halotropolis and Alnilam.

Atlandreous says, "I can't do this." The twenty-three year old looks straight at Cetrono and says, "I don't even know your daughter."

Cetrono asks, "Is there anyone in your life right now?"

Atlandreous replies, "Sir, my army is my love. I can't give you what you want. It is not in me to love anyone except my responsibilities. Your daughter will never be happy with my devotion to my kingdom. I cannot give the time needed for a relationship."

Icaras says, "Right now, you're at one extreme. It is time to balance your life. I want you to get to know Tess. Do you love your kingdom?"

Atlandreous replies, "Of course I do, sir."

Cetrono says, "She is nineteen and beautiful. Her personality is something you will love for the rest of your life. Give it a chance; you will have to at least court her for one year. Be seen in my kingdom with Tess. The idea of you courting my daughter will solve some of my problems in my kingdom. If you don't fall in love with her in one year, I will give you the opportunity to get out of this. By the way, did I say she can probably give you a challenge with the sword?"

Atlandreous is very upset with his new assignment. He had no say in the matter. He does not say anything about this to anyone. He keeps it totally to himself about not agreeing with the courting of Tess. The twenty-three year old follows orders. The Alnilam Supreme Commander is missing his men back home already. His role in life is changing. In accordance to his military work, he feels like it is about to lose everything he has worked so hard for.

A week later, Atlandreous is in Halotropolis waiting to see Tess at the Cetrono's palace. Even though the city-states are similar, Halotropolis devotes a great number of resources into their buildings. Each city-state has their own architects and every city has different building styles. Out of all the cities on the peninsula, Halotropolis puts the most details into their buildings with geometrical shapes and statues. Atlandreous feels as if he is in a whole different world.

Atlandreous is at Cetrono's palace. He is escorted to the ballroom by servants. No one came with him from Alnilam. In the room, there are over a hundred high officials and their guests. The twenty-three year old is really starting to get nervous. Not knowing the unknown is killing him. He stands tall and keeps his composure. In the back of his mind, Atlandreous wonders why him. He wonders if this will have any affect on the political situation in Halotropolis.

From Alnilam spies, Atlandreous has discovered Tess is going towards the new religion. The Alnilam Supreme Commander believes in the gods. In Atlandreous' mind, he wonders how two people with two different religions work out or even get along? Tess has said nothing to her father about her new belief. Atlandreous talks with a guest in the ballroom looking around to see if he can point out Cetrono's daughter. The people of Halotropolis are fascinated with Alnilam's Supreme Commander because of his accomplishments. Everyone in the room makes a point to talk to the young man from Alnilam.

After the Alnilam Supreme Commander gets acquainted with some of the high officials of Halotropolis, Tess is escorted by Cetrono into the ballroom. The two walk and intermingle with guests. Atlandreous looks at a distance and is flabbergasted by her looks. She is five-three with an athletic build. Cetrono's daughter is attractive, with thick brown hair, and brown eyes. With a white dress which fits her curves, it compliments her dark olive skin. Because Atlandreous is five feet ten inches, he wonders how she can even stand up to Atlandreous' sword like Cetrono said prior. To Atlandreous, she is striking. At the same time, he wonders how she is personally.

Tess is in the room smiling and talking with everyone she encounters. She smiles and includes everyone. She even says thank you to the servants. Atlandreous can tell she has good social skills. But at the same time, the twenty-three year old does not want to be here at all. Tess' personality flows in the ballroom.

Cetrono goes to Atlandreous and shakes his hand. In the audience's view, he hugs the Alnilam Supreme Commander as a brother. The two look at Tess as she speaks to a small crowd in the background.

Cetrono says, "Go up to her. She doesn't want this either, but you and my daughter have a great deal in common. Follow me, I will introduce you. Remember, after a year you have the right to walk away from this. If Icaras trusts you then, so will I. Icaras is a good man."

Atlandreous replies, "In my life, I thought I would fight for my kingdom and die with honor. I have talked to my generals, and they will be taking larger roles in my army. I need to be there, but I do trust my men to take care of affairs while I'm gone. If you think Icaras is a good person, you should meet my father one day."

Cetrono says, "Let us not talk about fighting. Icaras and I are friends. Remember balance. My daughter can give you that. One day, you will need that balance to make you who you'll become."

Atlandreous asks, "May I ask who that will be?"

Cetrono replies, "Icaras and I have a great deal of confidence with your leadership. Trust what is going on in your life right now. Tess has the potential to give you what you need to even become better. A real man will fight for family harder than fight for himself."

Atlandreous walks with Cetrono towards Tess. The Alnilam Supreme Commander is forcing himself to keep his composure.

They reach Tess, which is speaking to her political councilmen; she turns around and smiles at the twenty-three year old from Alnilam. She waits until Atlandreous says something first. For a brief moment, Tess does nothing but smile at him as she waits for some form of conversation.

Atlandreous breaks down and says, "Hello Tess. I have heard good things about you."

Tess grabs Atlandreous' hand and replies, "And, I have of you."

The two look at one another and wonder what to say next. Cetrono sees both of them smiling at each other.

Atlandreous says, "I know this little party was for us. Let us say we leave for a little while." He looks at Cetrono and asks, "Is it okay, sir?"

Cetrono, Tess, and Atlandreous pull away from the crowd to speak without any interruptions from the guests.

Cetrono says, "Do what you think you need to do." The Halotropolian King looks at his daughter with a cheerful look and says, "I love you Tess. You are royalty. Sometimes royalty is not what you expect to be. I told Atlandreous you have a year before you two decide any future thoughts. If you choose not to go on with this, you both can walk away. The courting starts at this moment. In the middle of the hottest month of next year, I will ask you both what you have decided and I will respect your wishes. At least this will be a learning experience. Both of you have been wrapped up with politics and leadership. It is time to know the other things in life."

Atlandreous and Tess walk towards the palace grounds together. They are both attracted to one another, but being forced into a relationship is hampering their natural instincts. Even though they know the other one is eye-catching, there is a huge wall built up between the two. At first, there is a great deal of silence, and Atlandreous tries to speak about small politics but stops after Tess only answers with short sentences. The tension builds up, and they walk further away from the palace. They get to the grounds where there are not as many people around.

Tess says, "Why do we really have to do this? I think you are attractive, and I know you have a good name with your people in Alnilam. With my responsibilities in my kingdom, I can't give the time for love. My father says a person finds it when he or she is not looking for it. It seems love is thrown in our face. What I am feeling about our courting has nothing to do with you. In my aspect, there is too much going on in my life to have a relationship."

Atlandreous replies, "I agree. My men are the most important thing to me right now. Protecting my kingdom is my love. It will be very hard for me to do this for a year. It is not that you're not beautiful, but I have other priorities that have been given to me. I cannot slow down. If I take a break, everything I have worked for will be destroyed. I have worked too hard to let that go. To court someone you have to give almost everything you have to that person. I can't do that with you or anyone."

Tess says, "In what we do for our kingdoms, I do not think we have the luxury of having time together to build anything meaningful. We both have too much politics in our cities to deal with. I do not have time for someone to really care about. Our politics will pull us apart."

Atlandreous replies, "I agree, but I am going to do what my king wants. We will spend time together. You will come with me to Alnilam to learn my people. You will see and understand my politics. We have accommodations waiting for you back in my kingdom."

Atlandreous and Tess stay at Halotropolis for two weeks. Tess shows the Alnilam Supreme Commander what she does for her people. Atlandreous can tell she is admired by her society. She is a gifted leader and knows what to say at the right moment. The politicians and high officials in the city show perfect obedience. Tess and Atlandreous eat at a different noble dwelling every night. The citizens of Halotropolis are very curious about the twenty-three year old.

Right before they are to go to Alnilam, Tess takes Atlandreous to a religious meeting. It is the teaching of God. They go into the temple. Atlandreous does not want to stay in the same room because he thinks he is disrespecting his gods. They go deeper into the temple. He feels uneasy as they talk about God. It is not much different in what Atlandreous has been taught in his religion, but there is only one deity. He cannot comprehend the thought processes of such a belief.

This is almost a deal breaker for Atlandreous. He can use the excuse of his gods conflicting with Tess' God to get out of this. But he stops himself out of respect of Icaras. Atlandreous does not want to tell Cetrono his daughter is a part of this religious movement.

After the congregation, Atlandreous and Tess walk down the streets of Halotropolis. They speak very little to each other. They glance at each other in an uneasy way. They try to talk, but something is really bothering Atlandreous.

Tess stops and says, "You do not approve of our new religious movement do you?"

Atlandreous replies, "I can't. I was brought up to believe in my religion. I felt as if I would go to hell if I listened to one more word coming out of that room. I have prayed in my head ever since I left that religious meeting."

Tess looks around to make sure no one is listening and says, "I had to show you what is going on in my city. Halotropolis is about to have a new religion. My father and Senate cannot stop it. Only the older people are not accepting God. There is a great deal of violence on both sides. My father does not understand what is going on here. Most of our leaders are of the old fashion religion. The younger generation wants to take over our government and give it to God. Because you are here, people have thought twice in attempting another uprising in our capital."

Atlandreous replies, "I'm glad it is not happening in my city. Our gods keep our city safe."

After Tess shows the city and culture of Halotropolis, they go to Alnilam. It is a culture shock to her as well. Atlandreous is not as religious as Tess. He shows her the city and how his city is growing. Every night they meet with Atlandreous' acquaintances. She is not happy being in Alnilam. All Tess can do is fret about her responsibilities she left behind. In the back of each other's mind, they both want to stop this and go on with their own lives. The only thing holding this together is the respect for both kings. Neither Tess nor Atlandreous want to be the first one to give up on this.

Back in Halotropolis, the religious movement is still going forward. Cetrono's government is giving false promises to the people who believe in one God. There are whispers of hatred towards Alnilam because of the courting between Atlandreous and Tess. Because the older religion of Halotropolis is almost the same as Alnilams, the younger generation from Halotropolis feels suppressed with Icares' involvement. Alnilam warriors are helping police Cetrono's city to stop any riots.

After two weeks in Alnilam, Icaras orders Atlandreous to his palace. A messenger says it is very urgent. Atlandreous takes Tess with him. The twenty-three year old thinks it has something to do with Halotropolis. Because there is an honor system between the nobles of the two city-states, Tess is safe in Alnilam because of the new treaty.

Atlandreous goes to the palaces and bows to his king. Tess does the same out of respect.

Icaras says, "Atlandreous, I need you to go to Khartoum with two thousand warriors. We have found a new tree which has more elasticity than any tree on the planet. A bow was brought back from the region and can shoot further than any of our own. We must transplant this tree for our military's future."

The Alnilam King looks at Tess and says, "I have told your father about the tree and where it is located. Because you have shared the discovery of steel, I told him we will share this discovery to help make his military stronger for your future. This is a ten month journey round trip. I have over a thousand men already there harvesting the new tree, but there are hostile inhabitants that do not like us there. We are taking it by force. The region is too far for us to govern, and the people there do not have the military technology as we do to keep it. Tess, you will go in your father's behalf. I know that you don't like what was presented to you with this courting idea. I have spoken to Cetrono about this, and we both agree you can get out of this after the mission to Khartoum. Tell me your wishes when you return. Tess, you will be safe with my warriors. They are the elite of my kingdom."

Atlandreous replies, "I will do as you ask, but may I suggest not taking Tess because of the danger involved. We do not want someone getting hurt and Alnilam getting the blame."

Tess says, "I'm going. This is important too my people. I will not take no for an answer. You don't know that I can fight. One day, Atlandreous, we will spar. I think it may be interesting."

Icaras smiles at the two and replies, "I have spoken to you father, Tess. He tells me you should go. Everything will be explained when you get to the delta. Cetrono trusts Atlandreous and says he trusts his daughter's life in his hands. Tess, you are a true leader. You will go to the delta and sail down the river until you reach the largest lake on the continent. You will go towards the largest mountain range until you reach the Khartoum's civilization. We are building our military power there. This can be a revolutionary weapon."

Right before they go, Atlandreous wants to see his father one last time before he leaves. He needs his father's guidance. Everything is going too fast for the twenty-three year old. Thanos just got back from Mintaka. Atlandreous is excited to see him. The Alnilam Supreme Commander goes to his father's home in Alnilam.

Atlandreous walks in Thanos' home and says, "I have missed you Father. How was your trip?"

Thanos replies, "It was good. Our trade in the region is getting more lucrative. I spoke to Tarasios. He has trained everyone in the region in your art of war. You will be proud. Tarasios misses you. He told me he can't wait to spar with you again."

Atlandreous looks at the ground as if he is ashamed and says, "So much has gone on in the last eight years. I don't even know what Tarasios looks like anymore. He is a ghost in my memory. I still love him as a brother, and he has my loyalty, but I have other issues right now. He should have come with me eight years ago. I need him."

Thanos puts his hand on his son's shoulder and replies, "Respect his decision. I have been informed of the situation at hand. I know about Tess and what is about to transpire. I believe in you, and I know you will make the right decisions. This is an important mission for both kingdoms."

Atlandreous looks away and says, "I know. It is too much for me. I don't know how to play politics, and I don't want it. I am forced to do something I'm not good at."

Thanos directly says, "Listen to me. I am not taking your side or Icaras'. Tess is a very good leader and a good woman. Treat her with respect and get to know her. Even if you don't come together later, you two will become very good friends. That friendship can save thousands of lives. Remember that. I will not say anymore. Go to your journey and remember my thoughts on the matter."

Thanos and Atlandreous give each other a hug and the twenty-three year old leaves the room feeling better.

Tess and Atlandreous get ready to go. Tess and the Alnilam Supreme Commander are out of the element even more now. Everything is moving fast. The responsibilities they had before is nothing compared to what they have to accomplish for their kingdoms. What they had to do before they met is like a dream now. The only thing they can do now is to go forward.

CHAPTER VII
THE POWER OF ADVENTURE

In a week's time, Tess and Atlandreous are at the mouth of the river. This is the beginning of their journey. Even though there is an outpost at the delta, most people from the peninsula do not go further than thirty miles up the river. It is too dangerous. The Iteru, meaning Great River, is the longest river in the world. It is the most powerful body of water on the continent. The tributary is a very treacherous watercourse to travel. It will take the representatives from Alnilam and Halotropolis almost three and a half months to arrive in the Khartoum Kingdom. Twenty-two people from the two city-states have already died trying to reach the kingdom in the last year.

Tess and Atlandreous are about to board a small ship to start their journey. Alnilam warriors escort the two representatives to a small ship. A person is there to greet them before they get aboard. Atlandreous and Tess look at their surroundings as they walk towards the small vessel. For being so far from the byland, the Alnilam docks and outpost are very well constructed. A great deal of materials and manpower went into building this station.

Suelarous, an Alnilam captain, salutes the Alnilam Supreme Commander before he boards his ship.

Suelarous says, "Hello sir. No one told me who was representing our kingdoms until today. It is a great honor for me to take this journey with you. I have gone up and down this river three times in the last three years. I'm here to make sure you get there safely. If you need anything, I am here to assist you."

Atlandreous salutes the captain and boards the ship. Being respectful, Suelarous helps Tess get aboard.

When Atlandreous gets his footing aboard the ship, he replies, "Icaras told me little of the situation here. He said I would find out more after I arrived."

Suelarous says, "The Khartoum people have tribes all over this continent and are on the brink of becoming a powerful civilization. They have pockets of strong armies. Because of logistics, they are fighting other kingdoms which are destroying their civilization one by one. These people want to trade technology for natural resources which can help our two city-states. They need our technologies to fight back their enemies. Their resources and discoveries will revolutionize our military and trade."

Atlandreous asks, "Why is Tess here?"

Suelarous looks at Cetrono's daughter and says, "Tess, the main reason you're here is to make sure the Halotropolis representatives are on the same page with Alnilam. If you do have a problem with the negotiations, you and Atlandreous have the right to stop this summit. You and Atlandreous are equals on this mission. There are over two hundred people from Halotropolis at this outpost. Your advisors are aboard these ships. They will give you the answers you need."

Atlandreous says, "I still don't understand why it is so important for us to be here. Couldn't our diplomats do a better job? There has to be something else."

Suelarous replies, "It has got to the point that your presence is required. Our diplomats have done all they can. Yes, there is something else. The Khartoum people have discovered new medicines which can fight infections and sickness. These new medications have cured some of our people back home. People that should have been dead are still alive because of these remedies. It can be very important in war and commerce to get these medicines. The Khartoum people want to trade their discoveries for ours. A Halotropolis team has been sent ahead of us with the know-how to make steel. Besides the molless tree and medicines, The Khartoum people also want the knowledge of ship building. A team of Alnilam ship builders have been sent two days ahead. With the Khartoum Kingdom having the possibility of being a very powerful empire, the byland kings think the Khartoum Kingdom can turn on us later. Because these people know how important you are to our kingdoms, the people on this continent will not do anything stupid."

Atlandreous and Tess start to float down the river. In the beginning, the landscape is breath taking. There are numerous animals which rely on the delta. It is more diverse then their kingdoms back home. While they look over their small ships, the representatives from Alnilam and Halotropolis almost forget their responsibilities back on the peninsula.

Back home in Alnilam, Atlandreous' generals are setting the standards. The Alnilam Supreme Commander's leadership has made true leaders of his generals. Icaras feels he has the right people in the right place. Even though Atlandreous is not present on the peninsula, his generals do not want to let their commander down when he returns.

To the Kings of Halotropolis and Alnilam, the mission in the Khartoum capital cannot fall short. With this new natural resource, Cetrono and Icaras can trade to the Alnitak people and put their trade deficit to a more lucrative one. With the molless tree and medicines, it will jump start a new revolution in trade on the peninsula. The whole economy of Halotropolis and Alnilam are counting on these resources for prosperity. Because the two city-states are trying to work together, it is very important for Atlandreous and Tess to be on the mission. The two representatives need to see first hand how the world is changing in trade.

There are diplomats from both city-states already in Khartoum. They are learning the native language and culture to help the representatives from the peninsula. A great deal of human resources from the two-city states is going into this mission.

As Suelarous' fleet of ships travel up the river, they have to stop and camp on the river's banks at night. It is too dangerous to travel in darkness on the river. The teams from the peninsula are on small ships with large sails. The ships have oarsmen to help with speed. The vessels have very little luxuries from home. Atlandreous and Tess are the only ones with a cabin. Their living quarters aboard the ship are only fifty-six square feet, which is nothing to what they are accustomed to back home.

On the second day on the river, Atlandreous is going over how to get to their destination. He wants to know where and how they will travel. Suelarous is showing a map to the Alnilam Supreme Commander with the details of the journey.

Tess walks towards Atlandreous and says, "Sometimes being

royalty is not so glamorous. If you have a quick second, I need to speak to you if I may."

The captain leaves them alone. Because it is a small ship, the two have to whisper to one another. The oarsmen keep rowing, and the people on the small vessel keep working to make good time.

Atlandreous asks, "I am yours. What can I do for you?"

Tess says, "I think you're a very good leader and good general, but, when we get back home, I am going to put a stop to this. You and I have been forced into in something I know we both don't want from each other. The way I feel has nothing to do with you. I totally respect you, but what your king and my father want from me will be impossible."

Atlandreous replies, "I totally understand. I feel the same way. I think you are the most beautiful woman on the peninsula, and very important to your society, but, it is like you said, we have been forced into this. When our adventure is over, I will concur with your decision. The only thing I ask is that we become friends no matter what."

Tess grabs Atlandreous' hand and says, "Respect is the stepping stone to friendship. We have the first steps of being friends."

Tess pulls away as she gives a smile to Atlandreous. They continue their journey up the Iteru River. The two are missing their luxuries at home. On the ship, the two have servants which tend to their needs, but Atlandreous and Tess are already missing their friends. At the same time, they know this is a good experience. They do not have to play the politics as they do back home. Even though they both hate politics, they miss it.

The word relationship is nothing they want to hear right now. They both want to make something of themselves and maybe someday have someone important, but that someone will only get in the way of their goals right now. Their lives are way too busy to love anyone. At the same time, Atlandreous and Tess respect each other's way of life, and try to make the most of their journey.

Two months into their adventure, the representatives of the peninsula have almost forgotten their lives back in their homeland. There are countless tasks to do in preparation for the trade summit with the Khartoum people. The people Atlandreous will encounter have a different culture and social structure than his own. The Alnilam Supreme Commander has guidance from his council to help with his future diplomacy, but one bad gesture can destroy the mission.

Seasonally, it is the perfect time to go up the river. It is not flood season for the Iteru River. The river's current is not strong and the vessels make good headway. On the way to the Khartoum society, the Alnilam captains trade with other civilizations on the Iteru River for supplies. There are guides to help with the language barriers. To the inhabitants around the river, Atlandreous' presence is very important to their trade in the future, and everyone from the villages helps in the process.

Atlandreous and Tess have said little on their voyage. Because Atlandreous feels his actions are rude, he decides to break the ice. He does not know if she will give short answers or allow a conversation. He goes to her in front of the ship.

Tess is looking over the water. Atlandreous can tell she does not really want to talk.

Atlandreous asks, "Can you help me? I am trying to understand the new movement of the religion in Halotropolis."

Tess replies, "It is not religion as you speak of. It is God. I also believed in the same gods as you do. I will not judge your religious beliefs. It is not up to me to judge. God is everything. I thought there were many gods to make things happen in this world. I realized one day there had to be a beginning of creation. Something started somewhere. To my mindset, it couldn't be gods that created the world. It could only be one. In a logical aspect, only one could have had the power to start life. With other gods in the mix, there could only be chaos. Your god of the earth would destroy the god of the sea. The sea and earth are still here. By now, there would have been a conflict, and both gods would have destroyed one another."

Atlandreous does not believe in her beliefs but says, "I see your point, but it is hard for me to see only one god wanting to make what we see and know. People work together; why can't the gods?"

Tess asks, "How many wars have taken place in the last one hundred years which destroyed whole civilizations and societies?"

Atlandreous replies, "At least five in my historian's point of view."

Tess quickly says, "Then if they were gods, gods would have destroyed themselves until there was only one. The earth would not be here, and we would not be breathing this air. Would you agree?"

Atlandreous says sharply, "I did not come over here to debate you. I understand we were sent here together. I want to learn about your culture and understand the world a little better. I am asking you if I can ask questions about your culture, and you can ask about mine. It will help benefit one another if we do so. Do you agree?"

Tess laughs in an embarrassing manner, "I'm sorry. I came off wrong. Because of the silence with one another since this journey began, I thought you were coming to attack my belief. Asking about religion is not the best way to start a civil conversation."

Atlandreous smiles and says, "I agree. So, every evening after we camp, we will talk about our cultures to help one another in politics to come. Politics and wars go side by side. If there is a political struggle with each other's city-state, we can avoid a war through understanding. With understanding and compromise there will never be a war."

Tess replies, "I agree with that last comment. Every evening we will learn from one another for that purpose."

For the next months of their mission, they start to become friends and the journey is going according to plan. There are some setbacks because of the Iteru River, but the weather has put the teams a week behind schedule. They have to take more chances with the river to make it on time. Suelarous is good at what he does, and they catch up to their schedule. The meeting with the Khartoum people will happen on time. Atlandreous cannot be late. When they are on the water, they take advantage of the day. Sailing up the river is too dangerous at night. Sleep is becoming a luxury to Atlandreous and Tess. It has been a rigorous trip so far. It does not help with the two representatives from the peninsula trying to become friends. With little sleep, they both know they are not at their best, but, they stay with their word and govern their emotions while they converse. Both of them are too tenacious with their honor and duty to make enemies with one another. Neither one backs down in learning from one another's society. Most of the time, they try to talk for at least thirty minutes. During one evening, Suelarous can tell the friendship between the two stubborn leaders is starting to grow.

Three months into the journey, they arrive at the last Alnilam outpost before they reach the Khartoum people. The representatives from the byland will take the last part of the journey by land.

The Khartoum society has lived here for thousands of years. War is the only reason the Khartoum Kingdom is not as advanced as Atlandreous' society. It has ripped their people apart. There is a lot of abhorrence between the people on this continent. This is the reason for the trade of the molless tree. The Khartoum people need better weapons, and steel is the answer to their enemies.

A Team from Halotropolis has brought materials and machines already to build steel. The Khartoum people will copy the technology to build their own steel refinery. Once that takes place, they will have the advantage to their adversaries. Atlandreous does not want to give the technology to these people. With all the turmoil on the continent, the Alnilam Supreme Commander does not want another potential enemy to have their technology.

Tess and Atlandreous finally reach their destination. Yorubas, the ruler of Khartoum, goes toward Atlandreous and Tess. The Khartoum King has interpreters to help with the language barrier. Atlandreous' teams get off their horses. The Halotropolis and Alnilam teams, which are already stationed at Yorubas' capital, start to greet their countrymen. Tess jumps off her horse and goes right beside Atlandreous to show she is in charge as well.

Using an interpreter, Yorubas says, "Thank you for coming. I hope one day we can trade with your kingdoms more freely. With your technology of ship building, I can see it happening in five years. This is a good trade between our kingdoms. I have worked very hard to get what you acquire from our kingdom. I have accommodations for you. I have servants to address your every need. We have harvested the molless trees to take back with you, and we have seeds to plant this tree in your own kingdom. What we need from you is how to make steel. I have also gone around other kingdoms to get the resources you need for medicines. We have melted alloys before, but we cannot get the temperature hot enough for such an alloy to make steel."

Tess says, "My people are here to help you. Whatever I can do, it will be done."

Using an interpreter, Yorubas replies, "I am at your disposal. My men are your men. We will one day be allies, and this is the way we want to start off. My kingdom has so much to offer. Give me two more weeks to expedite the harvest. I have men all over this territory extracting the molless tree. Do you think we can make the first batch of steel in that time?"

Tess asks, "Do you have the materials I've asked for?"

Yorubas replies, "Yes, and your men sent ahead of you have just completed the first furnace to make steel."

Tess says, "It will only take a week to produce your first sword."

Yorubas says, "Thank you. This technology will save our people from our enemies."

Tess says, "I am also here to learn your culture so we can be better friends in the future. I need to retire for the day. Will you show us our quarters."

Atlandreous just looks at Tess and says nothing. He knows she did the right thing. Yorubas' servants take them to their quarters. It is not what Atlandreous and Tess are accustomed to, but, they have better sleeping arrangements than on the ships. They at least have stone floors and heated water for baths. The representatives from the byland can almost relax at this point. There is a great deal of work that needs to be done, but it will not be as taxing on their bodies as their journey up the river.

Everything is going as planned. The trade is going beyond anyone's expectations. The next couple of days, Atlandreous and Tess speak with one another during the evening. They speak of the trade and culture they are encountering. To Suelarous, they are almost a team on this expedition. There are some arguments between the byland's representatives, but for the most part they see eye to eye.

CHAPTER VIII
FINDING GOD

In the middle of the Khartoum consultation, Tess looks at the mountains in the background for hours. She has been intrigued about them ever since she has been in this kingdom. Tess goes to Atlandreous' tent without escort.

Atlandreous is by himself looking at a map of the territory.

Tess says, "Have you seen the mountains to our west. I am going to climb those mountains. I want to see what is on the other side. Our business is done here. Yorubas needs another two weeks to achieve his objectives. He is working diligently, but he is having difficulties with such a hard task. The Khartoum people are doing more than we expected. If you want to see what I see in God, come with me."

It takes Atlandreous completely by surprise and he replies, "What? Even if we take horses to the mountain base, it will take us two weeks to go up and down those mountains. I don't want to go. My responsibilities are here. I can't go on some excursion."

Tess says, "We will never have a chance like this again. This will be the only chance in our lifetime to take an adventure like this one. It is an escapade. Our friendship has grown to this point. Let's take it to the next level and go on a fun quest."

Atlandreous takes a moment and thinks of the tribes which hate the Khartoum people. If Tess goes alone, it will not be safe for her. Even with her military escort from her city-state, Atlandreous cannot let her go on her on. Icaras said she is his responsibility. If something did happen to her, it could lead to war between the two city-states.

Tess can tell from Atlandreous' expression that he hates the idea as he says, "I will go. It is something I really do not want to do, but it will be done out of respect for your kingdom."

Tess replies sarcastically, "You don't have to go. I don't need you to do this."

Atlandreous goes towards Tess and says, "Why do you want to do this?"

Tess looks straight into Atlandreous' eyes and answers, "Adventure and discovering God's world."

This is something Atlandreous did not expect from Tess. Atlandreous thinks being away from her environment has brought the little girl out in her, and that she wants adventure. Atlandreous really thinks she is being immature.

Tess gets her people together to climb the mountain range. To Tess, the politics in this land have been very boring. To her, their work is already done. Atlandreous, on the other hand, hates the idea, but goes along with it. To Atlandreous, this is something to keep his mind off politics back home in Alnilam. The Alnilam Supreme Commander has no earthly idea what is going on in his kingdom. He can only hope his military is still doing what needs to be done to become better.

Tess and Atlandreous get to the mountain range. To get to the mountain's base, it only took two days. The guides from Khartoum will help them get up the mountain. The adventurers have brought a great deal of clothing and mammoth blankets to keep them warm. Tess had heard only high ranking warriors from Khartoum climb the mountain range. It is a test of bravery. Tess wants to get respect from the Khartoum people, and she thinks this is the best way to gain admiration from their new allies. It is something Atlandreous did not think of. Tess and Atlandreous think the exact opposite when it comes to foreign affairs.

The first day of the adventure is fairly easy, but the third day gets a little tougher. Going up the mountain starts to put strain on their bodies. At higher attitudes, there is less oxygen. The temperatures are well below freezing at night.

On the sixth night, and close to their destination, Atlandreous and Tess sleep in their mammoth tents. It is the coldest night of the adventure. Both use each other for warmth, and they talk to one another until they fall asleep. The next morning, Atlandreous and Tess get up rather embarrassed about their embracing the night before. They look at each other for a brief second and go on with the adventure.

About mid-afternoon, they reach a point where they can see the mountain ranges and peaks. There is not a cloud in the sky. The snow is bright from the sun's power. Atlandreous and Tess are floored at what they see. Even though it is almost freezing weather, they feel as if they can almost reach heaven.

Tess looks at Atlandreous and says, "Do you really think gods could have made these mountains, or God?"

Atlandreous responds, "Being on this plateau, I can feel and see what you're visioning. But my gods created this."

Tess says, "Only God can make such wonderment. God is love; he gave man treasures for the eye to make men love Him."

Atlandreous says, "You're a wonderful person. Maybe, mankind is evolving to the next step of evolution. In a social aspect, it could be man is going from many gods to one Deity to help him evolve to become greater. In our society, it could bring the city-states together rather than destroy them like our kings fear."

Tess replies, "I agree. I consider you a friend and an ally. Let us remember this day. Thank you for the compliment and your honesty. I can tell what you say is from the heart."

They have reached their goal, and they start to go back to the Khartoum Kingdom. It takes less time to go down the mountain as it took to travel up. The more they descend down the mountain the better it is to breathe for the conclusion of their adventurers. Atlandreous and Tess keep the images of the peaks in their heads as they travel back. What they saw at the top of the mountain will be remembered the rest of their lives.

Five days later, they are back speaking to Yorubas. The leader of the Khartoum people speaks to them differently, as if they are fellow countrymen. Atlandreous and Tess have honored their traditions of becoming warriors and leaders by taking the adventure. The Khartoum guides tell the rest of their kingdom that Atlandreous and Tess are brothers and sisters from a different land. The trade goes a lot easier. The shipment of the molless tree is almost complete so traveling to the Alnilam river outpost can begin. So the Khartoum people can build their own ships, the Alnilam ship builders have built models so they can make them on a grander scale. The first production of steel is concluded. It is up to the Khartoum people to make steel on a grander scale.

It is time for Atlandreous and Tess to go back to their city-states. On the way to the river outpost, the two talk with one another on almost every occasion. The friendship between the two is getting stronger. The molless trees are carried by mammoths. Atlandreous and Tess travel ahead of the shipment to make sure there is safe passage.

When they get to the outpost, the ships they use are fitted to carry huge shipments. A great deal of manpower was used to get their shipment back to the peninsula. Over thirty-five hundred people from Alnilam and Halotropolis are on this expedition. This is the largest joint effort between two city-states.

The journey back down the river takes three months. Tess and Atlandreous wish they could have met on difference circumstances, but it is too late. Both Atlandreous and Tess are going to stick to their first agreement to break this off. They are friends. But the excitement of meeting someone new and special is gone. Friendship is all they are capable of.

Two weeks before Atlandreous and Tess reach the delta; they are on ships with their consignment. Each tree is cut to fit into the ships. Each cut can make about twelve bows on average. The shipment has over two hundred trees. The cargo will be split between Halotropolis and Alnilam. This will make the two city-states archers superior than any army in the world.

Tess goes to Atlandreous at the front of the ship.

Tess says, "We are almost to our destination. I want to say that you are a good man, and I respect what kind of leader you are to Alnilam. Your men respect you, and so do I. I do not want to lose contact with you when we go our separate ways."

Atlandreous replies, "I see you as a very good friend, and I would give my life for you. I have to tell you something. When we went to the mountain top, I totally understood your thought processes of God. If it were gods, they would only destroy one another to get power. It makes me think. The wonderment of the peaks would have been the first thing destroyed by a jealous god. Your religious movement will change humanity for the better. I wished our city-state was going in the same direction in religion, but its not. In my land, what I believe could hinder my leadership.

Even though I feel the same way, I could never bring it to the table of my politicians."

Tess says, "You can be the beginning stage of God to your kingdom. Just spread the word to the people you trust. There are some who believe as I do in your city-state."

Tess goes to the back of the boat to speak to her councilmen. The weeks go by, and they always talk at the end of the day. The last night before they get back to the delta, the two byland representatives can tell it is going to be hard to be separated. The adventure has changed their lives forever.

The teams get back to the delta. It has changed somewhat. Even though it has been five months, there is no one in Halotropolian armor to meet Tess and her men. There are over three thousand Alnilam warriors to meet the ships. Before Atlandreous and Tess know it, ships come from behind them to trap their ships into the delta. Atlandreous tells Tess he will find out what is going on. Orion is there at the peer to speak to Atlandreous. The Alnilam Supreme Commander has no choice but to dock. There are too many ships for them to go forward or backwards.

After docking, Atlandreous and Tess get off the ship and go to Orion.

Atlandreous asks, "What is going on?"

Orion goes to Atlandreous and says, "Tess, your religious movement has almost taken over your government. Because Icaras said he would help keep your father in power, your God followers started hostility with our kingdom. In doing so, Halotropolis attacked our bordering outposts. Alnilam's military has retaliated, and we are on a brink of war. Tess, Icaras told me to take you to Alnilam until this conflict is resolved. You will be safe in our kingdom. The shipment will go to Alnilam until we settle this. We are on your father's side. This dispute is about factions, not your kingdom."

Tess asks, "What of my people here?"

`Orion says, "Most of your warriors attacked our people when the news started. There was a great deal of speculation on both parties. There were no orders from your father, but your captains decided to take matters into their own hands. There was nothing we could do. Your father, Tess, is a puppet to your military right now. Icaras sent me here to get Atlandreous back to Alnilam. There will be war between our city-states. In the meantime, Vasic and Masaba are getting involved. Masaba and Halotropolis will fight Alnilam. Oh yes, Atlandreous—Tarasios, our friend from Mintaka, is a general of the Masabaian Kingdom. In the last seven months, and because his family is from Masaba, Tarasios is leader in the Masabaian military. Tarasios is no longer an ally. He is our enemy."

Atlandreous says, "I will never make him an enemy. What you're telling me is that in the time I was gone, the whole world has went mad. I can understand Tarasios' decision. I hope I never have to fight him. Am I in command of Alnilam's military?"

Orion replies, "Yes sir, you are."

Atlandreous says, "Than these are my orders. I will take this up with Icaras later. Tess, you will go back to your people. Your father needs you. Orion, is Cetrono still the ruler of Halotropolis?"

Orion replies, "As of last week, yes, I believe so."

Atlandreous says, "Even though the war is going to happen, I will not let my word of honor stray away from me. Tess, I am sorry for your warriors' deaths. This is politics. Even though this is a bad situation, I have to do what I need to do in to honor my homeland. Your people are free. The ships here are at your disposal. I have a feeling we will fight one another in the near future. Our friendship has to end here. Your men are set free to go back home. Their weapons will be stripped from them. At the small island of Kroteir, I will leave swords and weapons there for your protection for when you get back to the peninsula. This is all I can do for you."

Tess says, "I understand."

Tess' men are stripped of their weapons and given eight ships to go home. Atlandreous sends a scout ship ahead to Kroteir to leave them weapons. Atlandreous is only doing what he thinks he needs to do to make things right. He is going against his king's orders, but he thinks he has enough merit to be forgiven. Atlandreous has learned the culture of Halotropolis. Now, he may have to destroy it.

CHAPTER IX
FOR YOUR KINGDOM

Atlandreous gets on a ship after making sure his shipment is safe. It is going to take two weeks for him to get home. The Alnilam fleet will take a longer route to escape a potential sea battle. During the voyage, the Alnilam Supreme Commander wonders what is really going on back home. His military is at high alert. The Halotropolian military is ruled by Baudan, who is a firm believer in God. The skirmishes between the city states started because of religious beliefs. Now, the military of Halotropolis is knocking on the doorstep of the Alnilam Kingdom. There is a high level of tension between Cetrono's and Icaras' cities. The city of Masaba has taken sides with Halotropolis. The only ally Alnilam has is the city-state of Vasic, which is not as strong as Masaba. Alnilam is in serious trouble with fewer men and cavalry.

At this point, Cetrono is a puppet to his Halotropolian military. Baudan has put martial law in effect. When the fighting broke out between the city-states borders, the Halotropolis Supreme General took full command of the civilian and military population. Some of the politicians from Halotropolis even took sides with Baudan. With the religious movement to one God, Cetrono and his Senate are not in good standing with his masses. Cetrono's political circle is still sticking to their traditional religion of gods. Now, the new religion is taking over Halotropolis.

Cetrono is still the main political figure of Halotropolis, but right now, the Halotropolian King is only a figurehead with little power. Before starting any assaults on the Alnilam Kingdom, Cetrono asks Baudan to wait until Tess is back on the peninsula, dead or alive. Cetrono is trying to buy some time. Because there are still a vast amount of people in Halotropolis seeing Cetrono as their ruler, Baudan agrees. Both leaders are walking on broken glass right now for power.

Atlandreous and Orion get to the peninsula and dock at Vasic. They are ordered straight to Alnilam. There are no details of what is really going on. They get on their giant elk and ride quickly to Alnilam. The giant elk are very fast and agile animals but hard to ride at high speeds for a long journey. Even though they have ridden these beasts thousands of times before, the giant elk take a lot out of the riders because of their size and strength.

Atlandreous and Orion finally get to Alnilam. They are greeted by Erasmus, Nieander, and Hamon. There are little pleasantries between them. Time is the essence. With their commander being back, there is an enormous amount of work to be done. Atlandreous goes alone, straight to Icaras' palace, to find out exactly what is transpiring between the two city-states. The Alnilam Supreme Commander is going directly to the source. He does not want to speculate anything before making plans for battle.

Atlandreous is escorted by the palace guards towards Icaras, who is in a meeting with his councilmen.

Atlandreous walks straight in and says, "Sir, I need to know exactly what is going on here."

Icaras says, "Councilmen, leave us. I'm glad you're back. Your people need your leadership."

Everyone leaves the room. Atlandreous is very concerned, but does not lose his composure. The Alnilam Supreme Commander has been waiting for weeks to get to this point. He is hoping not to go to war with Halotropolis and Masaba. He knows this war can destroy every society on the byland. Atlandreous is a changed man from his recent adventure. In a way, Atlandreous wishes he had not gone to the Khartoum Kingdom. It has affected his clear thinking of pure military values. The words, *what if*, goes through his head more often. While the Supreme Commanders wait for the room to clear, his mind is overloaded with the situation, and goes into a daze.

Icaras goes right to the point and says, "You have not missed much since Orion was ordered to the delta. You are in command to defend us from Halotropolis. I need to know where you stand. I can see your mind is clouded."

Atlandreous replies, "Sir, you tell me to court a girl from Halotropolis, and now there is a possibility I may have to destroy her society."

Icaras says, "This is something I didn't expect, and nether did Cetrono. Even though I think Cetrono is a good leader, he can't stop this religious movement. Now, his stature is lessoned with his people. There is going to be a big change in Halotropolis, and it may even destroy our way of life. The whole peninsula is in chaos because of God. The only city staying out of the fight is Alnitak. If Alnitak enters the fight, our kingdom will be taken over. Colligitar and his politicians are not so happy with our trade. Many of their high officials have been cut out of the loop because of our commerce. Colligitar's city was the only middleman on the byland. Now, Alnilam is a true competitor, but Alnitak has enough problems on their hands right now. Tarentum wants to expand. Baylonis' men are on the border with a high level of military activity of their own. Even if Alnitak wants to be on our side, they can't. With this new religious movement, it is turning the world upside down."

What Atlandreous hears from Icaras reminds him of the time on the mountain, and how he is starting to believe in the same God. It is a revelation to the Alnilam Supreme Commander. In Atlandreous' mind, he feels maybe mankind wants to go to the next level of evolution. He knows there has to be chaos before there is clarity. He wants to evolve into the doorway to God, but with the responsibility to his military, he cannot put what he thinks into the equation. Atlandreous goes back and forth between God and gods. With hard choices, he almost becomes an atheist towards all religions. His kingdom is counting on his military skills. Since his adventure, he also notices more of his own people changing to God. Even on the way to Icaras' palace, the Supreme Commander has seen two new temples in the name of God.

Atlandreous regroups his thoughts and says, "I will fight to protect our kingdom no matter what. The thoughts I had before are completely wiped away from my mind. You gave me a responsibility. I can't let emotion dictate my judgment. The world is changing. You are my king, and you have my complete loyalty. May I get my armies prepared for battle?"

Icaras says, "I have always believed in you. This is why you're in command. Do what you need to do. I concur with your decision of allowing Tess to return home. After I gave the order, I started to regret my decision of having her sent here. You're starting to become a very good politician and diplomat."

Atlandreous goes to his generals and captains. All of the men Atlandreous brought from Mintaka are at the Alnilam Military Hall. The Supreme Commander wonders how he had done as a leader before he went to Khartoum. Atlandreous gave his generals duties to perform in his absence.

Atlandreous goes inside the Alnilam Military Hall. He greets his generals. Inside, his military officers stand up and salute their commander.

Atlandreous walks in with a calm face and says, "You may sit down. I have been absent for over nine months. I need to know where we stand militarily, and what our spies are telling you."

Nieander says, "We have all come together in our quest to make our military strong, and we all believe in you, but we need to know how your mission went. I have heard you let Tess go back to Halotropolis. I am not judging your decision. We just need to know how to make things happen in your administration. Questions will be asked by our men."

Atlandreous pauses for a second and says, "Courting Tess was an experience I will remember for a very long time. You all know it was not my idea to court anyone. She is a good person and a good leader to her people, but it was the best decision to let her go back home. If I kept her under our guard, it would have given Baudan more of a reason to attack. I know their military has a great deal of politics to play with. Their government is upside down right now. The way our borders are currently, it will take three and a half weeks for Halotropolis' military to be ready for a preemptive strike against us. As Supreme Commander, I do not know where we stand in this potential battle. Giving you leadership before I left, I need to know what you have accomplished for the safety of our kingdom. I spoke to Orion, and he has already started on the construction of the new bow with the first shipments of molless. He has already five hundred bows completed. In two weeks, he will have another one thousand. He has every capable person on the project of the new weapon. With the shipment of the molless tree, I have sent half of the total consignment to Halotropolis. It will take a week to get there. This will give us three more weeks to produce this new weapon before our enemy can do the same. We need to show Halotropolis we are not their enemy. For the next two weeks, we will have the technological advantage. They will know that. By that time, I hope we can resolve our differences with Halotropolis."

Nieander stands up and says, "The giant sloth will protect the formation of our infantry. They have been tamed and trained. In the last six months, we have already grown to three hundred giant rhinos, two hundred giant sloths, two thousand mammoths, one thousand elephants, and three hundred giant elk. This is the largest cavalry ever created by our kingdom. With your leadership, we have hoped to surpass your expectations when you got home."

Hamon stands up beside Nieander and says, "Before the last shipment of the molless trees to Alnilam, I made crossbow carriages. All I need is the molless tree lumber to complete the new mobile weapon. We have tested the crossbow, and it can shoot over two hundred yards with great accuracy. Because of being light weight, the new weapon can be moved around the battlefield quickly. In one week, you will have two hundred such weapons, along with our catapults."

Erasmus stands alongside his comrades and says, "Everyone is trained to utilize our new steal swords. In the last six months, I have made them indestructible. The weapon cannot be broken on the battlefield. However, the materials are very hard to come by. I have worked on the problem, but I am falling short of what we need for this war. I have four thousand new swords for our front lines. I will have two hundred more in two weeks. I don't have the materials to build anymore than that."

Atlandreous says, "We have almost a hundred thousand Alnilam warriors. With Vasic, it gives us a hundred and forty thousand men total. So, we have a weakness to our enemy. The Halotropolian people will have better weapons inside their infantry and more cavalry. It is not your fault, Erasmus. We need to know where we stand before we go to battle. I am so proud to fight with you all. It is sometimes better not to micromanage people and let them blossom on their own. You all have done well."

Orion stands up and says, "Sir, Halotropolis has over a hundred thousand people to fight for them, and Masaba has close to ninety thousand more. In the last nine months, God has dominated their two city-states. The two cities say they will fight as one for God. We all know religion is a powerful weapon. Our planters say they have almost twice the cavalry and archers. We are outnumbered considerably across the board."

Atlandreous says, "Take this as a humble statement. When I went to Halotropolis, they saw me as something bigger than I am. They feared me. Therefore, I will use that against them. Now, go to your men to get prepared. We will leave in two weeks to show force. If Baudan wants a fight, we will give it to him."

Everyone is adjourned. All generals go their separate ways to accomplish their goals. The Alnilam military works on their new weapons. It is their hope to defeat a superior number on the battlefield. The civilians work night and day to get prepared for the possibility of war. Women and children work twenty hours a day. There is no one in the surrounding area of Alnilam that is not working on projects to protect their kingdom.

Atlandreous goes to his father right after the meeting. He needs his father's advice on what to do. The Alnilam Supreme Commander goes to Thanos' chambers. He has not seen his father for over nine months.

Atlandreous sees his father for the first time and says, "I have missed you Father. You would have been proud of me during my adventure."

Thanos stops him and replies, "I have always been proud of you."

Atlandreous asks, "What do you think I need to do next?"

Thanos put his hand on his son's shoulder and says, "It is not up to me anymore. I am leaving you to do your duty. I have brought you up to make your own decisions, but I have enabled you by playing your politics. I am not going to do that anymore. You're a grown man, and I know you will do the right thing for your kingdom. You need to have your own triumphs and defeats without me. This is the only way you can grow. I love you son. I will listen to you when you need to vent, but ultimately you will make your own decisions. I am going back home to protect your mother. My time is done here. I have created a leader. When you go to the battlefield, I know you'll be the leader you are. I heard what you did with Tess. It was a good decision. It would have been something I would have suggested, and you had the common sense to do it without me.

You have compassion, understanding, and direction. You are at the right time and the right place. You have everything a leader needs to excel and change mankind for the better. This war will make you immortal in the eyes of the people on the byland. Your name will be remembered to the end of time."

Atlandreous smiles at his father and replies, "I will need your guidance, sir. I will have this under control. Give my mother my love, and I will leave you to do what you need to do. Thank you. I hope I can be the father you are to me one day."

Atlandreous leaves the room almost in tears. He loves his father. He feels like a bear cub leaving his mother's den to take on the world alone. Atlandreous goes to his quarters to sort things out to himself.

Meanwhile, the Halotropolis Supreme Commander is meeting with his generals to start a preemptive strike against Alnilam. He knows he has the cavalry and manpower to overwhelm Atlandreous. Baudan is waiting on supplies and heavy artillery to take the Alnilam Kingdom.

After regrouping, Atlandreous goes into military protocol. He puts all emotion to the side to protect his kingdom, but in the back of his mind, he thinks of Tess. She is haunting his thoughts. She is a good woman trapped in politics.

Other than the two city-states of Halotropolis and Masaba, the rest of the world's majority believes in different gods. Atlandreous wonders in his own mind if he is wrong in his own beliefs. To the Alnilam's Supreme Commander, the most beautiful woman has faith in something totally different than most of his countrymen.

Three more days before Alnilam's military marches to their border with Halotropolis, Atlandreous goes to the Alnilam King. Icaras welcomes Atlandreous to his garden.

Icaras says, "What can I do for you? Are we ready for war? I don't want this. I feel it will be the destruction of our society even if we win."

Atlandreous replies, "With all the reports coming in, I don't think Halotropolis has all their militaries together. About forty thousand Halotropolian warriors are on our border. I think in the next two weeks the numbers will be quadrupled. I have my men ready. I need three more days of preparation. I gave our people the intangible. You never get what you want when you want it.

The extra three days will give us the advantage we need to take on our neighbors. I will not attack first. I will let them make the first mistake."

Icaras replies, "I totally understand what you are doing. Do what you need to keep this kingdom from our enemies. I am battling the Senate to allow you to do your task. They have their own agenda. Our Senate and politicians thinks the whole world can be renovated without violence."

Every Alnilam general who had a project comes forward with their accomplishments. It is not exactly what Atlandreous totally needs to fight this war, but it gives him the building blocks. Atlandreous' mind is going a hundred miles an hour. He thinks of a way a battle can ensue, but, Atlandreous thinks of ways to fight later down the road. With the numbers going to this battlefield, the war cannot be won on the first day. This war will last for days or weeks.

Orion works on his new weapon, using the molless tree. He goes to the site where the bows are constructed and works on them himself. With dedication, the Alnilam people work even harder because of Orion's leadership. This gives him the momentum he needs to accomplish his goals for battle. He has even developed a strategy to make more bows as the Alnilam Army marches to the battlefield. Orion's idea is to make bows on large carriages as they go to the border. Because it will take a week by wagon to get to the front, it will give him an extra two hundred bows. With the extra bows, it will give Atlandreous an extra reserve of archers.

Atlandreous knows what he needs to do. Scenarios are turning in his head, even when he sleeps. The Alnilam Supreme Commander gets little rest. He thinks of Baudan and what he may do. Atlandreous wants to go to Tess to see what can be done to stop these hostilities. It is a good idea in theory, but it will not happen. The Alnilam Supreme Commander may never see Tess again. The friendship was there. Now, it has been stripped away by war and politics.

The closer it gets to the departure from the city of Alnilam, the harder everyone works. Icaras' people work on their projects at a feverish pace. Atlandreous is ecstatic with the progress in such little time. He has given his friends a timeline, and they have over exceeded his expectations.

Atlandreous goes to Erasmus' home. The Alnilam Supreme

Commander wants to go over battle plans and to see how his friend is doing. He wants to make sure Erasmus has the confidence to lead his men into battle. The two meet, and there is a little small talk for a couple of minutes.

Atlandreous goes straight to the point and says, "I came here to apologize to you. I knew you were having troubles with supplies before I entered the military chamber. I had to exploit our weakness. When a person in command exploits weaknesses, it pushes the others to compensate with their strengths. We all work as a team. I want you to listen to me. I am giving you a new responsibility. I want you second in command right under me. I'm making you Rear General of our army. If I am killed or can't give orders, I need your leadership to take over the battle. It will be a hard task. You will be the first officer ordered to the front lines to offset weak spots in our army. To win battles, I will be sending you and our men in harms way. What do you think?"

Erasmus replies, "I have always loved you as a brother, and I will give my life to make yours better."

Atlandreous says, "This is why I am giving you this promotion. I know I can count on your loyalty and leadership."

Atlandreous goes over different scenarios which can happen. Before their departure to the border, the other generals wonder why Erasmus is higher in rank. They all work hard on their tasks, but Erasmus was the only general to fall short in what was expected of him. It really bothers Orion. Orion respects Atlandreous' decision but wonders why. It eats at him, and he goes to Atlandreous.

Atlandreous is working on plans with a supply officer. Orion looks at the military goods while Atlandreous gives the last orders to take them to the front.

Atlandreous sees Orion and asks, "How are your men? I am going over supplies and I think I can give you more carriages than what you asked for."

Orion says, "If you can give me an easier way to transport my supplies and build bows on transit, I thank you. I do have a question before we depart?"

Atlandreous says, "What can I do for you?"

Orion asks, "I am just wondering why Erasmus is higher in rank than your other generals. I will always obey your command. I am just wondering why?"

Atlandreous replies, "I am truly blest with what I have. You came to me. Do you think that Baudan has the same respect from his men?"

Orion says, "No, I don't. Halotropolis is in martial law. Baudan is taking full control. You could have done the same, but you haven't. Our military is on your side and so is our civilian population. With your leadership, you know martial law will only blow up in your face later."

Atlandreous says, "Our friendship is the best advantage in this situation we are about to encounter. We look at each other as brothers and respect one another. If we do have questions, we talk about it. Nothing can ever destroy us on the battlefield. I will give you the reason, and I know you will understand my thought process. I want you to remember this with the people you command. Erasmus is a good leader, and it is crunch time. There is nothing he can do to make more steel swords. He feels he has failed you and me. When someone feels this way and is a true leader, you have to give them more responsibility so they can forget their failures. You give them a purpose to keep those leadership qualities going forward."

Orion asks, "Why? If a person fails even if it is not their fault, a person can easily fail again, right."

Atlandreous asks, "Do you think Erasmus is a good leader? Do you think he wouldn't give his life for you or me? Because of our friendship, do you really think he would ever fail again?"

Orion says, "No, but his confidence is shot because of his failures. It will make him second guess on the battlefield."

Atlandreous says, "Actually not. He is second in command and the burden of failing is behind him. He has something to fight for. This is my decision, and I hope you can agree."

Orion says, "His confidence may not be there when it is crunch time, but I believe in you and your decisions. I will do whatever he says on the battlefield, even if it kills me."

Atlandreous says, "Remember this example of human nature. You will completely understand one day."

The Alnilam generals have done everything they can before they go to the borders. If they wait too long, Baudan will start a preemptive strike and take Alnilam. Atlandreous knows Baudan's ego will come to the battlefield. Everyone from Halotropolis knows Atlandreous is the best general on the peninsula, but with more manpower and cavalry, Baudan is confident he can take Atlandreous straight on.

With the potential war, Tarasios, Atlandreous' friend from Mintaka, is a general of the Masabaian Army. Atlandreous knows his friend is honoring his heritage, but the scenario the two friends may fight one another is haunting him. In the Alnilam Supreme Commander's mind, he thinks the whole world has gone mad, and God would not have let this happened. Atlandreous is going agnostic in his beliefs the more he thinks about it. The only person he thinks he can count on is himself. Atlandreous has to do his duty, but, he really does not know what is ahead of him.

Atlandreous arrives at the border of Halotropolis. Alnilam planters go back and forth telling what the enemy is doing. To the Alnilam Supreme Commander, the enemy is still not completely ready to attack Alnilam. Baudan's men and the Masabaian military are not in position for a decisive preemptive strike.

Atlandreous goes to his headquarters on the front line. He has all of his generals with him at the tent. Atlandreous has been chosen to be supreme commander over the Vasic and Alnilam military by both kings. His title is no longer the Alnilam Supreme Commander, but the Master of War. To the new Master of War, it will be hard to get the two city-state militaries together to fight as one, but, Atlandreous also knows it is difficult for Baudan to do the same.

Atlandreous stands in his tent and says little. While the new Master of War hears others talk about their battle tactics, he gets ideas of how his men are thinking. Atlandreous stands in the middle of his council and generals while he waits for complete silence.

Atlandreous says, "This is it. There is no turning back. We will have war. Even though there is no blood on the battlefield, it will end in bloodshed. The enemy has more than expected warriors here. We have to take every asset we have to create an advantage."

Nieander asks, "How are we going to win this war?"

Atlandreous says, "Alnilam fights as one on the front. We know how to fight together. The Vasic army, who is commanded by Roubertus, will take our flanks and rear center. I will use Vasic's cavalry together with ours and punch a hole in Halotropolis' Army. When the time is right, Baudan will make a mistake. Alnitak is still staying out of this war; they are watching their borders to their North."

The next day, Atlandreous asks Baudan to meet dead center of their two borders. Baudan accepts the summit of the two kingdoms. He wonders what Atlandreous wants. Does the new Master of War want to negotiate or buy some time for something else? Baudan also knows Alnitak is staying out of the fight. He feels betrayed. Halotropolis has tried to get Alnitak to take their side, but Colligitar does not want to get involved.

Atlandreous and Baudan meet horse to horse, dead center on the border alone.

Atlandreous looks at Baudan and knows he is overconfident because of his numbers on the battlefield. The Master of War knows he has to think differently to get the Halotropolian Supreme Commander to fear him. They just look at each other for over a minute. Atlandreous pulls on his reins and looks at the army behind Baudan.

Atlandreous points at the army which is in front of him and says, "Do you think your army will fight as one or will your religions conflict and unravel your troops?"

Baudan replies, "They will fight as one. This will be the last time we speak. What can I do for you?"

Atlandreous says, "Let us have one battle on equal ground and do this as gentlemen. Years down the road after this conflict, this peninsula will become one. If there is an honorable fight between us, the later generations will have no reason not to come together and make a powerful society. If we fight dirty, there will be generations of hate, and the majority of our people will not accept unity. Do you agree?"

Baudan says, "You're an honorable man. I wish I was fighting alongside you in battle. However, like you said, I am like you, and setting my emotions to the side to do my duty. There is no choice but to do this. There is no good general that loves war. If they do, they are mad. I will take you, Atlandreous, on any battlefield. Let us have an honorable fight. God will go against your gods. Let's plan the day after tomorrow in the Castin Valley."

The next day, they meet on opposite sides of the Castin Valley. Both generals will be able to see the fight in between the valley below. It is the perfect battlefield for a gentlemen's war. Both armies will meet the next day and fight until there is a winner.

The night before the fight, Atlandreous gets all of his generals together inside his tent.

Atlandreous says, "Is there anything we have left out?"

Roubertus replies, "I believe in you and so do my men. If we fight this war, everyone on the battlefield will lose. Alnitak has the largest army on the peninsula. Will they just take over our governments after this battle?"

Atlandreous replies, "They are powerful enough now to take complete control. But many people from Alnitak make good trade because there are separate city-states. The world is about to change and this battle will start it. We don't know what will happen to the world after this, but I do have confidence in mankind."

That night, Atlandreous cannot sleep. He thinks of Tess and God. God is still on his mind and he wonders if he is doing the right thing. Atlandreous wonders why God would still be in his thoughts. But his fate is sealed to fight in the Castin Valley. He will fight tomorrow and do what is expected of him.

CHAPTER X
THE CONSTELLATION OF ANTIQUITY
{PRESENT DAY}

Kyle runs to Duncan's tent and yells, "Wake up! Wake up! Get out of here!"

Kyle jumps into Duncan's tent and shakes his mentor. There are bullets flying all around. The Ugandan military makes a perimeter around the camp. The Ugandan soldiers still cannot see in front of them. With bad weather, the visibility on the mountain is only ten feet. Duncan's team cannot tell where the shooting is coming from. Bullets are hitting rocks and boulders all around the campsite. The people attacking are using silencers on their guns to prevent an avalanche. Kyle knows his attackers are well equipped and cannot be regular treasure hunters.

Rachael is still in her tent. A Ugandan soldier comes to her and drags her out. Right when she leaves, her tent is shredded with bullets. After being saved, she looks at the Ugandan soldier with great gratitude. They both go behind a boulder for protection while bullets fly by.

During the middle of the attack, Duncan is still unconscious. Kyle is trying to wake up the archeologist. Kyle looks at Duncan's closed eyes and notices his eyes are rolled in the back of his head. Kyle goes into panic and slaps Duncan in the face. He yells for him to wake up. Duncan finally becomes conscious and is unaware of what is going on. He has no earthly idea of the situation which surrounds him.

Duncan says, "What's going on? What's happening?"

Kyle yells, "We have to get out of here! There are people firing at us!"

In the background, the Ugandan soldiers try to find where their attackers are located. The Ugandan military finds the direction of the bullets coming towards them and fires back. Duncan and his crew are inside the Ugandan border. To him, Duncan thinks it could be the Congo Republic. Kyle does not know who is firing at their camp. In the background they hear a faint sound of someone getting hit with a bullet. Duncan's crew does not know if it is one of their people or their opposing attackers. Duncan, Kyle, and Rachael just wait until it is all over and let the Ugandan military take care of what they were sent to do. Duncan is really glad the Ugandan military came along. He knows his crew would be dead by now. All of a sudden the firing stops.

A Ugandan lieutenant runs towards Duncan.

The lieutenant says, "We got one of them. One of my soldiers wounded or killed one of our attackers on the spot. My soldiers went to investigate. I think the one we hit is still at his position."

Duncan is still in a daze from his sleep and asks, "Do you know who did this?"

The Ugandan lieutenant replies, "I don't know, sir, but it is not safe here anymore. We can't get supplies or more men up here for at least three more days. If this weather stays the same, we are sitting ducks. I—think—that is something you would say in America."

Duncan says, "You said it right. Thank you for your protection."

Right before the Ugandan lieutenant can turn around to give orders to his men; one of his soldiers runs to him and salutes his commanding officer.

A Ugandan soldier says in a stern voice, "You need to come here right now. You have to see this."

Duncan, Rachael, Kyle, and the Ugandan lieutenant walk towards the high ground. At a short distance, there are Ugandan soldiers looking at something behind a boulder. Duncan knows the answer of who attacked him is right behind the giant rock. They get to the site, and there is a body lying there. Duncan and the lieutenant look at the body more closely.

Duncan asks, "Who is this?"

The lieutenant says, "He is from the Congo military. His attire can only be issued from his military. On the map, we are only inches from their border. They knew our location. Being way up here, and the weather being so bad, they thought they could get the treasures we never found. The whole world knows we're here including the high officials of the Congo government. They can stage a fake find and say it came from their side of the border. They were expecting to find the treasures you found in Spain. With the bad weather, we can easily be killed and no one would be able to find our bodies. Are you ready to go back?"

Everyone looks at Duncan, and they are just waiting for him to say yes.

Duncan stares at the body and says, "No, there is something else here. I know it."

Kyle gets frustrated and says, "We have looked all over this area and there is nothing here."

Duncan says in a calm voice, "Kyle, you said you believe in me."

Kyle replies modestly, "I do, and I will do whatever you ask me to do."

Duncan says assertively, "I have awakened from the best sleep of my life. I will not be able to sleep for at least sixteen hours. When I do sleep, I need to sleep in the tomb we just found. I need to do this now before this vision leaves me. Lieutenant, I need you to protect this area. Your president said to do whatever I ask, and I am asking you to set up your men and keep this place from other invaders for two days."

That night, the lieutenant sets up a perimeter around the tomb and camp site. The lieutenant does not believe in all of this, but he does what is ordered. Duncan is concerned about the fog. Eventually, it starts to lift and it is easier to see. If his attackers come back with force, Duncan's life could be in jeopardy. Because Kyle and Rachael believe in Duncan, they stay. The two had the option to leave, even though it was dangerous in this weather. They both stand behind their mentor and friend. Kyle and Rachael have seen things from Duncan, short of being a miracle.

During the night, Duncan tells the tales of what he has seen in his dreams. He speaks of Atlandreous and why they are buried on the mountain. To Duncan, his visions have to be supernatural.

The next morning, the sky is clear. The weather is unexpected.

The archeologists can go back down the mountain, but they choose not to. They go ahead with what Duncan asks, even if their lives are in danger.

When Duncan feels safe, he goes into the tomb to find answers in his subconscious. He is ready for his next adventure. Duncan brings everything he needs to feel comfortable inside the tomb. He looks at the walls and tries to see what he can see in the writing of the ancient society. Then he starts to fall asleep very quickly. Duncan goes under with more control this time. It is like taking a nap compared to the visions before.

The next morning, Kyle and Rachael wait to see if he can wake up Duncan to get answers. Kyle waits and waits but cannot take it anymore. Kyle goes into the chamber to check on his friend. Duncan is barely awake and looks at Kyle.

Kyle asks, "What did you see?"

Duncan replies, "Everything I need to see. This mountain is full of answers. Give me a computer, a pencil, and piece of paper."

Duncan goes outside and goes to a computer to find a map of the mountain. He pulls up the constellation of Orion. Duncan feels the whole mountain is laid out with the heavenly body of Orion and each major star is an archeological site. At this point, he has no earthly idea why.

Right when he finishes his search on the computer Duncan asks Kyle to give him the global phone to call Mr. Callaway. Duncan does not care about his life, but he is responsible for his team. Immediately, Callaway answers the phone.

Because it is windy on the mountain, Duncan pulls away from the group to hear the tycoon better.

Duncan says, "Hello—Hello. I can hear you. I need more Ugandan troops up here. We have been attacked. Can you help us?"

Mr. Calloway says, "The weather is supposed to be good in the next couple of days. I will send over a hundred people to help. The Ugandan president said he will give us whatever we need. Tell me what you find when you have a chance."

Duncan hangs the phone up and pulls the teams together. He does not leave out the Ugandan military. He takes everyone to the computer and starts pulling things up on the screen. He goes to the Orion constellation sites like he already knows the answers, but he has to find a path to follow. He goes to a site and just looks at the screen.

Duncan says, "We have to go here on the mountain." As he points at the screen, his colleagues look closer to the picture on the computer. Then he says, "If we go straight down to this area we will find another answer to this saga. When the helicopters arrive, we will take the sword and a piece of clothing from the chamber to be carbon dated in France. The sword we found will be brought back to Uganda to be put into a museum."

They get to the location where Duncan had pointed to on the computer. Because the mountain is so large, they are not sure if they are in the right place. They search for hours until once again Rachael gets on her walkie-talkie.

Rachael says, "I've found something. There is something similar to the first tomb; it is a carved doorway into the mountain. If I hadn't seen the other tomb, I would have gone right by it."

Atlandreous says, "We'll be right there."

Duncan runs and climbs to Rachael's location. While they are walking, Kyle looks at Duncan and cannot believe what he is witnessing. This adventure started with the city inside the mountain in Spain and has brought them to this tomb in Uganda. It is as if Duncan has been here before. He has a clairvoyant sense of the people lost to time. It is something that cannot be explained.

When Duncan and Kyle get to the site, Rachael's team is trying to open the doorway. It is identical to the tomb they just found, but time is of the essence. If their attackers are pursuing the teams, the archeologists do not have the luxury of setting a schedule for a proper excavation.

Rachael and her team pry the door open. This is not as exciting as the door before because of the time issue. Everyone fears the people who attacked them earlier will come back with greater numbers.

Right when they start to enter the chamber, they hear helicopters coming towards them. They do not know where the noise is coming from. They are all hoping it is the Ugandan military. The Ugandan lieutenant runs to Duncan and orders his men to get in defensive positions.

The Ugandan lieutenant runs to Duncan and says, "With the mountain's acoustics, I have no way of knowing if it is my men or the Congo Republic."

Duncan says, "Everyone inside the chamber! Take your positions, Lieutenant!"

The archeologists go inside. Duncan is the last to enter. Right when he enters the lieutenant hears his walkie-talkie. It is the Ugandan military. The helicopters hover overhead. One by one the Ugandan military sends men by rope down from their helicopters. If the helicopters try to land, it could start an avalanche. Over one hundred fifty Ugandan men are sliding down ropes to the ground. A Ugandan officer from a helicopter runs toward his lieutenant and then stands at attention waiting for orders. Duncan feels more confident and knows he can go back to work and not be on a timed schedule.

One helicopter almost lands to retrieve artifacts to be carbon dated. The rest of the helicopters fly over the mountain to find the Congo military. Because everyone is on the side of the Ugandan border, the helicopters have every right to kill anyone who enters their domain without question. Duncan wonders if this will start a war between the two nations. War is something the archeologist does not want.

The archeologists go into the chamber and see it is another tomb just like the first one they found on the mountain. It has different writing, but they can tell the same society made it. It is also vacant of treasures except for another golden sword inside the male sarcophagus.

Because the tombs are so similar, it is a quick excavation. The archeologists will come back to this site and study it more closely in the future. There is too much going on for a thorough excavation. Duncan knows there are more sites on the mountain.

One hour later, they find the other two sites. The archeologists found their position to the first and second tombs. The third location was much easier. It is exactly like the stars on Orion's belt, and Betelgeuse represents the first tomb they found first. Duncan thinks the people buried lower down the mountain have to be less important to the person buried above.

The three tombs on the lower part of the mountain are simpler in construction than the first. After they go into each tomb, they find the same thing one man and one woman in stone caskets. Each one has a golden sword in each of the male's sarcophagus. All the writing is different, but it also seems to tell a tale of these people.

Duncan takes all three swords from the tombs and puts them against a boulder outside the last archeological site they found.

Duncan says, "They are all the same size. These swords were constructed by the same person. The writing is identical except at the handle. The engravings have to be the names of these people."

Rachael, look at the names more closely. "If I'm right, it will give you a clue to their alphabet. These people had to be the beginning fathers of the civilization we are looking for."

Kyle asks, "How did you know where to look?"

Duncan says, "In my dreams I remember someone called Orion, but he spoke in a different language. I don't know what role he plays in this story. Alnitak, Alnilam, and Mintaka are all in my dreams as cities. All three names are the names on Orion's belt. They are places in the civilization I vision in my dreams, and all three cities play a pivotal role in their history. When I looked on the map on the computer, I knew right away where the other tombs were located. There are no more stars except Bellatrix, Regel, and Saiph. The star, Bellatrix, is where we have to go next on the map of this mountain. But if you put the map where the star should be located, we will have to go around this giant rock to get there. The next site will be the hardest to find. There are multiple answers there. I know and feel it."

Kyle asks, "What do you think we will find there? You have been right about everything we have encountered so far. This is almost unbelievable."

Duncan says, "I have been blest by what I have seen, but there are numerous unanswered questions in my mind. I don't know what we'll find. I got us here to this point because of my dreams, and I know I have to go back to find out what happens in this tale. I wrote down everything I dreamed about in the first find in Spain. Now, I have to find another fitting piece to this puzzle. Orion was the key to finding more here. If I go back to sleep, I know I can find answers to what we seek. I hate this. I don't want it. I would rather not know the answers than have something telling me to keep looking. I don't have control anymore. I want my life back. I want to be a simple archeologist again. It is almost like a curse."

Kyle says, "It is not like a curse. There is a reason for you to know the next step. It seems the past is asking you to go forward for the next generation of humanity. Something happened to this civilization; their world is talking to us right now with these finds, and you're the ambassador."

The next day they go to another location. With snow on the mountain, it will be almost impossible to find anything. Where they are looking will take a while. There will be a great number of second guessing as to where to look. They have taken measurements of the map of Orion and the mountain. From the computer to the mountain, the location is not in a straight line like the belt of Orion. In some spots, the archeologists will have to dig into deep snow.

After hours, Kyle looks at the side of the mountain and says on his walkie-talkie, "I think I've found it. I've found another doorway to the past."

All archeologists run over to Kyle. It is at a location where they thought it would not be likely found. While Kyle looks at the site, the lines are on the mountain wall and the ground surface. It is like a jigsaw piece implanted in the ground. The doorway is over a thousand pounds. It is going to take everyone to lift the stone out of the mountain. Whoever constructed the doorway made sure it would be almost impossible for someone to break into. With no tools around, it would be out of the question for a straggler to open the doorway. A person would know to go here directly with the right tools. The people who constructed this site knew what they were doing.

Duncan and the team try to think of any way to open the entrance with what they have on hand. They try a couple of ways, but they keep failing. Everyone is getting frustrated at the obstacle. Then someone has the idea to inch the stone up from the ground with shovels and crowbars. They take one side and inch up with their shovels and then stab their crowbars on the other sides to move it up, using leverage from the mountain surface. Everyone works together inch by inch. It takes almost thirty minutes and a great deal of muscle.

It is time; they move the stone and there is a small opening going down into the mountain. Inside, there is a small staircase carved out from the mountain. No one knows what is down the corridor. The archeologists shine their flashlights down the hall, and they know it goes a long way. There are over twenty-five people just looking down the hallway waiting to go in.

Duncan says, "Well Kyle, it is your turn."

Kyle replies, "Excuse me, Rachael, I finally found something first, but if it were not for you, we would not be here. Rachael, you are the one that should go in first. You have given us the opportunity to be right here—right now."

Rachael is speechless, but says, "Okay, I'll take it. Thank you for being a gentleman. I will accept this and remember this for the rest of my life."

They all laugh and go down the hallway inside the mountain. Rachael's heart feels like it is about to explode with so much excitement. Everyone almost walks on their tiptoes going in. As the archeologists go deeper into the mountain, the hallway gets larger. The writings on the wall are not like the city inside the mountain in Spain. They go through the walkway and see a cavern fifty feet into the mountain. Duncan knows this is the doorway to his answers.

When they get inside the chamber, Duncan shines his light on the walls and glances around the large room.

Duncan says, "Remember the library inside Naissance; this place is very similar. Look at the tablets and writings on the wall."

Kyle shines his flashlight and goes to an artifact and says, "Look at the tools they used. This tool is similar to what people used during the Roman era."

Duncan replies, "I believe this place is between four hundred to six hundred years before Naissance."

Rachael asks, "What gives you this idea?"

Duncan says, "Look at the first tomb. It was very simple and so was the people who lay there, but someone dedicated so much time and effort in keeping these people's wishes of a simple place to rest."

In the room, there are more artifacts than in the library in Naissance. The archeologists pick up items as if they are in a garage sale. It is very overwhelming for Duncan's teams. There is a very strong presence of one God on the walls and artifacts. In Kyle's mind, Duncan has almost superhuman abilities to find everything and anything to the answers of these people. To Kyle, it seems as God has given Duncan a gift.

Then Kyle picks up an artifact which does not make sense to him. He studies it for a while even though there is a vast amount of other objects to look at first in the room.

Kyle says, "What kind of beast is this person riding on this carved stone?"

Duncan says, "It is a giant sloth which seems to be tamed by this civilization. This does not make sense at all. The giant sloth of this size was only indigenous to the Americas. There is no evidence this particular giant sloth lived on this continent." Duncan stops and pauses for a moment and says, "Okay, I have to tell you something, and it cannot go any further than this room. I have seen these beasts in my dreams even before we came in here. I tell you, I don't believe it myself. I am letting these visions take me over to understand this. I know I have to sleep here in this room to find out more details about this society. I will let you know everything I see."

Rachael says, "Look at this. This man is riding a giant deer or elk. Look at the antlers. The antlers are really funny looking."

Duncan replies, "I never thought man tamed these creatures. I only thought man used them as food. This is a giant elk, or really a descendent of a deer, which became extinct after the Ice Age. This is revolutionary."

Kyle says, "Look over here. I have found a small rhino carved from stone with a man riding him. Duncan, do you understand this?"

Duncan says, "Look at the size between the man and the beast. This is not a normal rhino. It has to be an Elasmotherium."

Kyle asks, "What is that?"

Duncan replies, "After the Ice Age, there were rhinos close to twenty feet long with one giant horn. The animal could weigh as much as four to five tons."

Rachael goes to the side of the chamber and sees something made of gold. It is a giant horn off some kind of beast. She tries to pick it up, but it is too heavy to lift off the ground.

Rachael looks at the golden horn closely with her flashlight, and Duncan and Kyle come to her side.

Rachael asks, "Can this be a mammoth's tusk?"

Duncan replies, "No, if I'm right, it is the horn of the Elasmotherium. It is something eclipsazoologist have never really found. If these people knew of these creatures, which means these beasts survived the Ice Age. In my dreams, I see these creatures as military weapons. This is why I think this is an Elasmotherium."

Kyle and Rachael know Duncan is right, but they do not want

to believe it. Looking at what the rest of the world would think; Duncan's visions seem to be impossible. They all want to understand how this civilization lived. All of them have their own thoughts of how this civilization prospered, but Duncan is on top of everything with his dreams. Kyle and Rachael accept Duncan's visions. They believe in their teacher, and are looking forward to understanding this with their mentor. They all keep looking around and find golden artifacts of animals of the day. So far, they have found golden mammoths, giant sloths, giant rhinos, elephants, and giant elk. The oddest thing to the archeologists is every artifact has a person riding these beasts. They all wonder to themselves how these people tamed such giant mammals.

Rachael looks at the writing on the walls of the chamber. She tries to use what she knows from Naissance to make sense of it all. The pictures are similar to all the tombs on the mountain.

That night, Rachael goes to Duncan's tent.

Rachael says, "I've looked at everything. I've tried to look at the writings at Naissance and these tombs. The only thing I can conclude is Naissance and these tombs came from the same society. With the pictures at Naissance, these people must have been connected somehow. The writing here is more primitive, but a great deal of writing is connected to Spain. With the tombs being so bare of treasure, these people put here were showing their world devotion, equality, and a lack of greed something I thought impossible during this time period. The people during the time of Naissance showed this as well, but I think this is almost five hundred years prior to the city inside our Spanish mountain just like you said. The reason I say this is because it would have taken centuries to build such a structure in Spain."

Duncan replies, "I saw these people in my dreams right before we got shot at the first tomb. I know these people here were the forefathers of the civilization in Spain. The person at the first tomb must have been the person to bring their civilization together. The others buried here are his friends, and they backed his ideas. When I go to sleep, I will see what happened. I know it's weird, but I just know. I tell you Rachael, I don't know if it is something I envision from something supernatural, or it is something I understand from the writings on the wall which I can only see in my subconscious. I don't expect you to believe me. I just ask you to respect my wishes in what to do next."

Rachael questions, "What are you asking?"

Duncan replies, "I need to stay in the chamber here for three to four days without interruptions. I will tell Mr. Callaway; he will understand. This is something the world needs to know. I need you to break the code to this writing to back my visions, but we can never speak of apparitions or dreams. The world does not understand the supernatural."

The next morning, Duncan calls Mr. Callaway.

Duncan says, "I need you to get the Congo Republic to back off."

Mr. Callaway asks, "What have you found so far?"

Duncan replies, "Some of the answers are here and some are elsewhere. If I don't do what I have to do here, the whole conquest of knowledge will stop here in Uganda."

Callaway says, "I will have to call Mr. Olson for help. He has connections to the Congo government. He is the only person in the United States which has the political know-how to help in this quest."

Mr. Callaway makes some calls. The tycoon calls Mr. Olson, and he does the unattainable. Mr. Olson stops the potential war between the two nations. That same morning a Congo military officer goes to make a treaty. He goes under a white flag towards the Ugandan military. Even though the Congo messenger is unarmed, The Ugandan soldiers keep their guns on the Congo officer.

The Congo military officer knows who Duncan is and walks slowly to the archeologist with his hands up.

The Congo military officer says, "Thirty years ago, this area was once ours. With new technology, it came under Ugandan's rule. Because there were political struggles during the time, our nation left it alone. Now my government wants to help with anything we can do. There will be no more disputes over boundaries."

Duncan replies, "I want knowledge, not war. This is too important for mankind to have such petty issues over land."

The Congo officer says, "There will be no more conflicts here. What will you need from my nation?"

Duncan says, "If you can, I need you to keep treasure hunters out of here. There is little gold here. There is some, but most artifacts are gold plated. It is not worth one life or a war."

For a couple of days, the archeologists work in the chamber.

They find things that amaze them. They now know the civilization from the past had a very strong military and had a great deal of technology for the day. Duncan and the archeologists cannot understand how this civilization did not make it over the course of time.

Inside the chamber, Kyle goes to an artifact on a table.

Kyle says to Duncan, "If this society had gone forward with new technology and survived, mankind would be to the stars by now."

Duncan replies, "Greed is the only answer here. Yes, they might have been wiped out by disease, but look at Naissance. This civilization was hiding from something. They needed refuge. Because the world has not really found any other technological civilization other than a few scattered like this one, we can see these people obviously were ahead of their time. I think the rest of the world didn't understand these people and destroyed them. It may be the rest of the world did not want to go forward with technology. Man did this in the dark ages. Technology was considered almost evil to the people of that time. Many religious leaders during the period had a great deal of power. Power was the true evil, not technology."

Kyle asks, "Do you think religion had a factor in these people's demise?"

Duncan replies, "Every war has to do with religion in some form or fashion."

Kyle asks, "What do we do next?"

Duncan says, "I am having dreams like I did in Spain. I need to finish what I started here. I will sleep inside this room tonight and sleep until this chronicle is complete in my mind. I need two days inside this chamber alone."

Kyle leaves his mentor to himself inside the chamber. Duncan goes in and waits to what took him before. For hours, he stays inside and nothing happens. He is so ready to go back to his dream world. It is hard to fall asleep. In his tedium, he tries to read the writings on the wall. After a couple more hours, he becomes tired and lies down. He tries to read and understand the writings, but finally falls asleep.

Chapter XI
Natures Intervention into Humanity

Two hours before sunrise, Atlandreous is still lying down trying to sleep. There is so much going on in his mind. He is so exhausted. The only thing keeping him going is his adrenaline and that is starting to wear off. He knows his body can only take so much. Being a leader to his generals and kingdom is really wearing him down. The Master of War turns over in his bed. All of a sudden the earth starts to shake. It is a severe earthquake. Atlandreous' tent falls right down from above him before he can even move. He is not hurt, but he gets disoriented for a moment. The earth trembles for over thirty seconds and starts all over again a minute afterwards. He struggles to get out of his tent and is thrown back down to the ground. A statue of the gods falls right on top of him during the second tremor. Because the sculpture is not really heavy and how it fell, the statue only startles the Master of War.

Soldiers run to Atlandreous' tent, and the aftershock throws them to the ground. Everyone is helpless. Horses and mammoths fall and break away from their confinements. During the animals' panic, the beasts run in terror over Atlandreous' warriors. Men run after the animals to calm them down. Tents around Atlandreous catch on fire. The camp site is in complete ineptitude.

Atlandreous finally gets out of from under his tent. He looks around and grasps the damage. To the Master of War, this would be a perfect time for Baudan to attack.

Atlandreous grabs the first soldier by the arm and says, "Find Erasmus and Roubertus right now. Bring them to me."

The soldier says, "Yes sir, I believe Erasmus is ordering a stronger perimeter around the camp, sir."

Atlandreous replies, "Tell him I don't care what he's doing. I want all generals to report here in twenty minutes!"

Right when the soldier runs off, Roubertus runs to the Master of War and stands tall and salutes him.

Atlandreous says in a stern voice, "Get your generals and captains here quickly. We don't have much time."

Roubertus yells, "This natural disaster could not have come at a worse time!"

Atlandreous yells back, "No—you don't understand. This is perfect. In the past, I have not believed in God, but now I do. Only God could have done this. You say this is a natural disaster. I say this is a natural blessing."

Roubertus says, "I don't understand. It was an earthquake; the worst I have ever encountered."

Twenty minutes go by; the Alnilam cavalry is under control. The fires are put out around the camp site. All generals and high officials are at Atlandreous' tent. Atlandreous is trying to put his tent back together. His generals report to him and help their leader. Except in repairing the tent, Atlandreous says nothing to his officers while he works.

After the finishing touches, Atlandreous stands up straight and takes a deep breath and says, "Everyone—inside my quarters."

Eight generals and twelve high officers walk into their commander's tent slowly. No one knows what the Master of War is doing. He is calm and collective. Atlandreous walks to a map on the floor and picks it up. The Master of War stares at the map and puts it on a table. Everyone looks at each other and tries to anticipate their commander's next move. Whispers are heard inside the tent. Atlandreous looks at his officers and waits until everyone inside his quarters is silent.

Atlandreous says, "Orion, leave now and go under a white flag. Tell Baudan I would like to speak with him at daybreak. Tell him I will meet him alone. This is the first step. Do not ride anxiously. Because of his tight grip with his civilian population, Baudan will be fearful of losing his power since he took martial law. It is a good time for the Halotropolian Senate to win back the power they lost. Now he is trapped between our military and the politicians back in his own kingdom. With the magnitude of the earthquake, all cities on the byland are either damaged or destroyed. I don't know where the earthquake hit the hardest. It can be Halotropolis, Alnitak, Masaba, Vasic, or Alnilam. Right now, Baudan is panicking. It is time to change the world as we know it. We must take care of this situation with Baudan and go straight home to assess our damage. Time is crucial here."

All officers and generals go their separate ways to go on high alert. Orion leaves and comes back an hour later. Orion goes straight to Atlandreous and jumps off his horse. Nieander is with Atlandreous going over the damage to their camp.

Orion says, "I spoke to Baudan personally. I told him that you want to rally with him. He agreed. He asked about you and asked why you didn't meet him yourself. You're right, he is panicking. He asked too many questions, and you could see he needed to get back quickly to his camp. He acted as if someone was going to steal something from him if he didn't get back quickly."

Atlandreous says, "If he came personally, he is desperate for answers to keep what he may lose if we attack. I will go to him as a desperate person, but turn it around. We will not fight this day. We need to go back home to help our civilian population. He will have to do the same to keep what power he has left. The Halotropolian Senate will be able to exert their power to take back what they lost before martial law. Cetrono's Senate does not want war. Of what I know and feel, their economy depends on Alnilam to prosper."

Nieander asks, "How are you so sure? What if Baudan needs to fight us for a moral victory? He thinks he can beat us. To him, he can go back to his people and say he took Alnilam under Halotropolian rule."

Atlandreous replies, "Manpower is the only thing that can help Halotropolis right now. If we fight and deplete that manpower, it can kill thousands of people Baudan swore to protect. He will be hated, and it will destroy him politically. Manpower is the only way to abate Halotropolis' suffering right now. Dead men on the battlefield can't rebuild kingdoms. Military leaders cannot lose the confidence of their civilian population. If Baudan fights us, he will not be able to rebound off losing men. Plus his men are wondering about their loved ones back home. Baudan has too much to lose at this point. This war we were about to have is the last thing on his mind right now."

At daybreak, Atlandreous and Baudan meet in the middle of the valley. Everyone from both sides looks at the two leaders who will either fight today or go home. Everyone from both sides knows they need to go home. Not knowing what is going on in each other's kingdom is the enemy right now.

Atlandreous looks at Baudan and says, "I humbly come to you. We can fight today if that is your choice, or we can go home to help our countrymen. There are no reports from my scouts or messengers of what city got hit the hardest from the earthquake. I hope to God people from both sides of the borders are safe. If in one month you still want to fight, we can. You have the molless tree, and you will have the same weapons. Because you have more men, you will have the advantage."

Baudan asks, "Is this a ceasefire? And did I hear you say the word God?"

Atlandreous replies, "For the time being, I don't want to fight you. Tess has allowed me see the light of God. You and I both have politics to play back home. Our civilian population we swore to protect is in danger not from war but from nature. It is time for you and me to not be warriors, but leaders to our damaged lands."

Baudan says, "I will leave ten thousand Halotropolian men here at the border to keep peace on my side of the border. I ask you to do the same. I will not attack or fight you for one month. Go back to your people, and I will do the same. Oh, by the way, Tarasios is still very loyal to Masaba, but he did not want to fight here today. Even though he is torn between you and his kingdom, this battle would have been brother against brother. I did not want to make him make that choice. Even though he is a good leader and would have done his duty, I put him in the back of the battlefield."

The Alnilam and Halotropolis military leave a total of twenty thousand men at the border. Atlandreous and Baudan rush back home to help their kingdoms. Atlandreous is exultant he did not have to go to war. He wonders how badly his kingdom is damaged after the natural disaster. He has not gotten any reports. He wonders what effect this natural disaster will have on the peninsula.

On the way back, Atlandreous gets reports that Halotropolis and Alnitak were hit the hardest by the earthquake. The kingdom of Masaba had some damage, but their buildings are made stronger than the other city-states. The King of Masaba put numerous resources into the construction of his city. The peninsula has had earthquakes in the past, but not like this one. Over five thousand people died in collapsing buildings in Halotropolis and Masaba alone. Because Vasic and Alnilam are farthest from the fault, the two cities had the least amount of damage from the earthquake.

The Master of War rides his giant elk back home. He rides ahead of his military. Atlandreous travels for twenty hours a day to get back to his capital in two and a half days. He rushes to Icaras' palace to speak to his king. Atlandreous goes through the streets and notices the older buildings did not stand against the natural disaster. Most of the Alnilam's new buildings are reinforced and have little damage. The Master of War goes by a hospital and sees hundreds of people outside the building. Physicians cannot get to the injured. It is devastating, but Atlandreous wonders how Alnitak and Halotropolis fared in the same catastrophe. Icaras is relieved that Atlandreous is back in the Alnilam capital. The Alnilam King can use his leadership skills to help pick up the pieces.

Atlandreous goes to Icaras' throne and says, "I have diverted aggressions between Halotropolis for the time being. How is the city structurally? What can my men do to help?"

Icaras says, "We had little damage except for older buildings and our fleet. Tsunamis destroyed half of our ships at sea. Because our ships are still coming in, I don't know the full extent this has caused our navy. Most of the city will be repaired within two weeks. If we use our military we can do it in seven days. Some buildings need to be leveled. We have the resources to rebuild our city."

Atlandreous says, "So that is the full extent of our damage from the ravaging earthquake. The earthquake was the most powerful I've ever felt. At Castin Valley, it seemed every city on the peninsula would have been turned into rubble."

Icaras says, "The mountain range which keeps our byland divided from the rest of the world is the power of the earthquakes. Masaba is damaged, but Halotropolis and Alnitak are the worst hit from the natural disaster. Alnitak is not talking about their needs. I have offered to help. Colligitar does not want anyone on the peninsula anywhere near his kingdom."

Atlandreous asks, "What of the government of Halotropolis? Are Cetrono and Tess still rulers of their land?"

Icaras replies, "That I don't know. I don't know if they are even alive. There have been numerous deaths inside Halotropolis. There is little communication between our two cities. I have got little information from the messengers of Cetrono's city."

Atlandreous says, "Let my men help Halotropolis. Let us use our military to make a joint effort to rebuild Cetrono's kingdom. This will let the tensions between our two city-states evaporate. You just said we were hit lightly. Alnitak and Halotropolis were hit the hardest. They need manpower. If Halotropolis was hit harder than the Castin Valley, the city is in a great deal of trouble. Halotropolis may be an ally in other future conflicts."

Icaras says, "Halotropolis will not let our military go in with our swords. I don't want another potential war."

Atlandreous says, "I will lead my men into Halotropolis unarmed."

In a stern voice Icaras says, "That can be suicide. I can't let you do that. I see your military and political mind, but what you ask is intangible."

Atlandreous replies, "Give me twenty thousand men to help. I believe Baudan will take me under a truce. He is about to lose everything. Baudan is a good general. If I help him politically, I think I can help make something of this disaster for the people on the peninsula. On the other hand, Alnitak has always been the black sheep on the byland. They will not ask for help. If they do, we should also help them as well. But Halotropolis is more likely to end up on a more positive note."

Icaras says, "I will give you fifteen thousand men to accomplish your goal. We cannot let our defenses down. I don't trust Baudan. The religion of their people will start a conflict between ours. If I let you go, it will only lengthen the time to rebuild our city. Fortunately, very few people in Alnilam were hurt. We have a surplus of medical supplies and physicians. I can't let any supplies go outside our kingdom until I am sure we are not in danger from the aftermath of this natural calamity."

Atlandreous says, "If we don't help, thousands of people will die within three weeks in Halotropolis. In our ranks I have some that believe in God. I will only take those people into Halotropolis.

There will not be a religious conflict. God is the new religion which I think will take over the peninsula. I don't think the rest of the world outside the byland is ready for the new religion, but going in the word of God will lessen the tension between our two city-states."

Icaras replies, "Religion is a fine line to walk on. I will not tell anyone of my true beliefs or faith. It is too dangerous. I have to comply with the masses and the politicians. Our youth is starting to change the world. Everything is about to change as we know it. I have to get our people ready for such a change."

Atlandreous asks, "What is your ideology of God?"

Icaras says, "Like I said, I go with the masses and politicians. I will not say anymore."

Atlandreous goes to the Halotropolian border with fifteen thousand men. He waits until a representative from Cetrono's kingdom. The Master of War tells the spokesperson of his intentions. This is too important for a Halotropolis speaker to make a decision. Atlandreous has been told a representative will meet him at the border at sunrise.

That morning, Atlandreous waits for the spokesperson from Cetrono's city. The Master of War does not know if Halotropolis will let him help. It is a faith of goodwill, but the King of Halotropolis may not have the power to let it happen. Atlandreous does not know if Baudan or Cetrono has control in the kingdom right now.

At the border that morning, five horses come towards Atlandreous. The Master of War waits for his answer. Then he sees something he did not expect. Tess is there to meet the Master of War. Atlandreous does not know what to say or do.

Tess is on her horse and says, "Atlandreous, what can I do for you? It is good to see you. Your people told the truth about the attack at the delta. That should not have happened. I am sorry my kingdom came to such a quick decision to attack your countrymen. The order did not come from my father."

Atlandreous stops for a second and says, "How is your kingdom? I have heard rumors that your city was hit hard from the earthquake. I have brought my soldiers to help rebuild your city. Alnilam is on schedule for reconstruction. We are fortunate. Icaras and I don't want hostilities between our kingdoms. This gesture is to help produce peace between our two city-states."

Tess says, "My people can use the assistance. My father needs all the help he can get. Our walls are badly damaged. Alnitak was hit the hardest, and the rest of the world outside our byland knows it. Colligitar has put most of his military to the main continent. I don't know if the Tarentum Empire is probing for weakness in Alnitak to attack. We offered to help, but Colligitar denied our request. No one from Halotropolis is allowed in Colligitar's city right now. With them being closest to the mountains on the main continent, I feel they are not letting the rest of the world know how damaged they really are. Colligitar is too stubborn and prideful to let anyone help him."

Atlandreous asks, "What of Baudan? Is your kingdom still under martial law?"

Tess says, "No, my father and the Senate have complete control. By you backing down, Baudan had to do the same. He came to my father and said he abated your threat. He is still in command and in good standing with our people. He is a very good military leader. Baudan was only doing his duty in protecting his kingdom."

Atlandreous asks, "The way you sound, time is of the essence to make Halotropolis stronger to ward off any potential war with the outside world. Do I have your trust to help rebuild your walls so you can protect your kingdom? It seems it may be in both our interests to make your defenses stronger."

Passive aggressively Tess smiles and replies, "Yes, let us continue our friendship. By the way, there were three days coming back from the delta that my men didn't have weapons. What if I had been attacked by some other foreign threat and there was no way to protect myself coming back to my kingdom?"

Atlandreous looks straight at Tess and humbly says, "It was not my intention to put you in harms way. Duty to my kingdom came first. I respected you, and I wanted you to go back to your father. I know you may be a little irate, but I think you would have done the same."

Atlandreous and Tess go towards Halotropolis. It takes five days with fifteen thousand Alnilam warriors to get to the damaged city. During their travel, they say little to each other. The skirmishes between the two city-states changed their outlook. They do speak of how to accomplish the goals in repairing Halotropolis. Atlandreous and Tess have too much on their minds to speak of friendship.

The Master of War is a little ashamed of taking the weapons and leaving Tess defenseless. Tess is also feeling guilty of being rude to Atlandreous when he gave his hand to help her city. Because of these emotions, Tess and Atlandreous avoid each other while they travel to Halotropolis.

Tess and Atlandreous get to Cetrono's city. The people of Halotropolis welcome the Master of War. With Atlandreous being in Khartoum during the bickering of the two city-states, the people of Halotropolis know he had nothing to do with the politics or skirmishes between Halotropolis and Alnilam. Cetrono made sure Atlandreous' name was in good standing with his people before he arrived.

Atlandreous goes to Cetrono's palace. The Master of War is escorted to the king, and Baudan is there as well.

Atlandreous walks to Cetrono with open arms and says, "I have brought my men to help. They are at your command. What needs the most attention?"

Cetrono says, "Our defensive walls are unstable. The shifting of the earth has put cracks in every part of our protective barriers. Any attack will have my walls tumbling down. They are going to have to be reinforced and reconstructed. I have the materials to do so. With your help, I can have this done in one week. Some of my Senate says it is ludicrous to let a potential enemy work on our defenses. I told them you have already seen these walls and know their weaknesses. My Senate and political circle fear you. Now that you're helping, you are looked upon as a hero and not an enemy. Right now, it is empires outside our peninsula which my Senate is concerned about. It is very important to ease the minds of my people. The Alnitak Kingdom may go to war with Tarentum. If Baylonis wins over Alnitak, I know their empire will not stop there. We have received reports of heavy activity with Alnitak's and Tarentum's borders. Something is up. As a leader of my people, I can't take any chances. This is why you're here."

Baudan says, "When we met on the battlefield, I told you I didn't want to fight you. I was only protecting my kingdom. Everything was escalating to war. I saw no choice. I respected you. Now, I respect you even more with the faith of goodwill. You and I may fight together down the road. If the tensions between Alnitak and Tarentum keep escalating, war will break out. We do not know the full extent of damage to Colligitar's city. If Alnitak's military can't hold off Baylonis' military, Tarentum may flood into our domain. Because there is little communication with Colligitar, we have to prepare for the worse."

Atlandreous says, "My men have brought tents to sleep outside your gates. My men need to seem humble to your people to show we are not a threat. Until we know more with Alnitak, our main concern is to rebuild your city."

On the first day, Atlandreous starts to rebuild the walls of Halotropolis. Cetrono's and Atlandreous' men work together. Both sides have been warned not to start any conflicts. If a conflict does start with the two societies, it has been stated that it will be punishable by death.

Because Atlandreous has used cement before back in Mintaka, it is second nature for the leader to make good time with the reconstruction. Halotropolis' Senate watches Atlandreous' men while they work. The politicians cannot say anything negative. Walls are quickly fixed and done with great quality. Everyone from Cetrono's city can tell Alnilam's men are working hard to make Halotropolis safe.

The Master of War was an enemy three weeks ago. Now he is helping the people of Halotropolis. If this was not so devastating of a disaster, Atlandreous would not be in Cetrono's kingdom. The opportunity of peace would never have happened this quickly.

The Master of War thinks most of the people on the byland want unity between the city-states. With God being such a dominate presence on the peninsula, it is bringing Vasic, Masaba, Halotropolis, and Alnilam together. Even though there are more than sixty percent of the people of the peninsula who still believe in the gods, a common religion is bringing people together. A natural disaster has made mankind more humble to their neighbors. Alnitak is the only city that is not a part of the group. The Alnitak society is more prideful. Colligitar's people feel they are the best on the peninsula and needing help will show weakness

Four days go by; Atlandreous is making good progress on the defensive walls of Halotropolis. Cetrono is very pleased with the effort of Atlandreous. Tess dedicates all of her time in the hospitals taking care of the people hurt from the earthquake. There are not adequate accommodations for the people injured from the natural disaster. More people die because of the lack of medicine and physicians.

On the fifth day since Atlandreous arrived, Cetrono sees over three hundred people from Alnilam riding to his gates. It is the physicians of Alnilam to help with the injured. Tess cannot believe what is going on. More of her people will be saved because of Icaras. Alnilam has brought every antibiotic and medical supply to help. Because Alnilam is the main supplier of medical supplies, they give them their surplus. It is a gift from the Alnilam King. Because of the difficult time, Icaras knows an alliance with Halotropolis is very important.

Tess goes to Atlandreous while he's instructing his men how to reinforce a wall on the east side of Halotropolis. Tess gets closer to Atlandreous so others cannot hear their conversation.

Tess says, "Can I speak to you, Atlandreous?"

Atlandreous stops what he is doing and replies, "What can I do for you?"

Tess seems to almost forget what she was about to say, but says, "I—have not been a very good host. When we met again a little over a week ago at our borders, I regret some of the things I said. I am a little ashamed with the way I acted to you. Because you left me and my men defenseless when we left the delta, I was angry. Everything I thought at that moment was wrong. Icaras has brought physicians to help my people. You are here to rebuild my kingdom. Most military generals would have let us die and take what is left of my kingdom. I—really appreciate what you are doing. Remember when we were about to go down the Iteru river, and I said respect is the building block of friendship. No matter what you do in the future, I will be that friend, and on your side."

Atlandreous says, "You showed me the way to God. I will remember that for the rest of my life. It was the mountain we climbed. It was a revelation to me. Climbing a mountain was the last thing on my mind at the time. I am indebted to you. In two days, I will be leaving to go back to my kingdom. I hope this will not be the last time we see each other. You were right; we are too busy to be more than friends. I see you with your people, and they need you. I still think you're beautiful and a good person, but responsibility to my people is the main objective in my life right now."

Tess says, "Before you leave, let us have a night to commemorate the new friendship of our two kingdoms. I would like to see you before you leave without the thought of work."

Atlandreous says, "That would be nice. Please let us try to not make this a spectacle. I am exhausted mentally with everything that has gone on in the last three months."

Tess replies, "I understand. Let us eat a ceremonial dinner at the palace with four guests each; not a lot of politics."

Atlandreous says, "Agreed."

Atlandreous keeps with his work. He is ready to go back home. With the will of good faith, he hopes the tensions between the two kingdoms are alleviated. The Master of War knows a war will destroy the peninsula in trade.

The day before the Alnilams are to march home, Atlandreous is at Cetrono's palace. The Master of War brings his highest officers. Tess has brought a couple of senators which believe in Atlandreous' intentions.

During the dinner Cetrono says, "Let us give a toast to our friendship. I am indebted to you and your men. Please tell Icaras I will return the favor when the time is right."

Atlandreous replies, "Thank you for letting us help in this time of trouble. I know you would have done the same. I know we are different in culture, but I realize we are from the same land and depend on each other in trade. I will leave tomorrow and go back to my people."

The dinner lasts for hours. Tess and Atlandreous talk about their adventure down the Iteru River. They stay outside the palace speaking as they did coming back from the Khartoum Kingdom. It seems as if their friendship never stopped. Cetrono leaves the two alone. Tess is a very good emissary to Atlandreous. In the last standoff, the Master of War was voted in leadership over Vasic and Alnilam's armies. The more the friendship grows, the less likely a war will start between the two cities. The war is abated, but it is not completely over. Some extremists on both sides are still mad and want vengeance.

When Atlandreous and Tess are in the middle of a conversation, Baudan goes to the Master of War. Tess excuses herself for the night. Atlandreous stands as she walks away.

Baudan says, "I wish you could stay a little longer."

Atlandreous replies, "My people need me back home. You and I have started a new friendship."

In a joking manner, Baudan says, "I still would have taken you."

Atlandreous replies and laughs, "We will never know how long you would have lasted."

Atlandreous and Baudan talk to one another about Tarentum and the war which almost happened. They speak as friends. There are no animosities between the two. They see each other as gentlemen and good leaders to their people. Atlandreous sees this act of good faith as a bridge between the two city-states. With the help from Alnilam, the bridge built here will never fall or be forgotten.

The next morning, Atlandreous goes back home. It will take Atlandreous twelve days to get back to his kingdom. Tess is a little sad to see him go. The Alnilam physicians stay for another two weeks. With the antibiotics and medical supplies, there are thousands that will be saved from certain death. Baudan starts to bring back his military from the borders, and Atlandreous does the same. Both leave two thousand men to keep peace between the two kingdoms. Neither side wants anyone to start an uprising again.

Icaras' city is starting to make new buildings where the others fell during the natural disaster. The two cities will live in peace for a good while. This new friendship between two city-states will help make the peninsula prosperous.

CHAPTER XII
THE EMPIRE OF TARENTUM
{FIFTEEN DAYS AFTER THE EARTHQUAKE}

Baylonis is talking to his generals at their main Tarentum Military Hall. Cainin, Tarentum's highest ranking officer, is there to go over the annexation of the Antares Kingdom. Tarentum diplomats and generals have been working on the details of the take over for months. Baylonis' military took the Antares society without any bloodshed. The new conquered land was the third largest kingdom on the continent. Because Antares was consumed with a civil war for the last six years, the depletion of manpower and economic stability was completely destroying the once strong kingdom.

Before the negotiations, Antares' nobles knew they could not hold off an attack from the Tarentum Empire. It was time for change, and Cainin came in with a solution of putting Antares as a state. Most of the Antares nobles will keep their power and leadership, but they will have to answer to Baylonis and pay dues. It is a much better situation than what Antares had before. The new state of Tarentum was destroying itself and needed solutions. Because Tarentum is an economic giant on the main continent, the people of Antares will be able to prosper again under the guidance of the Tarentum Empire.

Days prior, Tarentum warriors moved into Antares and put a stop to the fighting. Baylonis' military are known as liberators by their new conquered land. The Antares people were sick of fighting each other. Starting over and becoming something different was very appealing to Antares in the past negotiations to become a state. The civil war also took the pride out of the Antares society. Being taken over by a very successful empire, dignity will be given back to the people in the new state of Tarentum.

The Tarentum generals took leadership and control of the Antares' military right away. The Antares generals gave up their control to Tarentum to stop the civil war. With all the hatred between the two armies inside Antares, the fighting would not stop without the intervention of Tarentum.

With Baylonis' new state, Tarentum now has the largest army in the world. Because over twenty percent of Tarentum's military power was on the Antares' border before the take over, Baylonis' military was concentrating their military manpower on the borders between Antares and Tarentum. Now, the Tarentum military can be reorganized and become stronger. Because it was not a hostile takeover, only ten percent of Tarentum's military will have to be in Antares to keep peace and order inside their new state.

Because of good trade between Tarentum and Alnitak, war is not an option to the Tarentum Emperor. Even though Baylonis has already adopted Antares' military, he knows he cannot do anymore conquests for a long time. Reorganizing manpower and natural resources is the main objective for the Tarentum Emperor right now to make his empire stronger.

Two weeks prior to the meeting in the Tarentum Military Hall, Baylonis felt an earthquake. It was very weak where the Tarentum capital is located. Because the earthquake caused no damage to his kingdom, no one thought anything of it. Because of the distance from Tarentum to Alnitak, no scout or messenger had reached Baylonis to tell their emperor that Alnitak was hit hardest from the natural disaster.

Then the news hit.

The Tarentum messenger gets permission to enter the military hall. The messenger goes to his emperor and tries to salute, but because of fatigue and being out of breath, he trembles as he tries to stand up straight. Baylonis can tell the messenger has been up for days and traveled far. The Tarentum Emperor knows something is wrong somewhere but waits for the messenger to get his thoughts together.

The messenger catches his breath and says, "I have traveled for a week without sleep. I come from the Girulic territory where General Spenser is assigned. Sir, there is a great deal of movement from the

Alnitak military around our borders. Our spies say the walls of Alnitak are in shambles. A large earthquake hit the region. We have lost over two hundred men because of the natural disaster, and our army is over eighty miles from the center of the main destructive force. Our generals in Girulic think the Alnitak military is bracing for some kind of aggression from our empire. Majority of our spies cannot even get out of the Colligitar's kingdom because General Florick has thousands of soldiers patrolling the borders. The trade between Alnitak and our kingdom is nothing but a trickle. Colligitar's traders are saying nothing of the disaster. But there have been few Tarentum spies that made it back to our empire. The spies say Alnitak has lost tens of thousands of people from the natural disaster and majority of their buildings are destroyed."

Cainin says, "I don't think Alnitak knew we were taking Antares. If Alnitak's spies found out about the take over, it would have taken over two weeks to get back to the Alnitak King. It would take another ten days for King Colligitar to get a large army organized and deployed to Girulic. There has to be really something wrong in Colligitar's kingdom for him to build up troops in Girulic."

The messenger looks at Cainin and says, "General Spenser is waiting for your orders, sir. I must get back to him. He told me it is urgent to get back with instructions of what to do, sir."

Cainin looks at the messenger and says, "Messenger, I will relieve you, and I will send another in your place. Leave us now. Get some rest. Well done." Cainin looks at Baylonis and asks, "Do you think they want to attack us? Maybe they are thinking of a preemptive strike. If they think we might attack, they may attack us first."

Baylonis says, "No—The area around Alnitak has been known to have bad earthquakes in the past. If this is anything, it is out of desperation in hiding a bad situation. If we felt the earthquake here and Alnitak is over four hundred miles away, I can only imagine what happened to Colligitar's capital. Their main natural resources to rebuild their kingdom are in Girulic."

Berith, a Tarentum general, looks at Baylonis and asks, "What do we do now?"

Baylonis says, "We get more information. I want our troops in Antares to move closer to the borders of Girulic. We can't take the chance of a preemptive strike. Also assemble the Antares military in reserves. They do not know how to fight with our men and can be a liability if we fight together. If they are integrated with our warriors, confusion in ranks can destroy our military. But the Antares military will boost the morale of our military knowing someone else can back them. Colligitar's military is well disciplined and has good generals. Do not move too closely. It may be interpreted as aggression. If their society is wounded, any kingdom will fight back to protect themselves."

Two days later, more Tarentum spies come back and tell their emperor that indeed the walls of Alnitak are damaged and ten percent of Colligitar's population is dead from the earthquake. The Tarentum spies tell Baylonis that Alnitak's war machine is also severely damaged.

After the earthquake, the Alnitak military put sixty-seven percent of their military on the borders with Tarentum and Antares. Over six hundred thousand Alnitak warriors are at their northern borders with Tarentum and Antares. The main concentration of Colligitar's army is in Girulic. General Kentor of Alnitak is sixty miles east of Florick near the Alber Mountains.

Baylonis gets his military officers together at his palace. The Tarentum Emperor feels weird about the whole situation. In Baylonis' thoughts, why would the Alnitak King have three hundred and fifty thousand men in one area, and two hundred and fifty thousand in another region? Baylonis feels the Alnitak military could have been organizing for an attack against his empire before the quake. This can be the only explanation for the vast deployment of Alnitak warriors in so little time after the natural disaster. The time line of Tarentum taking Antares and Colligitar's army being in Girulic does not make sense to anyone. There is a ten day gap between Florick's army being so close to Tarentum. Baylonis wants to get the thoughts of his military before he can come up with his own conclusion.

Baylonis goes into the combat ready room. His generals and military advisors stand at full attention as their emperor enters the room.

Baylonis says, "I would ask you all to sit down, but I am asking you to stand to keep your senses. I know you all have come far to get here, but I need your full attention and input for this meeting. We have over three hundred and fifty thousand Alnitak warriors at our doorstep in Girulic, and another two hundred and fifty thousand close to Antares. An earthquake has damaged their kingdom as you already know. I have more reports of the devastation that took place in Alnitak. Why would they have such a powerful military at Girulic?"

General Akins says, "They know they're weak. If Girulic has the natural resources to rebuild their kingdom, wouldn't they try to protect it? If they are protecting with such desperate measures, their city must me in shambles. They are scrambling to rebuild quickly and use their military as workers."

Baylonis says, "I understand that. That is something I didn't think about. That is a simple answer. We all know nothing can be that easy. Is there anyone else that can help me understand this?"

Cainin replies, "I agree with Akins. In regards to what you're wondering, I think they believe we will attack while they're vulnerable. They fear us. It is like a gash in a warrior's stomach. Anyone is going to hold their hand over their open wound and hold their sword high. The earthquake must have devastated their city. Even though there is a peace treaty between our two governments, there has been a lot of give and take between our two nations. I think they are trying to hide something from the rest of the world. I don't think they want to go on the offensive. In their extreme anxiety, they are trying to protect their natural resources. Alnitak is using a façade of strength. It is like a teenager about to fight another peer. He sticks his chest out to show others he is stronger than the one he is opposing."

Berith asks, "What if we go on the offensive and take Alnitak? If they're weak, this would be the perfect time to attack Colligitar's military."

Baylonis replies, "If we try, we will lose more than what we will gain. They have the strongest military in the known world. If we win, it will weaken our military. We have enough to take care of in our own realm. Our empire will implode if we take anything else under our wing. I do not think we should even try to go that direction or even think about it."

Cainin says, "Sir, Berith is right. This is the perfect time to attack. Alnitak is scattered, and most likely their military is working to recover resources from the earth to rebuild. If that is true, their troops and armies are divided. In the last five years, Alnitak and

Tantalum have come close to war. We have never said it, but every time there is a summit, we have given up land and trade to please their imperialistic society. It is time to eliminate their ambitious state of mind before they decide to try and take our empire in the years to come."

Baylonis says, "Cainin, you are my best general. I agree, but what if you are wrong? I know I'm right. If we have to divert our armies for an offensive against Alnitak, rebellions will happen in our states. If we lose more than fifty percent of our military in a war with Alnitak, we will lose everything we have gained in the last ten years. Our military is the only thing holding our outer territories together. If we lose them, we will lose a vast number of resources which makes our empire what it is today."

Cainin replies, "We need to keep our military forces thirty miles from the Alnitak border. We need to be on a moments notice just in case they are thinking of a preemptive strike. We need to be ready for the worst. This is something the Tarentum Empire doesn't need right now with our new annexed state being so new."

Baylonis says, "I agree. But Antares is not a threat right now. We control their government. If we had gone to war with Antares, we would have had problems with rebellions. Now, we have taken the territory without bloodshed. There will be little upheaval from their extreme patriots. I concur with sending our military to our borders with Alnitak. This is too important for us not to go on the defensive. I need to know our strengths and weaknesses on our border with Alnitak. Cainin I am putting the trust in you to protect our Empire. Get your men together in the next two days. It will take six days to get to your destination. It has been sixteen days since the earthquake. Time is of the essence."

Akins looks at Baylonis and says, "I understand, and I will do whatever it takes in your name. Let us see what happens at the Alnitak borders. If we have to fight, I want to go in first to defend or attack them. Because we do have to reorganize, it would not be a good idea to think of attacking Alnitak. I totally agree in your wishes. I wish the earthquake could have happened at a later date. If it did, this meeting would have been different."

A little over three weeks after the earthquake, most of Tarentum's forces are thirty miles from the borders of Alnitak. Baylonis keeps some of his troops in his territories and states. There is so much riding on what the Alnitak military is thinking and doing at this point. Tarentum has no idea what Alnitak is up to. There is mistrust on both sides of the borders.

Cainin is thinking war will come now or in the near future with Alnitak. Even though the Tarentum Empire thinks they are the ones who put righteousness into humanity, greed and timorous faults are the main reason the Tarentum generals want to attack Alnitak. Baylonis has put all reserves in the defense of his empire. The Tarentum Emperor has sent representatives beyond his borders to see what is going on with Colligitar's kingdom. But if Alnitak is not talking about anything, there is little hope of diplomacy.

At the same time, all of the Tarentum generals do not agree with Baylonis. Their empire just took a kingdom which was the only obstacle to take Alnitak. In the past, even the Baylonis thoughts of attacking Colligitar's kingdom. Now, the Tarentum Emperor is backing down from conquest of taking Alnitak.

A couple of days after Cainin camps near his border with Alnitak, Cainin assemble his generals together to follow Baylonis' orders, but at the same time, Cainin wants to push the envelope a little. With the earthquake, the Tarentum Supreme Commander knows the Alnitak's military does not know about the annexed state of Antares. None of the Tarentum spies have come back to say Alnitak knows or even suspects. Cainin also knows Kentor is on the borders of Antares and Tarentum. The Tarentum Supreme Commander has a plan.

All Tarentum generals are at Cainin's military tent without Baylonis. The Tarentum Emperor has to keep his political circle in check in his capital. With the taking of Antares, the Tarentum politicians need to be kept at bay. With any conquest, there is always greed from the generals and politicians of any society.

Cainin stands at a map of the continent, while looking at his officers.

Cainin looks at Berith and says, "As far as I know, Alnitak has no idea Antares is a part of our empire. I know General Kentor of Alnitak is in that region. At Kentor's location, the geography of that region is the ideal place for them to attack us. Because it is all flat land, Kentor knows we will not have any high ground anywhere in the region. Kentor is known as an all or nothing general. We will keep our distance, but the Alnitak general can almost cause a war by himself. We need to keep him on the edge a little."

Berith says, "I understand. Kentor will be completely confused if he finds out Antares is a part of our empire. The fear might make him go on the offensive. Because of the distance to his kingdom, he has control to make the decision to attack if pushed."

Then Cainin looks straight at Akins and says, "Akins, I want you on our side of the Antares and thirty miles away from the Alnitak border. I want Alnitak to think Antares has become an ally not a state. It will bring more tension at the borders between Antares and Alnitak. Kentor knows you are the general who leads the spearhead into conflicts. It will make him think even more when his spies come back and say Antares and our forefront general is so close to his army. We are going to play mind games with Kentor to see if he makes the first move."

Berith asks, "What if Kentor doesn't make the first move?"

Cainin replies, "We will not go to war. We will not go against our emperor's orders. We will sit here until our emperor orders us to either attack or come home."

Berith looks at Cainin and says, "Sir, if the tides were turned, Alnitak would not give us the same courtesy. They would have attacked us already. These people are greedy, and they will not stop until they get what they want. Baylonis has given up so much land and trade to keep from fighting them."

Cainin replies, "I agree, but the orders stand. What Baylonis says will be obeyed. Yes, we are spicing up the fears and ego of Kentor, but we will not start any aggressions without Baylonis' consent."

All generals do exactly what Cainin orders. To the left of Alnitak's borders is the Antares Kingdom. It is only thirty miles in length against the Alber Mountains. With two hundred thousand Antares men so close to Kentor's army, it will make Kentor think there can be a possibility of war with the new Tarentum state.

Dead center where Kentor is camped is the Tarentum Empire. Kentor has the hardest area to cover. He has the manpower to defend his kingdom, but he is far away from supplies and reinforcements. Florick is over sixty miles from Kentor and there are only pockets of Alnitak warriors in between the two generals. Because a quarter of the army of Alnitak is helping repair their kingdom, Alnitak's military is spread thin. It is going to take almost two months before Alnitak can function as a city again. It will almost take two years to repair all the damage that hit Colligitar's city from the earthquake. The discipline from the Alnitak society is unbelievable. Colligitar's populace is determined to make their city great again.

On the twenty-eighth day after the earthquake, it is very quiet at the border. Tarentum scouts come back and forth and say there is little activity on Alnitak's border. The Tarentum spies do comment that the Alnitak's military is helping with extracting natural resources at a feverous pace to get it back to their capital. The chance of Alnitak attacking Tarentum is becoming bleak.

CHAPTER XIII
PLANTING THE SEED
TO DESTRUCTION

On the twenty-ninth day after the earthquake that devastated Alnitak, Cainin asks Berith to join him in his tent alone. Both Cainin and Berith want war. Berith has given up territories he has conquered for the Tarentum Empire. Good men have died to only have been given up in mediation to Alnitak. In summits between Baylonis and Colligitar, Alnitak took territories with diplomacy and trade. Because of Berith's military frustrations, he wants Alnitak knocked off the face of the earth. Berith believes in his empire. He knows it is a matter of time before Tarentum goes to war with Colligitar's kingdom. If war does need to happen, it would be the perfect time to do so while Alnitak is crippled.

Cainin also wants the trade inside the peninsula. The byland is in center stage to a great number of trade goods needed in the Tarentum Empire. If Cainin plays it right after taking Colligitar's kingdom, it will make him rich and powerful.

Berith enters the tent. At the same time, Cainin is ordering a messenger to take a letter to Baylonis. The messenger sees Berith coming in, and Cainin rushes him off.

Berith moves closer and asks, "What can I do for you, commander?"

Cainin asks, "I will ask you once. If it is too hard for you, I will not put you in harms way."

Berith says, "Ask me."

Cainin asks, "Do you think it is a good time to attack Alnitak and make the world a better place as we know it?"

Berith replies, "If we take Alnitak under our rule, we will have no adversaries. Our culture will go forward to make mankind better."

Cainin replies back, "So—we see eye to eye. I have a plan, but it could be considered treason. Do I have your word as a general to mention nothing of what I'm about to say?"

Berith says, "If it has to do with taking Alnitak, you have my word."

Cainin says, "We will go to war with Alnitak. I will make it happen. We have the most powerful military in the world. Colligitar's city is crippled. To save lives later, I think we should make Kentor start this war. We have been butting heads with Alnitak for the last five years. I can't see any other alternative but war."

Berith says, "I agree, but we cannot go against our emperor's orders."

Cainin says, "Right, but what would give us permission to attack Alnitak?"

Berith replies, "Alnitak would have to attack us, or we would have to be sure they are about to attack our military. Every one of our generals would have to agree to go to war. It would have to be life or death situation to go against the orders of Baylonis. If you give the order by yourself, you will be executed as a traitor."

Cainin says, "What if we make Alnitak's military seem that they attacked our lands? With Kentor on our borders, he will have no other choice but to go on the offensive."

Berith asks, "How? He has the same political situation as we do. We cannot fight unless we have no alternative."

Cainin says, "I want you to take your scouts and go inside the Alnitak border and take fifty Alnitak armor, weapons, and clothing. Do not kill anyone on the other side. It will be a difficult task. But in the cover of darkness, it can be done. If your scouts get into a confrontation, it will come back on us. This has to be so devious that no one can know from either side what we are about to do."

Berith asks, "What will we do with the clothing after we retrieve these items?"

Cainin replies, "Get what I ask, and we will go forward. If you want war, it will happen. The less you know the less you have to say if this does not go my way."

Berith gets a little anxious and says, "No, if I am going to be a part of this, I need to know right here and right now. You had my loyalty way before I entered your tent, sir. Right now, we are no longer innocent. I will be a part of anything to take out the Alnitak society. I hate everything Alnitak stands for."

Cainin says, "So be it. After you get the clothing and military weapons from Alnitak, we will stage a battle to make it seem Alnitak has already went against the peace treaty. On our side of the border, we have an outpost very close to Kentor's army. I will order those warriors to another location. The people relieving the outpost will be picked by me. They will be the criminals and the low life of our army."

Berith asks, "Why would you put undisciplined warriors so close to the Alnitak border? Are the ones you pick going to attack Alnitak to start this war?"

Cainin replies, "No, they are going to give their lives to save thousands of our fellow comrades in years to come. The undesirables will be killed inside our border. Later, our messengers or supply officers will find them dead. The Alnitak clothing and armor will be worn by our undesirable warriors. It will be staged to appear that the Alnitak military went into our realm and killed our men at our outpost."

Berith replies, "Now, I understand. I will give the order to the people I can trust. These people want war as well, and I will eliminate those conspirators to cover our tracks. I have people ready to do anything to start a war with Alnitak."

Cainin says, "This is why I picked you. We do not need to be known as traitors to our emperor. As of now, you are just as at fault as I am. There is no turning back from this point forward."

Berith says, "Agreed; I want this."

Berith gets his spies who he relies upon to find the clothing needed to stage the deception. It only takes two days for him to get the clothing and armor Cainin needs. At the same time, Cainin orders men out of an outpost close to Kentor's location. Then he orders the undesirables of the Tarentum military into the outpost. Cainin tells no one of this except the people he trusts. If Baylonis finds out, Cainin will be executed for treason.

On the thirty-second day after the earthquake, Berith orders his trustworthy guards to kill everyone inside the outpost close to Kentor's army. It is very swift. No one in the outpost had time to fight back. Cainin orders his guards to make it seem the outpost went through a major battle. Berith's loyal guards also kill three mammoths and an elephant and puts the insignia of the Alnitak's military on the beasts that lay dead. Cainin orders the clothing of the undesirables to be stripped off and the Alnitak attire to be put on. The stage is set. In the cover of darkness, no one of the Tarentum Army knew of the plot. The outpost is far away from any other Tarentum Army.

The next day after the staging, scouts from Alnitak find the outpost first. They look at a distance and notice dead warriors inside the fort. Arrows are everywhere and the outpost is still on fire. Because smoke is rising in the air, it will attract the Tarentum Army in the area. The Alnitak scouts do not dare get too close. It is too dangerous to be caught on the Tarentum side of the border. As the Alnitak scouts look at the outpost from afar, the scouts see their insignia on the mammoths and men. The Alnitak scouts run back to their side of the border as fast as they can. The scouts feel as if Kentor sent in his troops to start a war. The Alnitak spies ride back to Kentor to find out what is going on.

Two hours after the Alnitak scouts look upon the devastation at the outpost, a Tarentum messenger rides to the fort. The Tarentum messenger sees the outpost on fire and finds dead bodies of Alnitak warriors in and outside the outpost. In pure panic, he rides back to Cainin to report about the destroyed outpost.

After Cainin's messenger reports about the outpost, the Tarentum Supreme Commander puts all of his armies on high alert. He orders Antares to stand their ground and get ready for battle. Every one in the Tarentum Empire starts to get in a defensive formation. After Cainin's military gets organized for war, Berith asks to speak to Cainin alone.

Berith goes into Cainin's tent and says, "Everything has been put into place. Every Tarentum general is ready to attack Alnitak. No one knows of what really happened at our bordering outpost. Everything is going to plan. I am wondering if we are doing the right thing."

Cainin seems uneasy and says, "I go over it in my head every second and every moment. I will justify this the more I think about it. I know we are saving Tarentum lives. The Alnitak government is greedy and self-centered to the rest of the world."

Berith replies, "I have sent my warriors who collaborated in our plot to the Antares military. They will be the first ones attacked in the war which is about to take place. Kentor will eliminate the Antares Army first. He knows the Alber Mountains is where we will try to outflank his army. This is where they will strike first. After Kentor takes the Antares Army, our people will never know what took place here. After Alnitak's invasion, we will start our counter offensive to take out Kentor's army."

Cainin says, "That is most likely to take place. Kentor is about to be put up against the wall, and he will have no choice but to attack. My spies tell me there is sixty miles between Kentor and Florick. The gap is defended poorly between the two armies. The messages between the two will intensify more in the days to come. We must destroy their communication as much as possible. In doing so, the chances of them attacking will become greater. The fear of not knowing will cause them to attack. My best warriors will go in and take the messenger outpost inside the Alnitak borders without them even knowing. I have elite warriors which can speak the perfect dialect of Alnitak. We will confuse the communications between Kentor and Florick. With my warriors wearing their uniforms, my warriors will never be suspected. The two main Alnitak armies will be confused."

Berith asks, "What about their capital city?"

Cainin replies, "From what our spies say inside Alnitak, their morale is holding on by a thread. People inside the city are dying from dehydration. This is the sole reason for General Florick to be in Girulic. Colligitar is using his military primarily as a work force to restore their water system in Colligitar's city. The walls of Alnitak are still in shambles. Colligitar's people have put up patches in their defenses. With our artillery, their walls should come down in days rather than weeks. If we take Florick and Kentor out in the opening assault with the Antares, we will destroy their society with ease."

On the thirty-third day, Tarentum's military goes ten miles closer to the border to Alnitak. A messenger from Cainin was sent to Baylonis right when their outpost was staged to be attacked. Baylonis also knows the situation of the capital of Alnitak. Cainin has done everything correctly to make sure Baylonis gives the order to wage war against General Florick and Kentor.

CHAPTER XIV
ALNITAK'S POLITICAL SUICIDE
{ONE HOUR BEFORE THE EARTHQUAKE}

It is three hours before sunrise. Every one of the Alnitak military knows about the conflict between Halotropolis and Alnilam. Colligitar wants an emergency meeting before the battle starts. This will affect trade and resources from the two city-states on the peninsula.

The Alnitak Supreme Commander is at his estate in the center of the city. General Florick has a more lavish home compared to some of the senators of Alnitak. He has over twenty servants taking care of everyday duties. Two of them are at the estate's stable getting their master's horse ready to ride to the Alnitak Military Hall.

Kassandra, Florick's wife, walks into the room while her husband puts on his formal military attire. The Alnitak Supreme Commander is rushing to make sure he is not forgetting anything before he goes to the early morning meeting. Kassandra helps with her husband's formal armor. In the way Kassandra is acting, Florick can tell she wants to say something.

General Florick asks, "What is in your thoughts? I can always tell when there is something heavy on your mind."

Kassandra replies, "I—don't know why we are not putting a stop to the Halotropolis and Alnilam conflict?"

Florick replies, "It is hard politics, but if we do help, it will leave us vulnerable to attack by Tarentum. It would take half of our military to put a stop to the conflict between Icaras and Cetrono's kingdoms. After their war, Alnitak's trade will increase and everyone in our kingdom will prosper."

Kassandra says, "It is not right for us to become rich because of war and death."

Florick says, "I agree with you. When you became my wife, you knew I had to defend our country. Well—it is not just people who attack us. It is the well being of our kingdom. I also have to protect that aspect of our government. I don't like this part of military politics. However, I have to look at what it will bring to our sovereignty. Without any potential consequences, Alnitak did not start this war and cannot prevent it."

Kassandra replies back, "I understand the life of politics. At the same time, it still doesn't make it right."

Florick is ready to go. The Alnitak Supreme Commander looks at his wife and embraces her. He knows she is right. But like most military commanders, he knows he cannot do anything about it. He can say something to the king and Senate, but if he plays the wrong politics, he could find himself demoted. There is someone always wanting to take his place.

Florick's hands are tied. Politicians and kings are the rulers of his known world. The Supreme Commander goes to his stable. He pauses for a moment and thinks of the conversation which just took place between him and his wife. Florick gets on his horse to ride to Alnitak Military Hall.

In the Alnitak Military Hall, Colligitar is about to start a meeting with his military advisors. The Alnitak King is waiting for his Supreme Commander to arrive. It is early morning. There is almost two and half hours before sunrise. Colligitar has other concerns other than the conflict between Alnilam and Halotropolis. The Alnilam King will keep his spies on the peninsula to keep progress of the battle. Alnitak is also worried about the territories they have taken in the last five years. There have been countless rebellions in the new provinces. Some of the natural resources are having problems reaching the Alnitak's capital. Because Colligitar's city is growing very quickly, resources are becoming scarce.

Colligitar's goes into the military chamber. Florick arrives and is greeted by his officers. Everyone is looking at maps and sees their king entering the room. Alnitak generals and advisors stop what they are doing and stand at attention.

Colligitar says, "You may sit down. What can you tell me about both sides of our borders?"

Kentor replies, "We think Tarentum is thinking of taking Antares as a state. There are little facts in the matter, but some of our spies see high officials from both sides speaking in each other's territories. There are long talks and no aggression between the two. If Antares becomes a state, Tarentum will have a little less than three times the military as ours. Antares has over three hundred thousand warriors. Because of their civil war, they are all veterans and know how to fight. If the two combine, the new alliance will have over two million capable warriors. The continent's cavalry will be three times the size of ours. There are very few kingdoms which Tarentum doesn't have control over on the mainland. If they decide to attack our kingdom, it would be very difficult to hold them back. We need to be prepared for a war in the near future."

Colligitar says, "Our city walls are indestructible. The mountain range between our kingdom and the continent would put an army into a bottle neck. Even if they do attack, I feel we can defend ourselves with an acceptable loss. There would be heavy casualties on both sides. Baylonis cannot afford a war with us. The lack of trade between our two governments will destroy him politically."

Florick replies, "The main natural resource from Girulic is our main concern right now. We need to build more defenses just in case we are next on their conquest list. We need to build walls coming into the byland. We have talked about it before. Yes, it would slow down trade between us and the continent, but if we can't defend ourselves, we will not be able to trade with anyone. The mountains coming into the byland are ideal to build an indestructible defense."

Colligitar says, "I agree with Florick. I was opposed to the idea of building a wall for a long time, but now, I'm thinking differently. If Baylonis takes Antares under his rule, it will give him the strongest military in the world. Even though Baylonis has more warriors than we do, our superior training and tactics gives us the ultimate advantage on the battlefield. If Antares is a part of the Tarentum war machine, then we have something to be concerned about. The Antares has been in a civil war for the last six years. There are countless veterans in their ranks."

Protemous replies, "The trade between Tarentum, Antares, and the rest of world will be hampered. If we build walls coming into the byland, it will be seen as defensive and aggressive. They will do the same. The trade will not flow as it does now. Our treasury will not be able to cope."

Colligitar says, "Protemous, I agree, but being king, my main responsibility is to keep our people safe from foreign armies. I agree to make the wall. With the world right now, we have to consider an attack will happen in the next five to six years. We can't take on Tarentum and Antares at the same time."

Florick asks, "What if the continent sees our kingdom building barriers and decides to attack us? Building a wall coming into the peninsula can bring war. The summits we have with Tarentum have brought peace and prosperity to both of our kingdoms. The possibility of trade being cut off may cause tension between our two societies."

Colligitar replies, "If Tarentum is about to take Antares, they will have to reorganize for the next five years to even think of attacking us. If they are thinking of pulling together, time will be on our side if we build the wall right now. We cannot take any chances of them thinking we are vulnerable from this day forward."

Kentor says, "When will we start the project?"

Colligitar says, "Right away. It will take a great deal of manpower and natural resources, but we need to think about our next generation. Think about your daughters and sons. War will happen in our life time with Tarentum. It is time to start thinking of the survival of our society."

Right before anyone can say anything else, an earthquake starts to erupt. People are thrown to the ground. Stones drop from the ceiling and Kentor is hurt from a fallen stone. He is still able to walk, but is in great pain. Kentor's shoulder was hit with a ten pound piece of stone. He is scraped badly. The earth stops shaking and everyone from the room gets up completely stunned. Kentor grabs his shoulder to stop the bleeding and starts to feel the pain.

Colligitar gets up and yells, "Everyone outside!"

Right when everyone starts to evacuate the room and starts to get their composure, another tremor throws people around again. People try to crawl out of the room. This time the cracks in the walls and ceiling start to get larger. Every second, more and more stones fall to the ground. Even though the elite of Alnitak try to show intrepidly, the looks on their faces show otherwise. Florick gets up and drags Colligitar to his feet and moves him outside the building.

When all of the advisors and military officers run out the room, the ceiling collapses. If they had stayed another moment, everyone in the room would have been crushed under the stone structures.

Once outside, Colligitar says, "Thank you Florick. I would have died if you didn't drag me out. I am indebted to you. Now we have to figure out our city's damage. With the plans we just talked about, everything we said is null and void. It is still dark. It will take another two hours before sunrise and two hours into the day to assess our wounded city. We need to put out the fires first. Flames will be easy to find in the darkness. With our fountains on almost every street corner, water will not be an issue."

Alnitak is the hardest hit from the earthquake on the byland. Colligitar first orders no one to enter his city from any other kingdom. The Alnitak King also orders everyone from different city-states not to leave. The whole city is shut off from the rest of the world. He does not want other people from different kingdoms to see the full extent of this natural disaster. Right away he orders trade to be done twenty miles outside the city. Twenty percent of all homes and buildings are severely damaged. Out of almost eight hundred thousand people living in Alnitak, a hundred thousand people are injured or killed from the natural disaster.

Two hours after sunrise, reports come in to Colligitar about Alnitak's outer walls.

Kentor goes to the palace with his wound bandaged. It is a bad gash and blood is still seeping through his dressing. The second in command cannot let pain govern his responsibilities to his people. Because everyone of Alnitak is afraid of an aftershock, everyone stays outside their homes and buildings. Because the city's structures are damaged, another tremor could bring buildings to the ground.

Kentor rides his horse to his king. Colligitar is going over political situations of the earthquake with some of his Senate. The Alnitak King orders every servant of his kingdom to find the wounded and dead to prevent disease.

Kentor stays on his horse and looks down to the king as he is about to rush to find out more information.

Kentor says, "Sir, most of the walls are destroyed or need to be totally rebuilt. The southeast wall is completely demolished. Two of our military depots have completely collapsed. Over three thousand swords and shields are under rubble. Over seven thousand military personnel are injured or dead. If Tarentum wanted to sack our city, they could easily take us."

At the same time, Protemous comes to Colligitar by chariot.

Colligitar looks at Kentor and says, "Find out what we do have. I want a count of every sword, artillery, and asset we have at our disposal."

Protemous waits until the conversation is over with Kentor and says, "Do you have a quick second for me?"

Colligitar asks, "What do you know so far?"

Protemous says, "Our aqueducts are damaged very badly. Part of our city is taking in water. We have stopped the water flow, but we will have no water for at least a week. People will die from the lack of water. The cattle outside our gates have vanished. Some are dead, and others have broken their confinements and are lost to the world. Food will become a problem in four days. Because the lack of food and something as simple as getting a drink of water, there will be numerous riots"

Colligitar says, "I am not saying this against you. But the Senate is finally going to do some work for their people. I want to have a meeting within two hours."

Protemous replies, "It will be done. Sir, the death toll is rising. There is panic throughout this city. It will have to be controlled with our military."

Colligitar yells at a servant and says, "Find General Florick; I want a military meeting here in four hours. We will have a joint meeting with the military and Senate in six. We all have to come together. There will be riots in this city within three days if we don't put a stop to this before it begins."

First Colligitar gets his Senate together. Most of the building which can hold a large meeting is severely damaged. Colligitar wants to have it outside so some of his people can hear the speech and give direction to best handle this natural disaster. Nothing has prepared the Alnitak King against something so devastating.

Out of three hundred Senate representatives of the people of Alnitak, there are only two hundred and sixty-two that survived the natural disaster. Because the Senate lives in larger estates, the quake had a harder toll on their homes. Colligitar is going to have to get the Senate to work together to make something happen.

Colligitar is about to give a speech to some of the high officials and civilians. The Alnitak King cannot hear the conversations in the background of the crowd. All he can see are lips moving and the people shaking their heads as they cannot believe this is happening to them.

The Alnitak King stands on the highest structure in the center of his city and yells, "We have been wounded. Life is like taking steps. A person will go forward with two steps, and then that same person will take one step backwards because of circumstances in everyday life. Walking the steps of life is the same in societies and humanity. Right now, we are taking a step backwards. It was not our choice or fault, but it happened. Let's take our society to the next step. The only way we can do that is together. Even I will work to the bone to rebuild our great city. I will work alongside the rich and less fortunate. I will work day and night until it is done. To go forward, I need to know the full extent of our problems so we can do what needs to be done. I need everyone to become a leader right here and right now. Leaders compromise, work hard, take control, and look out for the weak!"

The crowd goes wild and claps for their king. Protemous is in the background of the crowd and walks forward to Colligitar after the speech and says, "Sir, our aqueducts will take three weeks to repair. The water flow has been cut off from the source. I need every cubic yard of concrete for the next two and half weeks to bring water to our city. This should be our first priority."

From the yelling to his people, Colligitar clears his throat and replies, "In order to have a society, we need water. We also have another problem. Water is also a component of cement. We will have to take water from our people so they can have water later. Add another week or two to that projection. Now, most of the other components to make cement come from the Girulic region and close to the Antares border, it will take at least two weeks to start the process of bringing natural resources on a grand scale into the city. We have a lot of ground to cover to get the resources we need to rebuild. How long will it take to get some water flowing into the city?"

Protemous says, "A little over a week, if we have the manpower. We have some mineral resources to start the project. We have three aqueducts coming into the city. The smallest one, which is the least damaged, will be operational outside of a week. The smaller one will be able to get at least some water into the city enough to ration to keep people alive. With the other two, they are so massive it will take almost six weeks to repair with the right manpower. We cannot take a chance of the cement not curing correctly. If we do not do it right, we will have major problems down the road. This is something we have to do quickly and pay attention to in detail."

Colligitar says, "Every military personnel will help in the transport of materials. Because of the possibility of attack from the Tarentum Empire, I will have most of my elite warriors extracting materials from Girulic. I will have Kentor sixty miles east close to Antares extracting other resources to get what we need."

Everyone, including high officials from Alnitak, goes to work. People start to work night and day. No one strays from their objective. The more the society works on their city, the more problems they find. It is very frustrating to Colligitar to find new obstacles, but the Alnitak King shows nothing but leadership to his people. He goes through a lot with himself. He does not want to fail, but he knows he has to be strong in front of his masses. Because the situation is so urgent, Colligitar cannot vent to anyone. People count on his leadership that much. It is almost destroying him mentally.

The first objective of the Alnitak King is the city's aqueducts. The defensive walls are secondary. If Colligitar does not get water into the city, people will die. The Alnitak Senate and advisors help their king with options and physical work.

In the first week, workers bring water by transporting it by foot from the lakes and rivers. It keeps people alive inside Alnitak but does not help in the production of cement to repair the aqueducts. It almost becomes a stalemate between the survival of Colligitar's population or rebuilding the city to make it stronger to sustain life.

Because of problems, work is taking longer than expected. Instead of a little over a week, it takes almost two to rebuild the smaller aqueduct. On the thirteenth day after the earthquake, the flow of water starts to trickle into the city. The people of Alnitak have hope now. People rejoice for hours after their first main objective is obtained. With the news of the smaller aqueduct being somewhat repaired, people from the far reaches of the city run to the water supply with their water containers. The citizens of Alnitak even start to fight for water. With military help, the panic to get water stops with force. Because there is some water flowing into the city, job descriptions change. People who brought water from outside the city are able to go to other projects to rebuild their city. The leaders of the city redirected manpower to the larger aqueducts.

Colligitar starts to trade with other city-states for food and tools to rebuild his city, but that also takes longer than expected. Because the other city-states are also becoming exhausted from the lack of food and equipment, traders from other kingdoms have nothing to trade to Alnitak. This is becoming a nightmare for Colligitar. As soon as he solves one problem, two more come up.

For a brief moment, Colligitar even thinks of attacking the city-states for materials and food and stripping them for resources. But the peninsula's city-states are not a threat to him, and the Alnitak King is worried about the Tarentum Empire on the continent. Because Alnitak cannot take on two fronts, the most powerful city on the byland has to be cautious.

On the seventh day after the natural disaster, Florick arrives in Girulic with his three hundred and fifty thousand military personnel. The Alnitak Supreme Commander starts to help with the extraction of natural resources to rebuild his kingdom. When Florick gets close to the Tarentum border, he is very fearful of enemy spies. Before the Alnitak military arrived at the mining site, orders were sent to patrol Alnitak's borders. In doing so, it is very difficult for the Tarentum spies to go back to their borders to tell what happened in the capital of Alnitak. Every square mile on the Alnitak border is patrolled. There are hundreds of Tarentum spies trapped in Colligitar's kingdom.

On the eighteenth morning, a group of Tarentum spies break through to their border. They are chased by the Alnitak military but escape to their side of the border. Florick's warriors do not know if it is civilians or spies. The Alnitak warriors chasing the scouts dare not to go beyond their realm. If anyone of the Alnitak military goes beyond their borders, it could be misinterpreted as aggression and war could occur. The Alnitak warriors who found the people running to the Tarentum border go straight to Florick. The Alnitak Supreme Commander is working hard with his men to transport natural resources back to Colligitar

A messenger runs to Florick as he is giving orders to a couple of military officers.

The messenger says, "Our patrol chased six people to the Tarentum border. We think they were spies. Tarentum will soon know of our dilemma. If Baylonis doesn't know already, he will know a little after two weeks."

Florick says, "Ride to Kentor. Tell him to watch his borders and not fight if he has a choice. I don't want this escalating into a war."

Florick cannot afford a war right now. His whole kingdom is in jeopardy. If a war starts, the walls of his capital will not be able to hold back the Tarentum military machine. Most of his men are scattered all over the borders of Antares and Tarentum. If the Tarentum Supreme Commander decides to attack, Florick will not be able to regroup and defend against such a massive army.

Just as Florick feared, the people who escaped back into the Tarentum kingdom were spies. The scouts who ran to their border went to General Spenser who is the highest ranking general of Tarentum in the region. The spies tell their commander about Alnitak's weaknesses. General Spenser is also told that Alnitak has large armies in Girulic. The Tarentum general sends patrols all over his side of the border. The patrols tell their general that there is a great deal of activity on the Alnitak's side of the border. Spenser orders a messenger straight to his emperor to report what is happening.

A month later, a different Tarentum messenger comes back from his capital. In the last thirty days, General Spenser has tried to bring a summit between Tarentum and Alnitak but did not receive a reply. The trade between Tarentum has ceased. Alnitak diplomats finally come out and explain there is a plague inside their kingdom and don't want the disease to spread. General Spenser knows it is not the case, but waits for instructions from his empire.

The messenger gets off is horse and goes straight to Spenser.

The messenger says, "I bring word from Cainin and Baylonis."

Spenser says, "Where is my messenger I sent to our capital?"

The messenger says, "Cainin ordered me to take your messenger's place. Your orders are to stay at your position. An army has been sent to protect your flanks. Antares' military has been sent to protect us from an attack if Alnitak goes alongside of the Alber Mountains. Our Supreme Commander will be here in two to three days. His army will follow. We know Alnitak is weak right now. This may be the strongest their military might be for years. If this is the case, Cainin is concerned of an all out attack by Alnitak. He said do not provoke a fight."

CHAPTER XV
THE STAGE THAT CHANGED THE WORLD

On the thirty-third day after the earthquake, the Alnitak scouts who saw the Tarentum outpost on fire go straight to Kentor. The second in command of the Alnitak Army is going over the natural resources being extracted in their territory. Because of the distance to his capital, he is having more trouble transporting materials than expected. It is a slow process but steady. He brings better ideas to expedite the materials needed to rebuild his kingdom. This is his main priority. Kentor can only think what his fellow citizens are going through at his capital.

The scout runs and salutes his general and interrupts while Kentor is giving orders to his officers.

The scout says, "I must speak with you alone."

Kentor replies, "What is so important, so—"

The scout interrupts again and says quickly, "Please sir, I have something to ask you. This will be the most important question I will ask in my lifetime."

Kentor, in an assertive voice, says, "Very well. Everyone give me a second with this scout."

Everyone starts to leave. Kentor's officers do not understand, and he can see it in their faces. The second in command of the Alnitak Army wants to ask what is going on, but waits until everyone is far away before continuing the conversation. If a scout is interrupting his superior officer in this way, it has to be very important.

Kentor's officers are at a distance and he asks the scout, "What is going on? My men will be wondering what was said here."

The scout says, "We had a reconnaissance mission on the other side of Tarentum's border. We found a Tarentum outpost on fire. We couldn't get too close. We found our men dead on their side of the border. Our army attacked them. I don't know if you gave a secret order to do so. If we did attack, it will bring war."

Kentor says, "No, we didn't attack the Tarentum outpost. I know my generals didn't either. Something is wrong. If we did not do this, who did? There have been reports of our clothing being stolen in this region. One of my supply officers reported it about two hours ago. I thought it was the inhabitants of this area. How many of our dead soldiers did you see at the outpost?"

The scout says, "I don't know, sir. We couldn't get close enough in fear of being detected. I saw twenty of our men outside the walls and a mammoth with our insignia. It seemed to be a long battle."

Kentor says assertively, "Get all of our generals and officers here right away. I want everyone to be in my tent within thirty minutes. We must find out what happened and prepare for the consequences."

Minutes go by. Every second Kentor waits seems to him like hours. He thinks he knows what is transpiring here. The second in command of the Alnitak military does not say anything to his officers as they arrive in his tent.

The last of Kentor's officers rush into the tent to see what is so important. The last officer looks around and sees nothing but empty faces from his fellow countrymen. No one is talking. Everyone stands in line at attention in military protocol. The possibility of war has been on everyone's mind, and the Alnitak generals and staff know they are not battle ready. The morale of the Alnitak military has been compromised because their capital is in shambles. Now after the earthquake, the Alnitak military has become more humble to the rest of the world.

Kentor says, "I have ordered a messenger to the Tarentum border. We have a problem. A Tarentum outpost has been attacked. I know the Tarentum generals know we are at our weakest. They have gone through the trouble to make it seem we have breached our treaty with them. I know for a fact that no one in this room gave an order to attack their outpost."

An officer asks, "Sir, why would we even think about attacking Tarentum? We are not battle ready."

Kentor says, "Like I said. I didn't say anyone here gave the order. I think the high command of the Tarentum military staged this. I think Baylonis doesn't want war, but his military does. Cainin has to have a reason to start an attack against us. Their outpost on their side just did that. Get me a messenger."

Before a messenger can come into the tent, another scout comes in and asks for permission to enter. The messenger is very silent and asks to come to Kentor. The second in command of the Alnitak military gives the okay and the scout whispers into his ear. The generals and officers inside the tent watch and say nothing while Kentor gets more news. No one can hear the conversation. The scout pulls back with anger and fear on his face.

Kentor says, "Thank you, scout, I need you to stay. I want you to tell everyone here what you just told me."

The scout clears his throat and says, "The Antares military is in great numbers thirty miles inside their kingdom. It seems the Tarentum and Antares is in this together. Both militaries are exactly thirty miles inside their borders with a massive force. They're waiting for something."

Kentor says, "It was feared Tarentum and Antares were about to come together a month ago. Now our fears are true. With Antares, Tarentum has the most powerful military in the world. Without walls or natural defenses, they have the possibility to destroy our army with pure numbers. The only way we can defend ourselves is with a preemptive strike. If they are going to attack, we must take them off guard to tip the balance. If we attack first, we can negotiate a cease fire and continue to rebuild our city. If we punch them in the face hard enough, they will think twice about attacking Alnitak. We have the strongest and most disciplined men in the world. Tarentum knows that."

Another of Kentor's generals speaks up and says, "If we attack, we will be the aggressors. If this is staged by Cainin, he still has to answer to Baylonis. We must get word to the Tarentum Emperor to stop this before it gets out of hand."

Kentor says, "It will take two weeks before we can get word to Baylonis and know the outcome. By that time, they will have already attacked. They give us no choice."

Kentor pauses for a moment and paces back and forth. Everyone in the room is wondering what Kentor is about to say. There are whispers across the tent. The possibility of war is not something Colligitar had anticipated, but the possibility of war is right now. The Alnitak officers do not fear death, but being vulnerable scares them. The earthquake has brought a wound to their souls. The only way to heal the wound is to make their capital great again. The pride has been taken out of the Alnitak common soldier.

As Kentor takes a deep breath, he stops pacing and looks at the messenger and asks, "Messenger what is your name?"

The messenger says, "Kobo, sir."

Kentor says, "I need you to take a message to our Supreme Commander. Take a horse and ride as fast as you can to Florick. I need you back in four days. I am giving you the most important assignment of your life. Tell him the same thing you told me. Tell our Supreme Commander I will be waiting for his orders. If I do not hear from him in five days I will attack Antares first to keep from being out flanked. Tell him why I'm going to attack. You understand politics and war. You are the only person I can trust to make sure Florick understands what is happening."

The messenger rides off. He is determined to make the sixty mile trip by horse in two days. It is going to be difficult because of the terrain, but Kobo is confident he can make the impossible-possible.

Two hours into Kobo's ride, he stops at an Alnitak messenger outpost for a new horse. He is the only person there except for five caretakers. Everyone in the outpost rushes to the messenger to help.

Kobo gets off his horse and says, "I need the fastest horse here. I have a very important message to give to our Supreme Commander."

A caretaker asks, "What is so important, if I may ask?"

Kobo says, "We are about to go to war. Stay steady. Be ready for a fight."

A caretaker takes the exhausted horse and guides the beast to a water supply. Another caretaker brings a fresh stallion to Kobo. Right before Kobo gets on another horse, he is stabbed from behind by one of the caretakers. Kobo tries to fight back before he weakens, but the wound is too great. Three days prior, the Tarentum military took and killed the original Alnitak warriors at the messenger outpost and took their insignia. The letter to Florick will not reach its destination.

On the thirty-third day, Alnitak scouts report to Kentor. They say the Tarentum and Antares armies are marching closer to their borders. In a day and a half, Cainin's army stops. The tension between Alnitak and Tarentum gets worse. Tarentum is only twenty miles from Kentor.

Four days pass since Kobo left Kentor's tent. The communication between the two Alnitak armies has completely stopped. Kentor is worried and cannot wait any longer. It is the thirty-seventh day after the earthquake, but the Tarentum and Antares armies have not moved forward. Kentor's men are exhausted, but they still continue to extract natural resources for their city. They wait until they hear from Florick to start an offensive.

On the thirty-eighth day, Kentor orders his men to stop working and to prepare for war. With two hundred and fifty thousand men, he will give the order for a preemptive strike. The second in command of the Alnitak military orders an investigation about what is going on with the communication lines between the two armies. Kentor's men go to the message outposts, and the Tarentum military knows what targets to take out or leave alone. The infiltrators inside the Alnitak territories go unnoticed. No one of the Alnitak military knows what is happening to their messengers. The communication between armies has been broken for five days. Kentor does not know what to do without confirmation to attack Tarentum. He brings his generals together.

Kentor orders another meeting and waits till every officer is in his tent and says, "Our communications are down between our two great armies. The Tarentum Empire has taken Antares under their rule, and they too are also twenty-miles to our border. Florick has no idea what is going on. We are the leaders of our army, and I will not make the choice by myself. This is too important for one man to make the decision. If we all decide to start a preemptive strike, I will take full responsibility. I hope Florick will understand and follow suit. I need answers."

Albertous, Kentor's best officer, says "If we start a preemptive strike, it has to be soon. We have lost all communication with our Supreme Commander. He could be in the same situation. We have to think this all the way through. If we do attack, it will bring war.

Our army to the East may not be prepared. If the Tarentum Army is ready, Florick will not have a chance."

Kentor says, "Then we send a team of messengers to Florick. We will send dozens of messengers at the same time in all direction to our other army. Let me ask you all. Do we attack if we do not hear back from Florick? What is the time limit before we have no choice?"

Albertous says, "Ample time is five more days. If we wait any longer, the war will be over. Tarentum will be prepared to wage war by that time. They are well inside their borders and close to their supplies. They have staged the reason to attack with their burning outpost. Because of politics, the Tarentum Emperor will have no choice but give the order to attack us. I would guess we have seven more days. Cainin will have the supplies needed for a full scale attack. They want war. If the Tarentum military cannot do it politically correct, they will make the excuse to go forward with their conquest to take us. We need to attack in five days. We need to be ready."

Kentor says, "We will make one valiant effort to make our intentions known to Florick. We are alone here. Tarentum will inch closer everyday until they attack. We must catch them off guard. We will send fifty messengers to Florick at the same time. The messengers will not stop to rest or even feed their horses until they reach their destination. One of those fifty messengers will reach our Supreme Commander. If we attack five days from today, it will give Florick time to follow suit. If the Tarentum military is twenty miles inside their border, it will take their military five days to get to our border to attack."

One of Kentor's generals stands up and asks, "What if we are wrong? What if this is a setup so we will attack and give justification for Cainin to start this war?"

Kentor says, "We have over two million enemy warriors at our border. Antares is a part of this, our communications are down, and we have been staged to already have started this war. What more evidence do I need to give? I don't want this, but what choice do we have here? I am going to give the order to attack. Who is against this? I need to know."

Everyone in the room agrees with Kentor. The element of surprise needs to be on Alnitak's side. If they are to hoping to punch a hole in the Tarentum lines, they have to take Tarentum by surprise. Kentor knows Cainin's men will not attack first for at least a week because of political issues. Alnitak messengers are sent to Florick to prepare for battle.

On the forty second day after the earthquake, Kentor will attack Tarentum to tip the balance of power. This is the only option on Kentor's table right now. Fear will bring war to Kentor's kingdom.

Chapter XVI
Finding the Truth

On the thirty-ninth day after the earthquake, Florick is still working hard bringing materials to his capital. He has been concerned with the communication breakdown between Kentor and himself. He has sent people to investigate. The trickery with the message outpost from the Tarentum military is working.

The Alnitak Supreme Commander knows the Tarentum Army is waiting twenty-miles inside their border. Florick keeps mining materials to repair his capital. Because so many Alnitak warriors are so close to the Tarentum border, Florick thinks the Tarentum Empire is only taking safety measures to protect their kingdom.

At mid-afternoon of the thirty-ninth day after the earthquake, a messenger from Kentor finally makes it to Florick.

Kentor's messenger goes to Florick while he is at the mining site. The messenger tells them about the situation at Kentor's location. Florick wonders why he is the only messenger to get to him, and why his own messengers are not returning.

Florick says, "Thank you for getting to us. I have been concerned with the communication breakdown between our two armies. None of my messengers have made it back from your mining site. I have my cavalry scouting the region between our great armies."

The messenger says, "When I had to rest my horse, I made sure I was alone. I also went ten miles south to stay away from the Tarentum border. I had no interaction with anyone for two days. Our messengers have not returned either."

Florick says, "Interaction is the key to our troubles. Our messenger outposts are the only contact our messengers have to and from our two armies."

The messenger says, "Kentor has already investigated the outposts between our two armies."

Florick says, "The reason I am Supreme Commander is because I pay attention to details. Some people think it is a flaw; I think it is a gift. I think the only reason you're here is because you did not go to our outpost. If I'm right, we are about to go to war."

At almost dusk, six more messengers from Kentor reach Florick. Every one of the messengers that reached him did not go to a messenger station. Florick is waiting on two patrol units which are to bring back caretakers from the messenger outposts. There are a total of ten messenger stations between Kentor and Florick. Every twelve miles there is an outpost to take care of the horses and men.

Two hours after dusk the Alnitak patrols come back with ten caretakers from the Alnitak messenger outposts. Florick asks to see them outside his tent. All ten are lined up standing at attention. He paces back and forth waiting for someone to flinch out of formation. Every caretaker stays steady.

Florick looks at all of them in the row and looks at the sixth man in line and asks, "Where are we stationed?"

The caretaker says, "To the first northern outpost between our two armies, sir."

Florick goes to the ninth caretaker in the row and asks, "Where are you from?"

The ninth caretaker says, "Alnitak, sir."

Florick asks, "What part of Alnitak?"

The ninth caretaker cannot answer the question. He stands at attention and says nothing. Florick takes his sword and stabs the man right in the chest. No one flinches. Other Alnitak guards start to surround their Supreme Commander.

Florick asks the patrol who brought the caretakers to him and asks, "Where was this one located?"

The patrol officer says, "Our first messenger outpost to our south."

Florick says, "Take the southern caretakers out of here. I want the northern questioned and taken into custody for interrogation. I want the other four to come forward towards me."

The four from the southern messenger outpost move forward and still no one flinches.

Florick says, "You are not who you say you are. I commend you for your bravery. I respect you as good soldiers, but you leave me no reason to keep you alive. I understand you are fighting for your country, but you are going to be the reason we will fight Tarentum. This is not a fight between countries. This is a fight against humanity. We will destroy your empire. Because of not making this a gentleman's war, I will destroy everyone of your kind. Patrol officer kill these Tarentum soldiers."

The patrol kills them all in seconds before any of them can say a word. Florick orders his patrol to go to all messenger outposts and take them under custody. He tells a servant to get him as many messengers as he can find. Within ten minutes, twenty messengers are at attention waiting for orders from their Supreme Commander.

Florick says, "You have two days to get to Kentor. I want you to tell him that we are with him. If the Tarentum military wants to play games and dirty war, we will give it to them. There will be no regrets to attack Tarentum. On the forty-second day after our natural disaster, we will attack General Spenser's army and spearhead northeast until we reach Kentor. We will take them by surprise. Now go as fast as you can go. Our kingdom depends on you. Go!"

Florick goes to his tent. All of his generals are there waiting on the commander's next move. Every general knows they only have two more days before war and there are no answers of how they are going to do it. The Alnitak Supreme Commander comes out of his tent.

Florick takes a deep breath and says, "Officers, come into my tent. We have a lot of planning. Get the mining gear off of our cavalry and get them ready for war."

Florick goes to a map and everyone looks at their commander. Everyone stands at attention in military protocol.

Florick says, "It is time to go back to basics. We all know what is going on with Kentor's region. The Tarentum high command wants war with us. They are tied up in politics to not do so. I don't know if it is the Tarentum Senate or Baylonis himself. The Tarentum military is forcing the issue. In the next seven days, word will go back to the Tarentum Supreme Commander to give the okay to destroy our way of life. Cainin will attack. We will attack him before he can do the same. I have given orders to Kentor to take on the Antares. Kentor's army will meet us fifteen miles inside the Tarentum border. Our two armies will meet and go east. Akins, I need you to take nine divisions of our best cavalry and warriors and protect our flanks. You have a hundred and seventy thousand men under your command. We will come around and take Cainin head on. You will be the last defense before Tarentum starts their attack against our capital. If I don't make it back to protect our kingdom, I am putting my trust in you. General Akins, you are in charge of Girulic until I get back."

Akins says, "What you are about to do is suicide. Even with your nine divisions, you are going against at least a half a million warriors just in the first initial attack."

Florick says, "Surprise is the best weapon. If I have a wooden spoon and you have a sword and a shield, I can sneak upon you with the spoon. I can take your life without you even knowing it. Your sword would be useless. With our cavalry, I will spearhead through the Tarentum lines until we reach Kentor."

Akins says, "I believe in you. I will follow your orders to the death."

Florick replies, "We will take Tarentum. I have sent a messenger to Colligitar to prepare for war. Our capital has over two hundred thousand men to protect our city. Even if we don't win, we will deplete the Tarentum Army enough so we can defend our capital city. The only drawback in attacking first is reconstructing our city in a timely fashion, but the way I see it, a preemptive strike is the only solution to take on the numbers which will attack our city anyway."

On the forty-second day after the earthquake, Florick is ready at Girulic. It is two hours before sunrise on the day Kentor is going to attack. General Akins has built a defensive perimeter at the Alnitak border. It is a very rudimentary defense, but until Akins is attacked, everyone under his command reinforces the defenses every day.

On the other side of the border, Cainin also gets reports of the Alnitak military getting ready for battle. The Tarentum Supreme Commander pushes harder by digging in except for one massive offensive move. He is going to let the Alnitak military attack him on his own terms. The Tarentum military is just waiting for the storm to come in.

On the same day as Kentor is about to attack, a messenger from Florick breaks through to the second in command of the Alnitak Army. He goes straight to Kentor as his men are on the border with Antares and Tarentum. Kentor is making last preparations.

The messenger says, "Kentor, you will go northeast and meet our Supreme Commander at Rigel. General Florick will go on your northeast and outflank Cainin. Make two armies and attack Antares and Tarentum at the same time so your army cannot be out flanked."

Kentor asks, "You are the first messenger to get to us. What are Florick's thoughts of me attacking Tarentum?"

The messenger says, "The main reason our messengers did not get through is a majority of our messenger outposts were compromised. Florick told me to tell you to investigate the nearest messenger outpost. He said to attack in four hours from now and he will do the same. We must make our enemy guess where our main thrust is attacking. Akins will set a perimeter at Girulic so Cainin cannot out flank our driving forces. Florick was against the war until he found out Cainin was not making this into a gentlemen's war. There is a great deal Tarentum treachery in wanting this confrontation, and they have already taken this to the next level. He told me to tell you that the Tarentum military has no honor and you will do the same. No prisoners. This war is to the death."

Kentor says, "Plans have changed. We will attack Antares with a hundred thousand men. We will take the remainder of the hundred and fifty thousand and explode forward until we reach Rigel. Take half of our cavalry to Antares so we can punch a hole and come around and take Tarentum. We need to reach Rigel in six days to meet up with Florick."

CHAPTER XVII
FIGHTING FOR YOUR BROTHERS IN WAR

Two hours after sunrise, Kentor goes beyond his borders into Tarentum. He takes his main force to spread out with his hundred and fifty thousand warriors. General Albertous, who is second in command of Kentor's force, starts to drive into the Antares Kingdom with his army.

The Alnitak invasion into Tarentum and Antares begins. The Alnitak military has little opposition for the first five miles inside Antares or Tarentum. Cainin stands back and waits for the Alnitak military to attack him. The treachery and deceit from the high command of the Tarentum military has worked. Baylonis, the Tarentum Emperor, only knows the Alnitak military is attacking first because of their imperialistic nature.

On the first day, the Alnitak armies reach seven miles inside Tarentum and Antares. Only Tarentum outposts are destroyed. Kentor, Albertous, and Florick make good time. Akins, which stayed in Girulic, waits and patrols the Alnitak borders.

The Tarentum military just waits for the ideal moment. There is no rush. Cainin orders Berith and other officers inside his quarters to uncover his battle plan.

When the Tarentum high ranking officers get to their Supreme Commander's tent, Cainin says, "They are in our territory right now. The Alnitak military will not make it out alive. They are a formidable force and have good warriors. Colligitar has put a great deal of training in each of his warriors, and they are well equipped. With Alnitak being the middleman to the world, they have put so

148

many resources into their military. We are going to lose men this week and the next, but we have the ultimate advantage. We are fighting on our land, and you know the weak spots of our terrain. We are going to hit Girulic with a large force while Florick and his armies are deep inside our borders. We are going to spread our enemy thin. We will pick off the Alnitak armies one at a time. We will let Kentor take on the Antares military while we take on General Akins at Girulic. I will take Florick's itinerant spearhead and hold him off. Berith, I want you and General Spenser to take on Akins at Girulic. I am giving you half of my army to knock out Akins. This has to be done quickly and efficiently. Afterwards, we will be able to take Florick and Kentor on two fronts. First, our two armies will surround Alnitak's spearhead and crush their military. After we destroy Florick, we will destroy the rest of Alnitak's military machine. Gentlemen, Colligitar's military are outnumbered three to one, and we have the luxury of having more cavalry."

Every order Cainin gives goes into play. Berith goes to Spenser and takes command. He has over eight hundred and fifty thousand warriors to take on a hundred and seventy thousand warriors at Girulic. Cainin has seven hundred thousand warriors to hold off Kentor and Florick's armies. Antares has two hundred thousand men protecting Cainin's right flank. After the Tarentum Emperor knows there is war, more than five hundred thousand more Baylonis' soldiers will be sent to defend their empire.

On the forty-forth day after the earthquake, Berith moves into position with his men. Spenser takes three hundred thousand men south of Akin's main army. Alnitak scouts tell their commander that he is surrounded. He gets his officers together.

Akins tells his officers, "We are outnumbered six to one. Our scouts say they have surrounded us. We will stand here and fight. We will give up our lives for the greater cause of our army. Take every mammoth, horse, and giant rhino we have and punch a hole through the south-west side of our enemy. We will go around and destroy as much Tarentum cavalry as we can. When you die on this day or the next, remember it was an honor for me to fight with such valiant warriors. We must give time for Florick and Kentor to take their objectives. If we can give them that time, they can come back and take back Girulic. Give me a messenger."

A messenger comes to General Akins and says, "You called for me, sir," as he salutes his commander.

Akins says, "I need you to find Florick and tell him that we are outnumbered here. Tell him we can give him three days to take his objectives. After that, we will be completely compromised. You will be the only person to survive from Girulic."

The messenger says, "I totally respect you and our kingdom. I have friends here. I am refusing your order, sir. I will die here with you. I understand the consequences of disobeying your orders, and you can kill me, but I will not take the easy way out. I will die here with my army."

Akins says, "So be it. I will not kill you. You will take command of our frontal defense. We need this kind of bravery on our front line. I respect your devotion to your kingdom. It would be a waste to kill you. Send me another messenger."

A younger messenger comes in and says, "Yes, sir. What can I do for you?"

Akins says, "Go to Florick. Tell him we will hold on as long as we can to the enemy force which is about to take Girulic. Right now I estimate close to seven and fifty thousand to a million men which will attack us. Tell him that there will be a large force coming around to surround him. Ride now."

The messenger rides as fast as he can before the territory of Girulic is completely surrounded. That evening, the Tarentum military arrives in Girulic. Because it is late in the evening, Berith can only probe in with his scouts to find the strength and weakness of Akins' defenses.

The next morning, Akins goes to his cavalry commander. The Alnitak Army at Girulic has a good and strong cavalry, and the Girulic commander decides to go on the offensive. Akins' cavalry spearheads right through the Tarentum forces, but is quickly pushed back with heavy losses. Because the Girulic territory is mostly forest, the Alnitak mammoths have a hard time getting through the terrain. Akins' heavy cavalry is not being used to its highest potential in the battle. In turn, Tarentum uses their giant rhinos inside the wooded area. Because the beasts are smaller and faster, they destroy most of Alnitak's mammoths.

On the third day, the Tarentum military puts their horse cavalry on the front line. Akins does the same. The Alnitak and Tarentum horse cavalries collide, and there is a stalemate for hours until the Tarentum giant rhinos back their light cavalry and completely destroy the rest of Akins' cavalry.

That afternoon, the hundred and fifty thousand Alnitak soldiers know they are completely doomed. Akins can tell there is fear in his ranks and decides to get his men together.

Akins gets in front of his army and says, "Every warrior here is to give their lives to our armies in Tarentum. Every life given here gives precious time for our armies to do the same to our enemy. I will not fear death. I will kill until my last breath. When I'm falling to the ground dying, I will be smiling at my enemy, not thinking of pain!"

The Alnitak Army yells and screams for their enemy to come to them. Spenser and Berith take everything they have and attack Akins. At dusk, the Alnitak Army at Girulic loses over a hundred and twenty thousand soldiers. Akins and about twenty thousand infantrymen and archers fight for another twenty-four hours before they are exhausted. The battle for Girulic is over and Tarentum wins. It is pure carnage at Girulic.

Tarentum loses over three hundred thousand men. One third of Berith's heavy and light cavalry was also compromised. It was a costly battle for Berith. Akins fought and did what he could for his kingdom. The Alnitak Army at Girulic fought to the last man. Not one of Akins' men surrendered.

Now, Berith and Spenser have over a half million men to proceed and go after Florick and Kentor. It will take Berith two days before he can engage Florick. Cainin's forces are defending their area waiting on Berith. Cainin loses some battles to give Florick hope so he can punch through and get to Rigel. The Alnitak forces in Tarentum do not know they are about to be surrounded. Unfortunately, General Florick is limited on supplies and weaponry.

To the west of Florick on the forty-third day after the earthquake, Albertous attacks the Antares Kingdom with one hundred thousand men. Kentor's second in command is outnumbered two to one, but he thrust his cavalry in the most vulnerable spot in the Antares military and completely destroys their lines. Because Albertous stayed steady with his attack, the Antares military could never regroup and counter. The battle took thirty-two hours, and the Alnitak force in Antares has taken control. Kentor's second in command orders his men to sleep for four hours before marching to Rigel. It will take a day and a half before Albertous can meet up with Kentor and Florick. Albertous loses over fifty-five thousand men but won a substantial victory. With forty-five thousand surviving warriors, Albertous rides tall to Rigel. Albertous' scouts come back and say there are no enemy armies in front of him. The march will be easy for Albertous' men.

On the forty-fifth day after the quake, Florick is still engaging in battle with Cainin. Florick takes the offensive, but cannot break through to Rigel. The messenger from Girulic reaches Florick. The messenger gets off his horse and reports to his Supreme Commander.

The messenger salutes Florick and says, "Our army at Girulic is or will be wiped out. The largest enemy army in history is or has taken Girulic. General Akins is giving up his life so your armies can regroup. The Tarentum Army will sweep around and cut our armies from any more supplies or reinforcements. I am ashamed I left my army behind to die."

Florick says, "How can you be ashamed of yourself? You gave up your soul to get to us. That's what is important. You have no shame here. Because of your act of sacrifice, you will save thousands here."

The Alnitak Supreme Commander knows he is in trouble. He tells all of his generals to report to him at once. Alnitak's army keeps the bombardment up with archers and cavalry against Cainin. Florick's forces do not want the Tarentum to change their battle plans. Florick knows Cainin will not start a full scale attack until Berith and Spenser can get into position. Florick has less than two days to either get to Rigel or change his strategy.

With all of his generals, Florick says, "We have lost our army in Girulic. We are about to be surrounded. We must get to Rigel to regroup with our other armies. I've got word that Albertous is winning at Antares. Most of his army is intact so far. Kentor still has a hundred and fifty thousand men. We must regroup. Time is not on our side. We will run out of supplies within two weeks. The main thing we have to think about is where the army that attacked Akins is headed. Are they coming around to attack our armies here or are they going to attack Alnitak? We have over two hundred thousand warriors in our capital. I know the enemy that attacked Girulic is afraid of having two fronts attacking them. They want me. The only way we can win this war is to unite as Alnitak brothers at Rigel and send in an all out attack. Do not let our enemy keep us at a stand still. Any army that is stagnant will die."

General Florick goes full force towards his opposition. He takes all of his cavalry and spearheads through the Tarentum lines. He is able to spearhead a mile and divert his cavalry so his infantry can break through. It is a total success for Florick and his generals. Because the Alnitak military does so well, Florick's generals ask to keep attacking. The Alnitak Supreme Commander says no, and his army marches to Rigel. Because the battle between Florick and Cainin was so decisive, the Tarentum generals had no choice but to regroup.

General Kentor also spearheads through another Tarentum line. The second in command breaks through and completely destroys his enemy. Because Albertous is to Kentor's left and Florick is to his right, the army that Kentor fights is surrounded and another victory comes to the Alnitak armies. Three lines of the Tarentum military have been broken. The morale is on Alnitaks side.

On the forty-eighth day after the earthquake, all Alnitak armies are at Rigel. Alnitak has a total of three hundred and sixty thousand warriors inside Tarentum. A force of five hundred thousand is coming to Florick from the south and seven hundred thousand is coming from his east. Florick regroups and finds out what he has to fight with.

The main reason to get to Rigel is for the small settlements in the area. However, it is very rocky and it is a formidable natural defensive area. The region is only a week away from the Tarentum capital. It is also the ideal spot to gain food and water because on the other side of Rigel is a lush forest with little inhabitants.

General Florick knows the Tarentum Emperor will not like it one bit that Alnitak warriors are so close to his capital, and he also knows Baylonis will send in his military to attack. The Alnitak Army has the advantage, but Cainin followed Florick and is stationed six miles from Rigel. Berith will reach Cainin in a day in a half.

General Florick gets his generals together. When Albertous and Kentor see their mentor, they hug Florick as a brother. So far, Florick has won battles, but not the war. Because of all the fighting and death, no Alnitak warrior thought they would have made it to Rigel.

General Florick looks at his generals and says, "General Akins gave his life to give time for our army. We will not let that go unnoticed. We have about two days to prepare for the Tarentum attack. I have reports most of our cavalry made it through. We are outnumbered five to one. I can take those odds. Most of the Tarentum military is not trained as our warriors. But numbers do count. We need to find the elite fighting group of Cainin's forces and take them on with our cavalry. We will spearhead through their ranks with our archers and cavalry. The other half of the Tarentum military will be easy to deal with. When I made my last thrust to make it to Rigel, I could tell their best trained soldiers were not there."

Kentor says, "When I went through their ranks to get here, I felt the same way. I think their best warriors were at Girulic."

Florick responds, "We don't have time. The army that beat us at Girulic will meet up with Cainin tomorrow or the day after. We must get ready for a defensive war until we are closer in numbers for a counterattack. Within a week, we will be able to have one decisive battle to tip the scale of this war. We must put a large dent into their military so we can go back to Girulic and take back our natural resources to make our city great again."

Albertous says, "With all due respect, what if we are not strong enough to take back Girulic?"

General Florick says, "Then our civilization as we know it will no longer exist. It is up to us right here and right now to take our enemy so our grandchildren can grow up as we did."

The next day, Cainin gets his cavalry together and waits for Berith's army to take on Florick. He cannot wait. Every Tarentum soldier in a two day march goes to the future battlefield. It gives the Tarentum Army another hundred thousand men. The next afternoon, Cainin will have close to a million and half men to take on the Alnitak Army.

On the fiftieth day after the earthquake that ripped Alnitak apart, Berith goes to Cainin and asks about the situation at hand. To most of Tarentum's military, it is Florick who attacked their land. Berith brings his cavalry and every beast Cainin has to the battlefield from his surrounding area. The Tarentum cavalry outnumbers Florick's cavalry substantially.

At Rigel, Alnitak has two thousand mammoths, eight hundred elephants, five hundred giant rhinos, and fifteen thousand horses. On the other side of the field, Tarentum has five thousand mammoths, nineteen hundred elephants, twelve hundred giant rhinos, and a twenty-six thousand horse cavalry.

The Alnitak cavalry is superior to the Tarentum cavalry, but neither Florick nor Cainin knows who will win. Both Supreme Commanders wonder if it is numbers or training which will win on the battlefield. At the battle of Girulic, some of the best Tarentum cavalry was destroyed by Akins. Florick thanks the gods for the bravery of his formal general.

The next day at dawn, General Florick is at the front lines. He turns around and sees his army. He knows every warrior and beast will give their lives for their kingdom. The Alnitak Supreme Commander is confident that his military will prevail in this battle. Florick looks at his background as sees the mountains which will keep any enemy army from being a threat. The Tarentum military can only attack in three different directions.

Two hours later, the Tarentum cavalry and infantry come towards the Alnitak lines. There is no deception of where Cainin is going to attack. The Tarentum Supreme Commander is going for an all out attack. There is no holding back from the Tarentum military on this battlefield. It is all or nothing.

Florick looks and sees a vast army. It is very impressive to the Alnitak Supreme Commander, but he is not afraid to die for his kingdom. Florick thinks of his wife Kassandra. He knows if he does not win here she will die in the weeks to come when the Tarentum attacks his capital.

The first attack comes from Cainin. All of Tarentum cavalry goes to the front of the Alnitak infantry. Then Cainin's heavy and light cavalry runs towards Florick's army.

Florick looks at the battlefield and says, "Pull back our cavalry. Put them into our infantry. All archers come forward."

All of Florick's orders are obeyed. All Alnitak archers are ready for whatever comes their way. Alnitak archers get in their position as the Tarentum cavalry rushes towards Florick.

On the Tarentum side, thousands of Cainin's beasts rush toward

Florick's army. Alnitak is ready for the attack. Florick orders his elephants and mammoths to move thirty yards in front of his archers and infantry lines. When the Tarentum military gets closer, they will see what they need to eliminate first. Right before Cainin's army reaches the Alnitak Army. Florick orders his archers to fire beyond his own cavalry. Arrows fly through the air. Hundreds of Tarentum beasts hit the ground. Some of Cainin's cavalry make it through, but are injured from the arrows. Some of the Tarentum cavalry lose their riders, but thousands of Tarentum beasts make it through the Alnitak's line of fire. Florick's cavalry rushes to counterattack. A massive battle between giant rhinos and mammoths go head to head from both armies. Within twenty minutes, Florick's cavalry gains ground and pushes the Tarentum cavalry back. The Alnitak archers and cavalry work hand and hand to destroy the assault.

Thirty minutes into the battle, Cainin orders a retreat. Over twenty percent of Tarentum's cavalry is destroyed. Florick starts to think everything is going his way. To the Alnitak Supreme Commander, the superior training and discipline of his men will win this war.

Berith rushes to Cainin and says, "We have the numbers, let us just send in everything we have, including our archers. Let our archers get close enough to inflict damage. We need to fight as one. I will take personal command of our archers."

Cainin orders every heavy cavalry and archer to the battlefield. Cainin's heavy cavalry of elephants, mammoths, and giant rhinos are on the front line. Right behind the heavy cavalry are the archers and then their infantry. Cainin orders his light cavalry to stay behind.

On the other side of the battlefield, Florick sees the Tarentum military formation. It is more massive compared to his army. Florick knows this is the battle in which his kingdom will live or die.

Kentor runs to Florick and says, "Let me die in honor. I want to lead our men into battle."

General Florick replies, "I have to think of you as a soldier, not a friend. You're the only person that can turn the tide on the battlefield. The chance of you being killed in the next hour is great, but I will be following right behind you to the afterworld. Tell the gods I'm coming."

Kentor says, "I need the light cavalry to back us and counterattack.

I will give the order for them to engage. I see their archers are right behind their cavalry."

Kentor rushes to the battlefield by horseback. Alnitak's horse cavalry gets right behind their heavy cavalry. Kentor gets off his horse and climbs on a giant rhino. Once he gets there he changes the formation of the light cavalry. The second in command knows he only has minutes before the Tarentum's heavy cavalry attacks his formation. Every Alnitak rider is calm and ready. Kentor looks at some of his men as he gives orders. Everyone is focused on Alnitak's side of the battlefield. Kentor's cavalry is ready for what is going to take place here. No one is expecting to live. However, they are hoping to destroy the enemy enough so their society can live on.

The Tarentum cavalry comes straight at the Alnitak defensive perimeter. Florick sees a small weakness inside the Tarentum formation and orders five thousand archers and ten thousand infantrymen to take advantage of the situation. The Alnitak Supreme Commander also orders five thousand more archers in reserve to back up his light cavalry. Even though he is confident his actions will work, General Florick knows he does not have the reserves to fight for more than three hours before the fatigue of his military starts to make them falter on the battlefield.

Kentor waits for his enemy. The fear of waiting is starting to sink in with the Alnitak warriors holding their positions. His men want to go forward to meet their attackers. The second in command wants them to get closer so his archers can help even the odds.

Two hundred yards before the Tarentum cavalry reaches the Alnitak position, Kentor yells at the top of his lungs, "Ride to your death or ride to glory!"

Every Alnitak beast runs forward. Kentor's archers do the same. When the engagement begins, Kentor's archers will be only a minute behind their cavalry. On the other side, the Tarentum archers will take over ten minutes before they can inflict damage to the Alnitak position. Right after the engagement, Kentor ordered all of his light cavalry to go through and destroy the Tarentum archers.

The fighting begins. On both sides, mammoths, giant rhinos, and elephants collide. Right at the beginning, the Alnitak heavy cavalry loses ground. Kentor is at the front on his giant rhino. One minute later arrows are heard going over Kentor's head. The Alnitak archers are firing sixty yards in front of Kentor's position.

Kentor sees his first target. He takes his beast and gains speed. With so much momentum, his giant rhino thrusts his horn right into a Tarentum mammoth's leg and puts the mammoth to the ground.

In the distance, Kentor sees hundreds of Tarentum beasts fall to the ground from the fire of his archers. He orders his heavy cavalry to regroup under the cover of fire. Kentor can only see within a hundred yards because of the massive dust cloud. The flying dust is impairing everyone's vision. The second in command of the Alnitak forces regroup with their cavalry and fight what is inside their archers' range. The Alnitak cavalry fights and starts to win the battle. Both Cainin and Florick cannot see what is going on in the main battle. Both Supreme Commanders can only hope.

Three minutes before Kentor destroys the last of what is inside his archers' kill zone, he hears arrows coming from the other end of the battlefield. Because there is a constant bombardment of firing from the Tarentum and Alnitak archers, there are arrows colliding with each other and falling to the ground and hitting the Alnitak cavalry. When the arrows fly by, Kentor sees his horse cavalry go by, and the arrows stop coming from his archers to avoid hitting their own.

For five minutes of the battle, the Tarentum's momentum stops except what was in the kill zone of Alnitak archers. Berith takes command and lets the first wave of Tarentum's cavalry get destroyed. Berith brings over forty thousand archers to his front.

Not knowing what Berith is doing because of the dust cloud, Kentor takes his giant rhino and finds another target. He sees his horse cavalry running past him to counter the Tarentum archers. The Alnitak horse cavalry goes through at full speed. What seems like the last of Alnitak's light cavalry goes through the main front, an arrow hits Kentor in the leg, and six other arrows hit his giant rhino. One arrow goes deep into Kentor's rhino's neck. The second in command knows his beast only has minutes to live. He takes his beast to his target and hits another Tarentum mammoth. The horn goes right through the stomach of the enemy mammoth. With Kentor's rhino interlocked with the horn inside the mammoth, the two animals fall, throwing Kentor to the ground.

Kentor gets up slowly and is completely stunned. He gets up with the arrow still stuck in his leg. Every time he tries to run, there is extreme pain that shoots throughout his leg. Kentor's adrenaline starts to kick in. He sees another Alnitak rhino without a rider. He jumps onto the beast and continues to fight. With three arrows inside his new giant rhino, it seems he was the lucky one of the two Alnitak warriors. The arrows inside his rhino are not in vulnerable spots, and the beast is not affected.

At Kentor's location, arrows are still flying over the battlefield in large numbers. It has the sound of screaming eagles fighting over head. It seems more arrows are coming from the Tarentum military. To Kentor, the Alnitak horse cavalry should have broken the ranks of the Tarentum archers. Because of all the dust coming from the battle, Kentor cannot see more than forty to fifty feet. No one on the main battlefield knows if they are winning or losing. The only sounds coming from the fighting inside the cloud of death is gallops, yells of pain, and arrows. Everyone from both sides keeps fighting without any direction.

Kentor stops his rhino to look for another target. All of a sudden, another arrow hits Kentor's left shoulder. He looks at his new wound and looks at his rhino. He sees an arrow inside the eye socket of his rhino. He shakes on the reins, and the beast does not move. The rhino falls face first to the ground, throwing Kentor against the animal's horn. From the impact, he hits his head and breaks his right arm.

With all the dust in the air, Kentor gets up and does not know where to go. There is nothing in front of him but a dust storm from all the cavalry galloping across the battlefield. He walks forward hoping he is going in the direction of his main army.

About a hundred yards, the second in command starts to see more clearly. He is still stunned from the blow to his head. When Kentor stops for a second to regroup, he finds out he was not walking in the direction he needed to go. The wounded general is walking in the direction of the Alnitak and Tarentum light cavalry battle. He looks and sees his light cavalry being slaughtered.

Berith's redirects his heavy cavalry to meet the Alnitak light cavalry head on. Right behind the Tarentum cavalry is fifty thousand archers firing into and beyond the dust cloud towards the Alnitak's archers. Alnitak's light cavalry cannot retreat. If they try, the Tarentum archers will destroy them before they even get back to Florick's men. The Alnitak archers had to pull back before they would have been completely destroyed by the overwhelming numbers of the Tarentum archers.

Kentor turns around and sees the cloud of dust is starting to lift all over the battlefield. He can see his heavy cavalry retreating back, but with less numbers. Kentor's heavy cavalry destroyed what was inside the pocket with his archers, but another division of Tarentum's heavy cavalry is right in the middle of Alnitak's horse cavalry destroying their lines. Kentor knows the rest of Tarentum's cavalry will turn around and go after General Florick's formation. Kentor starts to walk back to his Supreme Commander. There is dust still in the air. He is still disoriented from his concussion. When Kentor gets half way back, a Tarentum warrior is returning back to his army and sees a wounded Alnitak general. Kentor cannot do anything because of his injuries. The general cannot put up a fight. The Tarentum warrior sees Kentor is an Alnitak general and puts a sword right through his chest. The second in command of the Alnitak military is dead.

Florick looks on and can see the dust lifting and sees that most of his horse cavalry is destroyed. The Alnitak Army at Rigel has lost seventy percent of their heavy cavalry. Florick only has a handful of mammoths, elephants, and giant rhinos against thousands of Tarentum cavalry. There is nothing but carnage on the battlefield.

Minutes go by; there is no Alnitak light cavalry alive on the battlefield. The Alnitak warriors get into a defensive position with what is left of their heavy cavalry. Florick's archers are right behind. Without any hesitation, the Tarentum military builds their lines to finish off Florick.

Florick looks at Albertous and says, "We have lost one of the best generals in Alnitak's history. You are the one to take his place. You will die here in honor as second in command of Alnitak. Take your position with our heavy cavalry."

Albertous says, "Before I go, can I say something, sir?"

Florick replies "Go on."

Albertous says, "No thank you, sir. I am not going to take the honor of second in command. I do not deserve such an honor. I respect the idea of Kentor, and I do not want to take his place even after his death, but I will give my life and loyalty to you and our army. Thank you, sir. I will follow your order and fight to the death."

Albertous gets to his heavy cavalry before the Tarentum military starts their attack. Albertous is outnumbered fifty to one and is ready to die here. With that kind of leadership, his cavalry is ready to die as well.

The battle begins, and Tarentum goes on the offensive. Florick knows within twelve hours his military will be destroyed. He left scouts outside his camp to tell his king of the events which are taking place at Rigel.

Albertous stands tall and goes forward to meet the Tarentum cavalry. Within an hour, the Alnitak heavy cavalry is completely destroyed. Albertous dies a courageous death. The Tarentum horse cavalry goes towards Florick's formation without any formidable defense. The Alnitak military at Rigel counters everything back with their archers.

After about four hours, Florick's archers run out of arrows. Alnitak's infantry is also exhausted. Hour after hour, the Tarentum Army beats Florick back. Tens of thousands of Alnitak warriors die. The Tarentum cavalry destroys every defensive perimeter Florick makes. The Alnitak Supreme Commander runs out of orders and counter moves. Florick sees the men he led here die a horrible death. At the end, Florick gives unattainable orders and his military still fights and gains some ground, but only to be taken back by Cainin's army, but exhaustion becomes more of an enemy than the Tarentum military. After about six more hours, Florick has only ten thousand infantrymen. He takes one last offensive and dies with his men.

The Alnitak scouts, looking at the battlefield from a distance, see their commander's military destroyed. They ride as fast as they can to the Alnitak capital. It takes them almost a week to get to Colligitar. When they get to the gate of the Alnitak capital, the scouts do not know what to say to their king. They stop and contemplate on what to tell their king. Their whole army just got wiped out. The Tarentum military still has one million two hundred thousand warriors which will probably attack Alnitak next. Colligitar will face six to one odds with his defensive wall still damaged. Even though Cainin lost most of his cavalry at Girulic and Regel, he still has ten times the number then Colligitar's city.

CHAPTER XVIII
IT ALL COMES DOWN
TO NUMBERS

On the fifty-third day after the earthquake, Atlandreous has another week before he arrives back in his city of Alnilam with his escort. He rides ahead of his main military which helped rebuild Halotropolis. The Master of War thinks about Tess and the leaps and bounds which have taken place on the byland. Right before sundown, Atlandreous crosses a stream on his giant elk. A Halotropolis messenger rides fast on horseback towards Atlandreous.

Right in front of Atlandreous, the messenger stops abruptly and says, "Your presence is needed back in Halotropolis."

Atlandreous asks, "What is so urgent for your city to find me? I didn't tell anyone what path I was going to take to get back home."

The messenger says, "Alnitak's military just entered the Tarentum and Antares borders. Tarentum just attacked their main resources in Girulic. War has broken out on the continent."

Atlandreous asks, "Who started the war?"

The messenger says, "Florick and Kentor, sir. Other than Alnitak, all kings from the city-states are on route to Halotropolis. Icaras, Richcampous, and Lopatheous, will meet in Halotropolis tomorrow to discuss options."

Atlandreous asks, "Where did you get this information?"

The messenger responds, "The messages were reported to Alnilam from your main port on the continent, and it was communicated to the rest of the city-states. All kings are on route by sea to our port. From there, they will ride to our city. By the way, Colligitar is also asking for our help."

One of Atlandreous' escorts says, "Colligitar did not want us around his city a month ago. Now, he wants our help?"

The Halotropolis messenger says, "Alnitak was almost destroyed from the natural disaster. The water supply inside their city is almost nonexistent. They have one aqueduct operational and another channel is only forty percent efficient. Colligitar's grandest aqueduct will not be functioning for another six months. Alnitak's food supply is cut in half because of the lack of water. The natural resources to make cement from Girulic have ceased. The once great city is now starving. With Colligitar's city having the largest population on the peninsula, the lack of water has affected hundreds of thousands of people, and people are dying."

Atlandreous asks, "What source did the situation of Alnitak come from?"

The messenger says, "He told me to tell you that an Alnitak senator asked for refuge for himself and his family inside Halotropolis hours after you left. I went three hours to find you after Cetrono granted asylum to the senator."

Atlandreous looks at his escort and says, "I will go alone. I need you all to ride as fast as you can to Alnilam and tell Erasmus, Orion, Nieander, and Hamon to meet me in Halotropolis. Go now."

Atlandreous' escort follows his orders; they go full speed to Alnilam. The Master of War goes back to Cetrono's city with the messenger from Halotropolis. Atlandreous does not know what to expect when he gets to Cetrono's city. He wonders if the Alnitaks are winning or losing the war with Tarentum. With the devastation of Alnitak, the supplies and manpower to take on Baylonis' military is not obtainable. Atlandreous wonders if the Tarentum Empire provoked the fight. He knows Florick and Kentor would not go to war unless they had the resources to do so.

Within thirty-six hours, the Master of War goes straight to Cetrono's palace. Atlandreous has not slept for two full days. He is exhausted, but he keeps a straight face as he rides through Halotropolis. There is a great deal of movement from Cetrono's military moving throughout the city.

Tess knew Atlandreous was about to arrive, and she decided to wait on him. Outside the palace, Atlandreous gets off his horse.

The first person he recognizes is Tess. Cetrono's daughter is at the top of the platform of the palace. Tess walks down.

They meet at the middle of the stairs. Tess smiles and says, "You were not gone long. It is good to see you again."

Atlandreous asks, "Are all the kings here?"

Tess says, "Everyone except for Lopatheous. He just got to our port and will be here tomorrow. Messages are coming from the continent that war has broken out between Alnitak, Antares and Tarentum. No one knows exactly what is going on except Florick and Kentor. By the way, the Alnitak King is asking for help from all city-states on the peninsula."

Atlandreous asks, "What are the kings saying?"

Tess says, "My father and the other kings are in favor of sending military aid to Colligitar."

Atlandreous asks, "What do you think the city-states should do?"

Tess says, "I have no say in any of this. The decisions are up to the kings."

Atlandreous says, "You just answered my question. I don't think they know the full consequences of helping Alnitak. Don't go inside. I don't want you a part of this. Helping Colligitar is a noble deed, but it is militarily impossible."

Atlandreous is escorted where the kings are meeting. It takes him almost five minutes to get to Cetrono's grand balcony over looking Halotropolis. When the Master of War gets to the kings, he does not know what to say. A million different scenarios go through his head. Atlandreous wishes he had his father to help in this political situation, but now he has to do it on his own.

Atlandreous goes to the doorway to Cetrono's balcony and everyone stops talking as he is about to enter. The Master of War looks around and can tell there are no clear answers for the discussion at hand.

Atlandreous looks through the doorway and says, "Hello gentlemen. May I come in?"

Icaras looks and walks towards Atlandreous and says, "I'm glad you're here."

Atlandreous says, "Thank you, sir. Hello King Cetrono."

Cetrono says, "Thank you for coming and thank you for being humble coming into my home. But this is not the time to be humble. The city-states need you. We are going to help Colligitar's kingdom."

Atlandreous says, "Sir, may I ask for someone to catch me up of what is happening on the continent? I just found out how badly the situation really is inside Colligitar's city."

Richcampous says, "We are lagging ten days of knowing actual events on the continent. It takes our scouts and messengers that long to get to our capital for us to find out information. Akin's army has been compromised at Girulic. Kentor and Florick are inside Tarentum battling Cainin and the Antares Kingdom."

Icaras says, "Florick and Kentor are good generals. They would not go into Tarentum unless they had the advantage or no choice. Colligitar is asking us to help protect the city of Alnitak just in case the Tarentum military, which attacked Girulic, goes south and attacks the peninsula. The army that sacked Girulic has close to a million men and can take on the peninsula by itself. Alnitak only has two hundred thousand men to protect their walls."

Atlandreous says, "Gentlemen, no. Neither Kentor nor Florick would have gone to war unless they knew there was no other choice. There is something wrong here. The military, which attacks Girulic, will not go south. This is a planned attack. The army you think is an immediate threat will go north and take on Florick and Kentor first. After taking the Alnitak armies, they will regroup and take Colligitar's city. Whatever happened at the borders to start this war was planned from the beginning. I don't think it was Kentor or Florick to make such a foolish move. I feel Florick and Kentor saw no alternative but to attack. On the other hand, we cannot help Colligitar. If we combine our forces on the byland, we will have over five hundred thousand warriors in and around Alnitak. Even with Alnitak's two hundred thousand warriors, we do not have the resources to help their king. Colligitar's city cannot even sustain itself. There is no way they can supply our armies around Alnitak. Our food stores are getting low, and we do not have the supplies needed to be inside Colligitar's city for more than two weeks. The supply lines are too long. Every mile we are away from a strong hold decreases our chances to keep an army strong. Our strongest point is here at Halotropolis."

Cetrono asks, "So, what do we do? Do we let Alnitak get destroyed?"

Atlandreous says, "Yes, because of the earthquake, we too have little food in reserves. I respect all city-states militaries, but we do not know how to fight with one another. If we fight with Alnitak, we will lose tens of thousands of men just trying to correlate on the battlefield. We need time. Alnitak is dead. It is noble to try to save Colligitar's city, but it comes down to numbers and time. If we fight with Alnitak against the continent, we will lose."

Icaras says, "Atlandreous is right. We would have two weeks of food and water before we run out of supplies in Alnitak. Our supply lines will be stretched. Between Alnitak and Alnilam, it would take my kingdom two weeks to build up the supplies needed to keep our army fed and armed for only a week. My food stores are on a thin line. It will also take us three weeks to get our artillery inside Colligitar's city to help defend it."

Atlandreous says, "We have to take Tarentum by surprise. We have less than two months before the Tarentum military can attack our four city-states. If they went to the extent of going to war with Alnitak at Girulic, they will not stop there. If Antares is on their side, they have no enemies to worry about on the continent. Total conquest is in the hearts of the Tarentum generals right now."

Cetrono says to Atlandreous, "After the earthquake, your kingdom came to our aid to rebuild Halotropolis. I thank you for your time you spent away from your own politics at home. Even though our city-states were about to fight one another, I think you should lead our armies to defend against the continent. I, myself, will give my armies to you. They are under your command."

Atlandreous says, "Let us start today. I do not want Alnitak destroyed, but there is no alternative. We have to worry about what is possible. I have seen you all as an enemy and a friend. From this point forward, we will only come together as one to make our city-states better for the future of our children. We need to become one to survive the elements of the rest of the world."

Within thirty minutes of discussion, all the kings agree with Atlandreous. The only king that has not had a vote is Lopatheous. With Atlandreous taking the position of Master of War against Masaba and Halotropolis, the rest of the kings do not think it will be a problem for him to bring the militaries of the city-states together to protect the byland.

The next day the kings of the city-states meet with Lopatheous without Atlandreous, and the Vasic king agrees with the decision to put Atlandreous as Supreme Commander of the peninsula. To make his plans go forward, Atlandreous is still waiting on his generals from Alnilam to arrive. By ship, it will take his generals eight days before they arrive. For the time being, Atlandreous can only wait to see what is happening with the war on the continent.

After a couple of days, the new Supreme Commander of the peninsula gets his thoughts together. Atlandreous wastes no time. He asks for a meeting with the kings again.

Atlandreous says, "We are on borrowed time. I need all of the armies to meet in Mintaka in two weeks from today. That gives us time for messengers to get to each city. Mintaka is almost the center of our four cities. With the reports from our messengers saying the army that attacked Girulic is headed north, it will give us more time to prepare. After the war with Florick and Kentor, we will have a little less than a month and a half to prepare for a formidable defense."

Cetrono says, "After Tarentum takes Alnitak, they will come after my city next."

Atlandreous says, "Yes, and we will be prepared. When Tarentum attacks Colligitar's city, it will take Cainin at least a week to take Alnitak. Because of the earthquake and lack of food and water, Colligitar's city is in no shape to fight a war. After Tarentum destroys Alnitak, we will make a stand six miles north of your city in the Floortatum Province. We will not use the cities as a defense. I have ordered all of my city's artillery to move into Floortatum. It will take two weeks to arrive. I am also ordering all of the city-states artillery to the area. I need a full division of Halotropolis to organize the province. We have a lot of training to do. We have to work as one to fight our enemy."

Richcampous says, "If we leave our defenses down at our city-states, we will leave our civilians defenseless."

Atlandreous says, "If we let them fight city to city, the Tarentum military will win. We have to come together and surprise our enemy. Tarentum will be expecting us to fight apart. After they take Alnitak, they will try to take Halotropolis first. We will have an army to meet them. They will think they are attacking Cetrono's men. After a small confrontation, that army will retreat to Floortatum. They will try to destroy the diversionary army and we will be waiting for them. The rocky area can hide our armies until Tarentum comes to fight on our terms."

Icaras says, "I have confidence in your battle tactics, but this is a gamble, and you're putting the possibility of cultural extinction. What if we are outnumbered three to one? We cannot bet those odds without walls."

Atlandreous says, "Surprise is our best weapon. We will come together as brothers and not let one of our cities get sacked. We will pull together and die together. Does everyone agree? There are no safe answers here. Taking our enemy off guard is our only true weapon."

All the kings agree. Cetrono does not want his city to be hit first and destroyed. All kings know Masaba would be next and then Vasic. Because Icaras' city is at the end of the peninsula, Alnilam would be the last objective of the Tarentum military. If they decide to defend each city one by one, Alnilam might survive after the depletion of Tarentum supplies and manpower. Atlandreous' city would have the best chance of surviving the war. If the kings went forward with the plan to defend city to city, Atlandreous would have the best chance to come out alive. The Supreme Commander of the peninsula is showing sacrifice to the other city-states.

Atlandreous stays in Halotropolis until he gets more information of what is going on with the war. He does not know what to expect. The new Supreme Commander of the peninsula waits on information where the main battle will take place on the continent. A scout comes back and says that Florick is at a stalemate with Cainin and his other armies are winning ground. The scouts say also the main objective of the Alnitak military is to meet up at Rigel to reorganize and fight on. At this point, Atlandreous knows what to do. He asks the kings to come together one last time before he goes to Mintaka. They all meet at Cetrono's balcony one last time before Atlandreous starts on his military objectives.

Atlandreous comes in and says, "Florick has the manpower and tactics to obtain the Alnitak's main spearhead through Tarentum. The Alnitak military will converge at Rigel. Florick will have enough resources and momentum to get to the best location for a defensive battle against Cainin's military before he goes on the offensive, but he is wrong. I think Tarentum's best warriors were in Girulic. Winning battles inside Tarentum has given Florick a false sense of hope. Cainin is surrounding Florick to deplete Alnitak's supplies. The battle at Rigel will be swift and decisive within a week, but not in the Alnitak's favor. After that, we have exactly a month to stage the battle in our favor. I will have everything ready at Floortatum. We have the time."

Cetrono says, "Some of us do not agree with everything in what you're planning. We need to regroup with Colligitar's military and fight with them. It will give us another two hundred thousand soldiers to fight the continent."

Atlandreous says, "I know it is hard to see. But I can envision everything in my head of what most likely will happen. It is not magic to see the stages of warfare, but it is who I am. You can agree with this and live, or disagree and let our societies as we know it become extinct."

Icaras says, "I am one of those people that disagree, but I have seen what you do on the battlefield, sparring matches, and political matters. I retract the statement of not going forward with your plan. If you think it is impossible to save Alnitak, I will take your side."

Cetrono says, "I have sent messengers to Alnitak. The women and children can come to our cities for refuge. I will not let the innocent die."

Richcampous says, "We will make sacrifices to help in other matters than fighting with Colligitar's city."

Atlandreous says, "It is not me letting the Alnitak population become nonexistent. With our food stores getting more and more depleted because of war and the earthquake, the saving of a few lives will jeopardize each city of resources needing to survive. It is a noble thing to do, but like I said before, it comes down to numbers. I am looking out for our four city-states. We will be flooded with refugees. Because the Alnitak civilians do not have supplies to get to any of the cities, they will die in transient. There will be panic in the months to come from your own cities not having the food to survive. With us defending ourselves, it will accelerate food consumption. In the process of leadership, I have diverted my generals from Alnilam to Mintaka."

Atlandreous understands the politics of the kings, but he has no time to think about anything else other than destroying his enemy.

The Supreme Commander of the peninsula knows he will have over a million men to fight.

Atlandreous arrives in Mintaka before his generals and the main armies on the peninsula. His father is there to greet him. Thanos goes to his son and they embrace as father and son.

Atlandreous says, "It has been a long time Father."

Thanos says, "I have thought about you every day. I am proud of you."

Atlandreous says, "I need you, Father. I have the most difficult decisions to make. I need your guidance."

Thanos says, "As a father, you can have my guidance, and I will be there for you, but I have the confidence that you will make the right decisions. Messengers have gone back and forth telling me of what is about to transpire here. I am still in the outside loop of Alnilam politics. All of the peninsula's warriors will be here in the next three days. You have this under control. All of the kings on the byland have confidence in your tactics and leadership."

Atlandreous says, "I have been very humble to the kings. At the same time, they put me in charge of all the armies on the peninsula. Then they doubt my thoughts of what to do."

Thanos says, "That is human nature. The kings have numerous people to answer to. They do not doubt you; they have learned to be careful. Scouts have told me of what you are thinking of doing, and I agree with a stand at Floortatum. Son, I had to leave you a couple of years ago in Alnilam to make you a better man. If I stayed, I would have enabled you. I played your politics at the beginning, and I had to step back. What you have done so far has astonished me. I will be here for you no matter what. The people on this peninsula believe in you, and so do I."

Atlandreous says, "Thank you Father, but I am overwhelmed. My circle of friends should be here in the next couple of days. The circle will be complete in my life to go forward and beat back our enemy."

Two days later, Erasmus, Orion, Nieander, and Hamon are home in Mintaka. They ride to Thanos' estate. The young men have not been home for years, and the village has turned into a small city. Their village has ten times the population as it did when they were teenagers. Atlandreous is going over some documents to try and find out how many supplies he has for this war. It is not looking good to the Supreme Commander of the peninsula. Then he sees his friends ride up on their giant elk. Atlandreous walks towards his generals. All of his friends go into military protocol and salute their commander.

Atlandreous says, "At ease. We have so much work to do. Every army on the peninsula will be here tomorrow or the next. All artillery will be at Floortatum next week. Hamon, when everyone arrives here, I want you to take their artillery personnel and ride to Floortatum. I will give you the details of our defenses tonight. I have the confidence in you to get it done. No matter what, you are in command of artillery. Find out the other city-states' artillery commanders and make sure they will not be threatened by you taking over the task at hand. Everyone wants to be in command. No one wants to be a soldier. If you cannot get them together and become a team, politics inside our city-states alliance can be just as deadly as our enemy."

Nieander asks, "How are General Florick and Kentor doing on the continent?"

Atlandreous says, "As far as we know, the Alnitak force in Tarentum is at Rigel. It looks like Berith took command of the army which attacked Girulic. Berith will reach Cainin in two more days. I give the Alnitaks a week before they are defeated and a month before we will fight on our own soil. Florick overextended his supply lines. As for our plans here, Erasmus and Orion, you two will be here for ten days before heading out to Floortatum. In twelve days, Nieander, you will follow with the heavy and light cavalry. It will take you less time to get to the future battle zone."

Orion asks, "Are we in complete command of the peninsula's armies?"

Atlandreous says, "No one is ever in complete command. To take control, you have to show leadership. Leadership will win over people and wars."

Orion asks, "How are we ranked on the battlefield? Are we higher than other generals of the city-states?"

Atlandreous says, "No, because of politics, Baudan and Roubertus will be higher ranked. No one has told me who is in command of the Masabaian military. They will be taking orders from me. No matter what, you will obey their command. Do I make myself clear on that matter?"

Hamon says, "If they make the wrong decision on the battlefield, thousands of lives will be destroyed."

Atlandreous says, "We need to have outside heroes in this battle, gentlemen, we cannot take all the glory when we beat back our enemy."

The next day, the armies of Halotropolis and Alnilam reach Mintaka at noon. The Vasic army arrives almost at dusk. Atlandreous waits and takes in information from his scouts about every detail of the battle on the continent.

When every general and Supreme Commander from each city-state arrives, they meet that night. A familiar face comes into Thanos' estate. It is someone Atlandreous did not expect to see.

Atlandreous sees his friend from his teenage years and says, "Tarasios, it is good to see you. I can see you are the Supreme Commander of the Masabaian Army. I know what you can do as an officer. But this is sudden."

Tarasios says, "After they made you commander of the four city-states. I was granted Supreme Commander of the Masabaian Army. It will be good to fight with you and not against you. My men respect and will die for you because of our alliance."

Atlandreous says, "We have not seen each other in over eight years. I have missed you. In that time, the friendship and respect of who you are never went away."

Tarasios replies, "When we were teenagers, I regretted not going with you to Alnilam, but I am a firm believer in God. We have come together for a reason, and God is the one who truly knows. The odds of us fighting as brothers are beyond me. I still remember the day you left Mintaka; I see it as if it were yesterday."

Atlandreous says, "The full circle is complete. I have had affiliations with everyone here in one way or another. I respect every person as a general and a leader to make this byland better for our children. We have to put all past and present differences aside right here and right now. I know you may not forget about them, but your children and your grandchildren will."

Orion asks, "How are we going to stop the Tarentum Army?"

Atlandreous says, "I have tactical scouts in Tarentum and they should arrive in four days telling of the battles in complete detail. Tarentum will take Colligitar's city. In the mean time, I need everyone on the peninsula to learn to fight with Alnilam's battle tactics. General, Roubertus, Tarasios, and Baudan, you are the leaders of your armies. Orion, Erasmus, Nieander, and Hamon you all are at their disposal. My generals will teach and adapt your armies to Alnilam's tactics. We need to take one step at a time. We will not know the force coming to our lands until my scouts report back to me, and we will have to adapt when they take Alnitak."

Everyone goes to their duties and Orion, Erasmus, Nieander, and Hamon teach the other armies the tactics of the Alnilam military. Everyone learns from one another and the other generals of the city-states are glad they did not have to go to war with Alnilam.

On the fourth day of training, a tactical scout comes to Atlandreous as he is going over battle tactics with the Supreme Commanders of the city-states.

The scout gets off his horse and says, "Florick and Kentor's armies are destroyed. The armies of Tarentum are turning south towards the peninsula."

Atlandreous asks, "How many Tarentum men and cavalry are on their way?"

The scout says, "Baylonis has pulled in his reserves, and they are also going south. The Tarentum military has over one million three hundred thousand men. Their heavy and light cavalry are going to out number ours five to one."

Atlandreous says, "Thank you, keep me posted."

Roubertus asks, "How are we going to take on that many men and beasts?"

Atlandreous says, "The Alnitak city will destroy over three hundred thousand of the continent's warriors. Alnitak will also destroy some of the Tarentum cavalry, but the most precious attribute is time. Roubertus, I need you and Hamon to go to Floortatum and get our artillery in place. The other components to our army needs more time here."

Roubertus and Hamon go to Floortatum. Orion starts on the training of the city-states army's archers. With Halotropolis and Alnilam getting the molless trees, their archers will have a huge advantage on the battlefield. Over ten thousand bows have been made from the molless tree which gives arrows a sixty yard advantage over most archers.

Atlandreous works on the city-states' armies for a week, and a person comes to Atlandreous while he is inspecting his cavalry.

The scout says, "The whole continent's armies are a week away from Alnitak. Baylonis has another two hundred thousand men on his side. He has asked every kingdom from the mainland to take us out."

Atlandreous says, "Bring all the generals to me."

Within thirty minutes, all of the generals from the city-states go to Atlandreous. The Supreme Commander of the peninsula is getting everything in place with the supply officers. Other military officers tell the generals of the situation. When everyone is in Atlandreous' presence, he just smiles at the commanders and keeps directing supplies and manpower to Floortatum.

Orion looks at Atlandreous and asks, "We have a million and a half men about to attack with five times the cavalry, and you smile while giving orders."

Atlandreous says, "That's right. It is time to go to Floortatum. It is time to go to work. I have the confidence in all of you to take on our enemy. This can't get any better. I know you all do not have the same religion as I do, but I am asking you to say a prayer for the Alnitak society. God is on our side. I know after this war God will be the true religion on the byland."

All of the city-states' military forces go to Floortatum. It will take Atlandreous' infantry a week to get there, but the armies of the city-states have time to get into position. Atlandreous and his generals are a little ashamed of not helping Alnitak, but being a military leader, you have to make decisions that are not always morally right.

CHAPTER XIX
NOBILITY OF A KING

On the fiftieth day after the earthquake, Colligitar finds out about the destruction of Akin's army at Girulic. There is panic in his Senate. The Alnitak King has found out why Kentor and Florick went to war and he tells his military advisors. The treachery of the Tarentum military couldn't have come at a worse time for the Alnitak Kingdom.

In Colligitar's city, the water is starting to flow from two of the three aqueducts. The water supply into the city is forty-five percent at full capacity. The last of the shipment of natural resources to make cement from Girulic is making its way to Alnitak.

In the last two months inside the Alnitak Kingdom, the weak and sick have died. There are over two hundred thousand people either buried or cremated to keep disease from spreading. With the destruction of the army at Girulic and deaths inside Alnitak, Colligitar has lost almost three hundred and fifty thousand people.

After finding out about the destruction of Akin's army, Colligitar assembles his generals and Senate together for an emergency meeting. Because Alnitak was on its way to recovery, the morale and hopes were coming alive from the civilian and military population until the defeat at Girulic.

Colligitar goes in front of the Senate and military advisors to get everyone's mindset in the right place.

Colligitar says, "The fight between Tarentum and Alnitak has started. General Akins and his army have given their lives for our kingdom. Kentor and Florick are going into our enemy's realm to lure Tarentum's military away so we can build a better defense here in our capital. Kentor and Florick are giving our city time for a defensive war."

A senator gets in front of the crowd and says, "Who started this conflict?"

Colligitar replies, "There is a great deal of deception from the Tarentum military. From what we have gathered from our armies in our Northern Territories, Baylonis has no earthly idea what his military has done to start this conflict. Our kingdom had no choice but to go to war. Tarentum's military thinks it is a good time to attack our kingdom at our weakest. Cainin is kicking us while we are on the ground. It is up to us to let them keep kicking us or to get up and fight back. To the Tarentum people, we are no longer a formable force as we were three months ago. Now they want to destroy our kingdom. The main construction project, as of right now, will be to repair our walls. We need to build a good defense against our enemy. If Florick and Kentor cannot beat back our enemy in Tarentum, Cainin will surely attack our city."

Colligitar only has two to three weeks to get his military together, and he knows he will never see Kentor or Florick again. The Alnitak King needs their expertise to defend his kingdom.

Colligitar is going towards a younger general to give command for Alnitak's defenses. When warriors speak of bravery and skill, the name Omar comes up in conversations. The young general has been under the command of Florick for over five years. He has moved up in rank very quickly.

Colligitar orders Omar to his palace. While the king is going over rebuilding the walls with his architects, Omar enters the king's chamber.

Omar stands at attention and asks, "Sir, you sent for me. What can I do for you?"

Colligitar says, "I have four generals ahead of you in rank. Those four generals are very cautious of what they do. They are not as aggressive as Kentor and Florick. You are young, but I need your energy to take on our enemy when they attack our city. We have less than three weeks before they attack. I need you to figure out the best way to defend our kingdom. I will take charge in repairing our walls. I need you to get our men ready for war."

Omar asks, "Can I say something, sir?"

Colligitar replies, "Yes."

Omar says, "We still have control outside our city. We have a very powerful cavalry. We need to move them outside our gates thirty miles east and west from our capital. When Tarentum does attack, our heavy and light cavalry can take their rear flank. Our walls will be able to sustain their initial attack. In doing so, they will not be able to regroup while we take out their weakest side. It will not win the war, but it will make them think twice to move forward in this conflict."

Colligitar says, "You have been thinking about this scenario before you came into this room. This is why I chose you. I needed someone who will have the guts to think of something so cunning. Get your cavalry officers together and make it happen."

Omar says, "I am putting Deus in command of our outside forces and Barrenious to take command of a small cavalry division which will stay here for defensive purposes."

It takes General Omar three days to get all of his cavalry together. Knowing he is young, Omar is very direct to his officers and men. If he shows any aspect of being youthful, his men will not respect him as a general. Omar gets all the Alnitak officers together to correlate all offensive and defensive plans. In the meantime, Colligitar puts all his efforts in reinforcing Alnitak's walls and outside defenses. Every tree outside the city is being cut down and being made into barricades and arrows.

On the fifty-ninth day after the earthquake, Colligitar finds out Florick and Kentor have lost at Rigel. Alnitak has lost over five hundred thousand warriors. The Alnitak King knows he only has maybe two weeks before the Tarentum Empire attacks his city. Colligitar has reached out to the four city-states to ask for military help, but it gets denied by the bylands. Colligitar feels alone in this war.

Omar orders Deus' heavy cavalry to their locations outside the gates of Alnitak. Omar will stay inside his capital to take command of the archers and artillery. Colligitar orders ten thousand infantrymen to protect both divisions of Deus' heavy cavalry. It leaves Alnitak with only two hundred thousand men, including their youth reserve inside their city.

One week before the enemy reaches Alnitak; Colligitar gets his Senate and military advisors together one last time.

Colligitar says, "We have about a week before our enemy attacks our city. We have done everything so far to reinforce our walls, but our defenses are still not up to par. We as a kingdom may fall. I, myself, have failed you. About three months ago I could have intervened with the conflict between Halotropolis and Alnilam. I did nothing. In turn, they will not fight beside our kingdom. I was concerned about everything else in our realm to be a leader to our fellow city-states. If I had given a military presence, the byland city-states would be here today. As a king and leader, I should have stopped the madness of the potential war to our brothers on the peninsula. Now, we have no allies. We are alone. The byland city-states have granted our women and children refuge inside their kingdoms. I will stay here and fight our enemy with our military. We have the army and the tactics to beat back Cainin's forces. I am asking the innocent to go to our neighbors. Whoever cannot hold a sword needs to leave until this war is over."

Everyday, thousands of people leave Alnitak towards the other city-states on the peninsula. Three months prior, the people of Alnitak thought they were better than the others on the byland. Now, with all the death inside Colligitar's city, most citizens are more humble and thankful to be alive. Thousands of Alnitak civilians are going to have a hard time making it across to other kingdoms. Colligitar took all the horses for their military light cavalry. At this point of urgency, the military has main priority. The civilians take little with them as they go deeper inside the byland. Without horses, the civilians cannot carry enough food and water for their journey. The Alnitak weak will die within three days while trying to go across the peninsula.

On the seventh day after the earthquake, General Omar only has three more days before the bulk of the Tarentum military is outside the Alnitak walls. The general gets his commanders ready in the Alnitak Military Hall. Colligitar is also there to give support to his new commander.

Omar walks towards his advisors and generals and says, "Reports have come back from outside our walls. There are close to a one and half million beasts and warriors about to attack our city. We only have two hundred and fifteen thousand men with our youth reserve and older veterans to protect it. The civilians that decided to stay have little military training. Everyone in this city has a sword, and we will not give ground to our enemy. We have the advantage in protecting our homeland. Let us get the final preparation in stopping our adversary."

Colligitar walks towards Omar and looks towards the crowd. The Alnitak King says to the audience, "We will not stop until we are dead or our enemy leaves for home. Right now let us be leaders as our fathers and forefathers were when they had the same situation. Our military values will be on the battlefield."

The audience cheers.

Omar yells, "We will not have a discussion of how to make this work. Commanders and generals, you have been trained for this. I am putting this on you to get your positions ready for the attack against our city. We have three days. I will come around to each position to see your progress. When the battle begins, I will know every strength and weakness of our city. Now go."

Everyone cheers for Colligitar and Omar. Every official and military commander leaves the room to start on the final preparations. Every leader of the city lifts up the morale of his men to work harder and more quickly than they had before. For the next forty-eight hours, every soldier works until they fall to the ground from exhaustion. Colligitar and Omar give specific orders to let their men sleep so they are ready for the next day. It is a life and death situation, and an exhausted army is a dead one. Because the Tarentum Army will have marched for almost two weeks to get to Colligitar's city, it gives the Alnitak military the advantage of more rest.

A day before the Tarentum military reaches the capital of Alnitak, Colligitar asks Florick's wife to come to him. Kassandra goes to Colligitar's palace. Florick's wife has no idea why he has asked for her.

Kassandra goes in the palace and says, "Sir, you asked for me?"

Colligitar responds, "I want to say that I am sorry about General Florick. He was my best general. I would have felt better if he was protecting these walls"

Kassandra stands up straight almost in tears and says, "Thank you, sir."

Colligitar says, "Right before the Alnilam and Halotropolis' military were about to fight one another, Florick told me you were against us not intervening and stopping it. I am here to say you were right. This city will not stand in the battle to come. It is my fault the other city-states do not want to fight with us. Other than that, I need your help."

Kassandra asks, "What can I do for you, sir?"

Colligitar says, "I regret some of the things I have done in the last three months. My daughter, Anastasia, has decided to stay with me to the end. It is very noble of her. I can't allow her to do that. I know the outcome of this conflict will not be in our kingdom's favor. She will not leave unless there is a higher purpose. That purpose is you. I am using you to get her out of here. I am putting you in charge of my elite guard. As you know, there are over eight thousand elite soldiers. Atlandreous is in charge of the four city-states' defenses. Because the kingdoms of the peninsula are giving my people a chance to live, I am sending our best warriors as a token of their generosity. I should have shown more leadership before the earthquake, and I regret that decision I made. After our city is destroyed by Tarentum, Cainin will not stop here. Our enemy will take over the known world. For me to fight my best, I want to think my daughter is safe. It is not logical with the odds against our kingdom and the city-states of the peninsula, but it will make me feel better."

Kassandra says, "I will make it happen."

Right before she leaves Colligitar's palace, Halamik, the commander of the elite guard, asks to enter.

Colligitar says, "Kassandra, stay for one more moment. Halamik, I need your leadership. Do you know Kassandra?"

Halamik says, "Yes, sir." The commander looks at Kassandra and says, "I am sorry about your loss. General Florick will be missed on this battlefield." Halamik looks back at his king and asks, "What can I do for you, My Lord?"

Colligitar says, "You will not be here to fight in this battle. I spoke to the Senate and they are leaving to take refuge inside the four city-states. I need a protector for our government's leaders and a military presence outside our city to give pride to our civilian population. In military situations you will be subjected to the peninsula's defense. All of our Senate and Alnitak leaders are preparing to leave. In three hours I need you to escort those representatives to Alnilam. For Alnilam to give refuge, I am giving our most brilliant minds to Icaras' kingdom. The best of our race will not die here. You will escort three thousand people and protect them at all cost."

That night, Halamik does what is ordered from his king. The Alnitak warriors, who stay behind, watch while their elite commander starts to escort the senators out of the city. There is nothing but silence coming from the protectors of Alnitak. Commander Halamik feels like a coward leaving his kingdom behind. Anastasia and Kassandra also leave to Alnilam with the Senate. Colligitar's daughter knows she will never see her father again.

The next night, Colligitar looks beyond his city's walls thinking of his daughter. He thinks back of when she was a small girl and he cannot get the picture of her glowing smile out of his head. The Alnitak King knows the chances of anyone on the peninsula surviving the war are slim to none.

Alnitak scouts go back and forth telling their king how close the Tarentum gets every hour of the day. About midnight, Cainin's main forces are six miles from the gates of Alnitak. Colligitar's warriors look over the horizon and see tens of thousands burning torches coming towards them in the distance. Everyone knows the battle will begin the next day. No one from Alnitak can leave now. In six hours, the whole city will be surrounded. Because the Tarentum military does not know what to expect, they are conscientious while their scouts check out the area.

The next morning, the Tarentum military has completely surrounded Colligitar's city. With Tarentum having one and half million warriors, Berith and Cainin contemplate where to attack first with their artillery. Cainin orders their smaller artillery and rams to charge towards the city. Cainin studies the Alnitak city and sees where he will put up his offensive weapons to tear apart the Alnitak walls. Berith moves forty of the most powerful Tarentum catapults into position. Even though the Alnitak artillery has the higher ground, the power coming from the Tarentum artillery is superior. Just in case Alnitak counterattacks with their heavy cavalry, Berith reinforces his artillery with the mammoths, giant rhinos, and light cavalry. To reinforce Tarentum cavalry and artillery, Berith's archers and infantry are also to the rear. Colligitar looks and can see it will not be long before his walls are destroyed.

Right before the Tarentum giant catapults are in place, Deus takes the Alnitak cavalry which was stationed over thirty miles away from Alnitak, and attacks the Tarentum rear. It takes Cainin and Berith by surprise. Because the Tarentum cavalry is in position by their offensive weapons, Cainin's infantry cannot guard against the force coming towards them. Deus destroys twenty thousand Tarentum infantrymen within twenty minutes. Berith counters with his archers and keeps Deus at a stand still inside the ranks of the Tarentum infantry. It gets to the point of urgency of hard choices. Berith gives the order to kill his own infantry in the line of fire by his own archers.

In the Alnitak city, Omar can see his plan working. Deus moves his cavalry to attack the Tarentum archers. The Alnitak cavalry outside the gates looks very small compared to Cainin's army. It seems Deus' cavalry is inching slowly to the Alnitak walls, but his Deus' army is getting smaller and smaller by the minute.

Cainin rides to his cavalry commander and orders a counterattack. The cavalry commander takes three fourths of the Tarentum cavalry to take on Deus directly. Even though there are over six thousand Alnitak heavy cavalry attacking, it takes an hour before Deus' cavalry is no longer a threat. Deus kills as many enemy men as he can before he is also killed.

As Colligitar is looking over his walls, Omar goes to his king's position and says, "We must breach their army with the rest of the cavalry inside our walls. Barrenious will not stop until he destroys the Tarentum artillery. He will give his life and men to protect this city. Because of Deus' offensive, Cainin's military formations are disrupted. This is a perfect time to confuse our enemy even more. Their Tarentum heavy artillery is in place. We must take our cavalry to the rear of Alnitak and go around their strongholds. Barrenious' cavalry will go under the protection of our archers. If we do this, we have to do it now."

Colligitar says, "Make it happen."

Omar orders his giant rhinos, mammoths, and elephants to the rear of the city. It will not be where the Tarentum military will expect an explosion of cavalry. Omar orders his horse cavalry to stay behind. His light cavalry will be used more efficiently inside the city if Cainin is able to breach the walls. General Omar also orders his reserve archers of five thousand to give more cover fire for his offensive.

Omar gives the order. His reserve archers rush to the rear gate. Barrenious' heavy cavalry gallops with their riders down the streets of Alnitak to their destination. There is no hesitation from anyone in Omar's ranks. Omar rides his horse to the rear gates. All Alnitak archers are in place.

Omar yells, "Fire at our enemy!"

There is an eruption of arrows coming from Colligitar's city. The archers fire their arrows and destroy the ranks of Alnitak's enemy infantry. There are no Tarentum heavy cavalry in sight. When a hole has been made outside the city by Alnitak archers, Omar orders the gates to be open. Thousands of Alnitak archers are ordered to run up the walls to be able to give Barrenious' cavalry cover fire. One hundred and twenty-three giant rhinos run out the gate destroying everything thing in their sight. Right behind them are one hundred elephants and two hundred mammoths going through six different gates to fight their enemy. The Tarentum infantry and archers cannot compensate, and are over run by Omar's offensive.

Berith is at a distance and sees the Alnitak's second offensive moving from the city. He orders all heavy cavalry in reserve to counterattack. The horns blow and the Tarentum infantry makes a path for their cavalry. It takes fifteen minutes before Tarentum's forces are organized and on their way to intercept.

In the meantime, the Alnitak heavy cavalry destroys the lines of the Tarentum infantry. In the middle of battle, the Alnitak cavalry can see the giant catapults a mile away. Barrenious rushes towards the Tarentum catapults. When the Alnitak front cavalry gets a half mile from Cainin's giant artillery, they get intercepted by a front line of Tarentum giant rhinos. With the backing of the Cainin's cavalry, the Tarentum archers and infantry regroup and counterattack Barrenious. Animals from both sides clash with one another, but because of overwhelming numbers, the Tarentum cavalry is destroying Barrenious' forces.

In the background outside the walls of Alnitak, Barrenious can see the Tarentum catapults firing at his walls. The Alnitak cavalry is getting slaughtered, but is still able to fight towards their objective in trying to destroy Cainin's artillery. The Alnitak archers regroup to give cover fire for their cavalry, but the Tarentum cavalry sends in their reinforcements. Cainin waits until Alnitak's cavalry is outside the Alnitak archers' range.

Within thirty minutes of the Alnitak offensive, the battle is over. The Tarentum cavalry has heavy losses. Cainin's catapults keep pounding at the Alnitak walls. Over eighty-five percent of the Alnitak cavalry is destroyed. In three hours, the Tarentum will put enough damage into the Alnitak walls to breach the city. Omar's hope to take out the catapults is stripped away from reality. Now, it is a matter of time before Cainin's men are inside Alnitak.

Two hours after the Alnitak cavalry is destroyed, Omar's archers are keeping the Tarentum military at bay, but the Tarentum giant catapults have damaged one wall to the point that it is about to collapse. Omar orders his men off the damaged structure. In doing so, there is a gap of firing solution towards the Tarentum infantry and cavalry.

Berith sees the gap, and the Tarentum infantry runs with ladders to the wall. Cainin's giant catapults stop firing. Alnitak's infantry come outside their gate to meet their enemy head on. Colligitar's warriors are giving everything they have against their foe. Outside the Colligitar's city, it comes down to hand to hand combat.

Omar sees his infantry outside the gates gaining ground. He decides to try and send the rest of the heavy and light cavalry outside the gates of Alnitak. Out of nowhere, Omar has one more chance to take out the Tarentum giant catapults.

The order is given, and Alnitak's light cavalry goes first and punches a hole through Cainin's men. Within forty minutes, Omar's light cavalry reaches the catapults and builds a wall for his heavy cavalry to knock out the catapults. Omar looks over the wall and sees his heavy cavalry knocking down the giant artillery. The archers firing from the wall of Alnitak cheer. The momentum seems to be in Omar's tactical favor.

On the other side of the battlefield, Berith is side by side with Cainin waiting for orders.

Cainin says, "We have given them false hope. Their heavy cavalry will be destroyed completely, and their light cavalry is minutes away from being shattered. Give the order to move our heavy cavalry and finish them."

Berith responds, "Yes, sir."

The Tarentum heavy cavalry runs to take on the last of the Alnitak cavalry. There have been heavy losses on both sides of the battlefield, but Tarentum still has hundreds of thousands of men in reserve. Luring the Alnitak forces away from the safety of their archers will give the advantage to Cainin's military.

The battle begins, and the Alnitak cavalry starts to lose within twenty minutes. Right when Cainin's elephants have superiority on the battlefield, they form a line and rush right to the Alnitak damaged wall. The Alnitak archers fire at the Tarentum elephants, but there are hundreds of them all in one line. Some of the Tarentum beasts fall to the ground from the Alnitak arrows, but more than sixty elephants hit the wall close to the same time. Because the wall is damaged, it starts to fall on its own weight killing some of the Tarentum elephants and the men riding on them.

Cainin sees the wall falling and says, "Send in our infantry and archers to support our cavalry."

Berith says, "We just achieved our first objective."

Cainin responds, "Yes, it was time to take down the wall. The Alnitak commanders just shortened this war by sending out their cavalry. This is why we were hitting the lower portion of the wall. I wanted them to defend and protect their weakest defensive area."

Omar goes to the breach and orders sixty percent of his infantry to the rubble of rock which used to be their wall. The Alnitak military is almost in shock, knowing the wall has been there all their lives. The Alnitak archers fire and hit their targets, but thousands of Tarentum infantry rush the wall to gain access to the interior of Alnitak. Cainin's men climb the rubble and the first three waves of infantrymen are held back by Omar's archers. Then it seems one by one the Tarentum military gains ground inside Colligitar's city. Both sides are frantic to defend themselves and attack each other. Thousands die on both sides, and the dead start to pile up.

Colligitar moves to the breach he swore to protect at all cost. He tells Omar to go behind the lines. If Omar does not move back, he will not see the whole picture of how to move his men to best defend against his enemy. To the Alnitak King, it is very noble to fight on the front lines, but yet a young decision by Omar.

Colligitar and Omar go to the second wall to assess the situation. Omar orders his archers to go to the secondary fortification inside the city. The Alnitak archers have higher ground and it is harder for Tarentum archers to use their arrows effectively hitting straight up to its defenders. It takes ten Tarentum archers to kill one Alnitak with a bow in their hand. Omar and Colligitar take different positions to correlate Alnitak defenses.

For the first two hours, it is a stalemate. The Tarentum military has secured the breach and use their mammoths to pull away the rubble from the destroyed wall. Inside an hour, Cainin's cavalry will have full access in and out of the first wall.

During the impasse, Omar goes to Colligitar and tells him the Alnitak infantry and archers can only hold their position for another two hours. Omar knows his city is doomed.

Omar asks, "Why did you give me command, sir?"

Colligitar responds, "You are young, loyal, and a good commander. What you have done is not to save our society. You are giving a chance to Alnilam, Halotropolis, Vasic, and Masaba. It is our society which started this war, and we will die defending our bad decisions and our kingdom. I will die here with you as a soldier. The reason I gave the peninsula our elite guard is to say I am sorry to put them in this position. This is our kingdom's fault, not the bylands. The elite guard will fight with the peninsula's commanders. I knew you would not flee to save yourself. You are an Alnitak warrior, and you will die as one here today or tomorrow. We must show nobility to the bylands, so we will not be forgotten in time."

Omar says, "You are right, I would have not left if you had given me the order. Sir, this will be an honorable death. I gave an oath to protect this city at all cost to you and our people. You are a true king and a leader. Even though there is no way of winning here, I can't think of any other way to die but for my kingdom. I will protect the three hundred thousand civilians that did not want to leave their homeland."

The fighting continues for another four days. The Alnitak warriors fight to the last man. Omar and Colligitar fight and stand at the front lines until they die by the sword. Everyone who stayed behind is either killed or becoming a slave to the Tarentum Empire. Over a hundred fifty thousand Alnitak civilians will go back to Tarentum as servants to Baylonis' empire. Cainin loses a quarter of a million men and twenty percent of his light and heavy cavalry. Cainin strips every asset from Alnitak to be taken back to Baylonis.

When Alnitak is secured by the Tarentum military, Berith goes to Cainin which is inside Colligitar's palace.

Berith says, "This city has been severely damaged by our military and the earthquake. It will take us years to get it back to its glory. It will destroy us economically to bring this city back to life."

Cainin says, "It will cost our government a lot in manpower and trade. But it is not this city which will bring us prosperity. It is the other city-states we must take one by one to make this profitable for our empire."

Berith says, "We need to stop here. We have lost over a three hundred thousand men already in taking Alnitak. The other states inside our empire will be hard to manage without military presence. It is a good victory and our people will remember this battle for centuries."

Cainin says, "I am not doing this to be remembered. I am doing this for the future of our empire. If we didn't start this war, it could have been millions of our warriors dead. This war would have started five or even twenty years from now, but we took our enemy before it could get a stronghold on our continent."

Berith responds, "Agreed, Now what do we do?"

Cainin says, "The four city states are ready for us, and we do not have the luxury of a natural disaster to help. Our spies have told me that their walls are strong and will be harder to breach. Most of the city-states do not have more than a hundred thousand men to defend their walls. We will take Halotropolis first and go from there."

Cainin orders all treasures in Alnitak to be taken to Baylonis. All civilians of Colligitar's city start their march back to Tarentum. The whole city is on fire and there is not much left.

Cainin goes outside the city with his army. The Tarentum military is standing at attention. Cainin and Berith look at their army and turn around and see the byland, and they are ready for the next step to take the known world.

CHAPTER XX
COMING TOGETHER AS WARRIORS

On the eighth day after the earthquake, Atlandreous reaches Floortatum. The defenders of the peninsula only have four more days before Cainin's military reaches the area. Atlandreous lets the Tarentum scouts see his military at a distance. The Peninsula Supreme Commander is enticing Cainin to fight. Because of the rocky terrain on the future battlefield, it is easy to hide the full extent of Atlandreous' army. Many of Atlandreous' infantry is hidden inside Halotropolis. Every residence in Halotropolis has a different warrior from a different city-state inside the civilian's homes.

The Peninsula Supreme Commander is the last commander to reach the future battleground. He lets all of the generals and his commanders make the final preparations. In doing so, Atlandreous puts leadership into his men and accountability. With so vast of an army, the Peninsula Supreme Commander cannot take on every task by himself.

Right before Atlandreous can go to his quarters to freshen up to see his generals, an Alnilam scout rides to the Peninsula Supreme Commander.

The Alnilam scout says, "Halamik is twenty miles east of here going towards our homeland. He has over eight thousand elite soldiers escorting over three thousand Alnitak civilians."

Atlandreous responds, "Icaras has sent messages to me of an Alnitak escort leading people to Alnilam but he did not say anything of an army that large. I need three hundred light cavalry to meet here within an hour. Get me the generals of the city-states."

Atlandreous goes inside his tent to freshen up. He eats and

waits. The generals from the city-states come one by one to his tent. The Peninsula Supreme Commander changes into a fresh uniform. Atlandreous goes to the main room of his tent and the generals from the city-states wait for orders.

Atlandreous says, "Tarasios, Baudan, and Roubertus, you have another day to get prepared without me. I hope my commanders have helped you get our armies together to fight as one."

Baudan responds jokingly, "Remember when I told you I would have taken you at Castin valley. I do not have officers with the talent of Nieander, Orion, Hamon, and Erasmus in my army. There is no doubt with your military commanders it would have taken a couple more days to win at Castin."

Atlandreous replies, "I'm glad you're in good spirits, I'm taking you with me."

Baudan asks, "Where are we going?"

Atlandreous responds, "We are going to Halamik of Alnitak. He is still alive. He is twenty miles from here, going to my kingdom. Colligitar has given his best minds to our kingdom with his Senate. My kingdom does not really need politicians. To achieve our objectives in this war, I need Halamik's eight thousand warriors. With his background in battle, he will be an asset to our cause."

Roubertus says, "Our rules do not apply to Colligitar's men. Alnitak's elite are there to keep order in their civilian population."

Atlandreous responds, "I don't think escorting civilians is his favorite thing to do right now. I know Halamik is ready to fight a war. He just got the worst task a commander can have protecting politicians."

Baudan asks, "What do you need with me?"

Atlandreous looks straight a Baudan and responds, "Halamik's men are really the best fighters on the peninsula. I have a feeling Colligitar sent his best commander to help keep pride in their destructed society. It was suicide to protect Alnitak. It will be up to us to make Alnitak's citizens feel welcomed, and Halamik fight at Floortatum."

Baudan and Atlandreous ride with their three hundred light cavalry to meet Halamik. It is a fast gallop, but takes the generals two and half hours to catch up with the Alnitak elite. Atlandreous has enough confidence in his other generals to get things done for the battle. The Peninsula Supreme Commander has little time to achieve his goal. He knows he needs to show leadership before the battle begins.

Right in sight of the Halamik's force, Atlandreous and Baudan stop. Ten men are sent out from the Alnitak cavalry to investigate. Atlandreous humbles himself and waits until the Halamik's scouting party comes to them.

When the Alnitak scouting party reaches Atlandreous, the scout says, "May I ask who you are, and what I can do for you, sir?"

Atlandreous says, "I would like to speak to Halamik."

Even though Baudan and Atlandreous are in general attire, the scouts do not know their identity. The scout asks, "Excuse me, who are you?"

Atlandreous says, "I am Atlandreous; the Peninsula Supreme Commander."

The scouts are shocked to see Atlandreous only has a small escort and wants to talk to their commander. The scout responds, "Come with me. If you would, please leave the escort behind. I don't want to scare our civilians."

Atlandreous and Baudan are escorted to Halamik. Right before they reach the Alnitak general, the Peninsula Supreme Commander does not know how to start the conversation, knowing he is the one who did not want to give military aid to Alnitak. Atlandreous knows he might be going into a hornet's nest.

The Peninsula Supreme Commander reaches the Alnitak general. Halamik is surrounded by warriors. An Alnitak scout introduces Atlandreous to his commander. At the same time, Kassandra and Anastasia ride to the meeting.

Halamik says, "I have heard so much about you. It is good to meet you. The last order from my king is to do what you ask of me. I am under your command. But I cannot leave my people unprotected if you want us to fight with you."

Atlandreous responds, "I thought I might have to beg you to help defend the byland. People ask me who I would not want to fight in hand to hand combat. I always give them your name. I have a great deal of respect for you. I am giving you a choice to ride forward to my kingdom or fight with me. I need you and your expertise as a general. In regards to your people going towards my kingdom, I will use my escort of three hundred light cavalry to do the task. Your people will be safe. Give them your food and water.

Because of the weight, the three hundred horses I brought will be used to transport your civilians' basic needs to reach my kingdom. It will take ten days to get to Alnilam by foot. My warriors will walk beside your people as family. I need every horse you have to be used in the defense of the byland. I need you in my army to counter when the time is right. Some of your men will die, but your men are warriors at heart. I hope they will take their sworn oath to protect what is left of your society and protect them at all cost. This battle will do that."

Halamik responds, "When I left Alnitak, I felt as if I was running away from death. Even though I am following orders by my king, I need retribution from feeling like a coward. I saw what my men felt as they left Alnitak. They were more embarrassed to live than to die as a soldier. In their minds, they are dead anyway without a reason to live. At Alnitak, they were stripped away from dying in honor for their kingdom. If you can give my men reprisal to fight our enemy, we will fight alongside your army."

Atlandreous says, "Your civilians will be escorted in honor to my homeland. You and I have two days before our enemy attacks Floortatum. You will get the satisfaction of fighting the people that destroyed your kingdom."

Kassandra yells, "Wait! I am in command of this elite division. I agree with Atlandreous, but I also want to fight our enemy. My husband died by the hand of a Tarentum sword."

Anastasia says, "I am not going to go with the civilian population. My people need heroes. Because my father is of royalty, I must fight to give pride back to my people. If we win this war, it will be very important in the transition of societies to have that hero. I'm going. My life is nothing unless I can prove leadership to my Alnitak refuges."

Atlandreous responds, "Agreed. We are no longer separate people; we are one and we will not separate sexes on the battlefield."

Halamik says to Atlandreous, "In politics, I have to get permission from our Senate. Kassandra and Anastasia also need to go through the political chain. There is so much emotion here. Give me a minute. I will make this swift."

Halamik goes to the head of his Senate. Within twenty minutes, Halamik rides back to Atlandreous.

The Alnitak elite commander says, "It is done. The gesture of your men walking aside our government officials has won them over. I told them you gave us a choice to fight or escort them to your kingdom. Our Senate wants us to fight to give back pride to our people. I will represent my people on the battlefield."

Atlandreous' three hundred light cavalry get off their horses. The elite guard gives all food and water to the civilians of Alnitak. Atlandreous' men walk with the Alnitak civilians to Alnilam. Right when Halamik starts to get his men in formation to leave, all the Alnitak civilians start to cheer for Halamik and his men. Halamik feels good about the new alliance.

The byland generals and Alnitak's elite make haste to Floortatum. Because of the situation, there are no animosities between armies. Halamik and his men want a purpose, and Atlandreous is overwhelmed, and needs all the help he can get. Atlandreous orders a messenger to ride ahead to have all the generals and commanders ready for a meeting when he returns.

When Atlandreous gets back to his army with Halamik's elite group, all city-states' armies cheer for Halamik as they enter the camp site. With all the death and destruction, the Alnitak general feels good to fight with the peninsula's men. Atlandreous brings Halamik, Kassandra, and Anastasia into the meeting with his generals and commanders in his tent. All generals and Atlandreous' officers are ready to hear what their leader has to say.

Atlandreous says, "We have the absolute best warriors from the Alnitak Kingdom with us. Everyone here should know Halamik. With Halamik's eight thousand light cavalry, we have a total of twenty-four thousand light cavalry to fight our enemy. It will out match our enemy. As far as our scouts say, Cainin has thirty-six thousand light cavalry. I am giving Halamik a thousand riders from each of our four divisions. He will be the spearhead of our counterattack. Nieander, I need you elsewhere. With Halamik coming aboard, everything has changed to our advantage on the battlefield."

Nieander asks, "Sir, would you think I would be more vital on the battlefield commanding the spearhead?"

Atlandreous responds, "I have a different task that no one else could do right now. I will give the details after this meeting."

Kassandra asks, "What of Anastasia and me?"

Atlandreous responds, "Halamik, you are in charge of your

cavalry. In the spearhead, Halamik will lead the counterattack, and Anastasia and Kassandra will command the left and right flank of that spearhead. Anastasia, you are well respected in your society as a warrior. Kassandra, your people loved and would die for your former husband. My men will fight for you. In the peninsula's culture, women didn't fight on the battlefield. Now, you two will be the first to change military protocol. In the future, we will need every man and woman on the battlefield to keep our enemies from destroying our lands. In the past, women have been known as the weaker sex. That is no longer going to be the case."

After the meeting, Nieander goes to Atlandreous.

Nieander asks, "Sir, I am wondering why you took me away from the offensive spearhead?"

Atlandreous responds, "You are my friend, but I am not taking you away from the danger. I am putting your expertise in a different area. I know where Cainin is going to attack our formations. I will set it up so he thinks he has the advantage. You are going to take command of the infantry defense with a small number of heavy cavalry with our giant sloths. Along with the two hundred and twenty sloths, you will have one hundred elephants, one hundred mammoths, and one hundred giant rhinos under your command. Cainin will come after you, and you better be ready. Remember, we are outnumbered, and he will think at some point to finish us. I have a plan, and I need your mind to make it happen."

Nieander says, "Thank you, sir. You are a friend and a good general. I need you to be strong."

Atlandreous says, "Now, you only have two days to get it together. You have a time crunch, and you better not disappoint our army."

The next day, Cainin's army is getting closer to Halotropolis. Atlandreous sends out a hundred thousand men ten miles closer to Cainin to lure him into Floortatum. After the diversionary force leaves, The Peninsula Supreme Commander is going over some plans with Roubertus, Tarasios, and Baudan. Atlandreous hears a familiar voice as he is looking at a map.

Tess says, "Hello Atlandreous."

Atlandreous stops everything he is doing and almost stumbles and says, "Hello Tess. Why are you here?"

Tess responds "In the last month, I have gone village to village to find new soldiers to fight against our enemy. I have brought over five thousand warriors for this campaign. I even went into your realm to meet the void."

Atlandreous says, "I don't have any doubt about your abilities, but we cannot have royalty fighting in our battles. In all of history, kings and their family are the ones who govern the civilian population. If someone of royalty dies in battle, it would tip the balance of power to your Senate."

Tess asks, "Can I speak to you in private?"

Atlandreous responds, "I have a quick second. Everyone leave us and come back in five minutes. Gentlemen, think of ways to destroy our enemy."

Everyone leaves and Tess and Atlandreous look at one another.

Tess says, "In what you just said, our society needs change. Anastasia is fighting, and that just changed it all. I will take on your best sparring generals. If I win, I lead the people I brought to the battlefield under your command of course. Remember, my father told you I can be a lady, but I could give you a challenge in sparring. I will not embarrass you in front of your men."

Atlandreous says, "Don't worry about my ego. Okay—done, Erasmus will fight you. He is almost as good as I am. We will do it right now."

Atlandreous yells for Erasmus, and Erasmus enters the tent.

Erasmus says, "Yes sir."

Atlandreous asks, "Erasmus, are you ready for a challenge?"

Erasmus responds, "Yes sir."

All the generals and advisors go outside and watch Tess and Erasmus spar. The first one to hit the breast plate with the sword will win. The two get into position. Erasmus starts off with an offensive and Tess counters. It goes back and forth for over a minute. Atlandreous looks at the two and is impressed with Tess. The Peninsula Supreme Commander had no earthly idea Tess was this good. When Erasmus is caught off guard, Tess goes on the offensive and trips Erasmus and kicks his sword out of his hand. Tess just stays right above him without any emotion and points her sword at his chest.

Atlandreous says, "Enough. I am impressed with your technique and balance. I'm glad I don't have to spar against you."

Tess responds, "I was brought up as royalty and a lady, but my father insisted that I learn to protect myself. Being a woman, I have more balance with a sword than most men. It is how God made us."

Atlandreous says, "Take the men you have and you will protect the rear left flank of our army. Erasmus and Roubertus will reinforce your position. With what my scouts said at the battle of Rigel, Cainin will most likely try to attack against your position."

Erasmus goes to Atlandreous and says, "I did not expect that one. This is going to be a very interesting battle. Either we are all going to die, or we are going to change humanities' way of thinking right here and right now."

Atlandreous responds, "To make mankind better you have to change. Sometimes, battles or natural disasters can change the thinking of any society. I hope after this battle I will not get exiled off the peninsula. If Tess dies, it will be on my shoulders, and war can break out between Alnilam and Halotropolis. As stubborn as Tess is, I bet Cetrono doesn't even know she's even here."

Erasmus says, "I agree. The kings are very conservative in politics and beliefs. Either you're going to be hated or loved. There will be no in-between after this conflict."

Atlandreous replies, "This is one battle of thousands which will plague humanity. It is either the right time for mankind to change or not. This is a milestone for women to have a say so in military matters. These three women are the leaders of a new idea."

That night, Cainin camps outside where he thinks Atlandreous' main army is located ten miles from the main byland's fortification. Atlandreous' warriors are combing the area behind their lines and taking out Cainin's scouts.

The same night, Atlandreous' four diversions of one hundred thousand warriors leave all the torches and campfires burning. At a distance, it looks like the entire city-state's army is stationed there ten miles north of Atlandreous' main fortification. In the middle of the night, the diversionary force goes back to reinforce Atlandreous' army.

The next morning the Tarentum scouts come back to Cainin and tell him Halotropolis has retreated. It confuses the Tarentum general, but without fear, he moves forward to his first objective.

CHAPTER XXI
THE WAR THAT ENDS ALL WARS

On the eighty-fifth day after the earthquake, Atlandreous and his generals are looking over the horizon and see Cainin's army approaching seven miles from the Floortatum's main defense. Cainin is more precautious now seeing the byland's military outside their walls. The Tarentum Supreme Commander is stopping outside Floortatum until he can find out more information to go forward.

To the inhabitants of the peninsula, the depth of warriors coming towards their stronghold is unbelievable. Atlandreous' mind goes into overdrive. He thinks of every detail. One last order is to clear a path for his cavalry to have complete access inside their main defense. Every rock has to be moved so the horses can move quickly. He sends a messenger to get it done. All of the peninsula's warriors make their final adjustments for the battle to come. Atlandreous knows it will be difficult for the Tarentum Army to attack his position at high speeds with their cavalry because of the rocky terrain around Floortatum. It will slow down the Tarentum's main offensive. To Atlandreous' generals, the Peninsula Supreme Commander has a systematic way to take on his enemy, and they have complete confidence in their commander, but as they look over the hill, they become concerned with the death toll.

A thousand thoughts go through Atlandreous' head about the men and women he trusts to defend against his enemy, and what his enemy will tactically try to accomplish. To the Peninsula Supreme Commander, everyone has strengths and weaknesses. He is hoping he has put the right people in the right places. As for the enemy of the byland, their military has a great deal of moral. Because Cainin defeated Alnitak with acceptable losses, the rest of the conquest should be easy.

From a military standpoint, Cainin is going into the byland blind. Because the hills of Floortatum are so rocky, it will hide the full bulk of the peninsula's army from being seen by the Tarentum military. It will conceal the full magnitude of peninsula warriors which is defending Floortatum.

Because it is getting dark, the war will not start for a couple of days. With the hundred thousand warriors Atlandreous sent ten miles the day before, it will give the byland another two days to prepare. People in Floortatum are still scrambling to get everything in place.

While looking at the Tarentum's massive army with his generals, Atlandreous says, "Cainin will position his men and attack our defenses as he did at Rigel. I need all of our artillery to protect our rear. Florick had mountains behind him at his battle. We do not have that luxury. But the Tarentum's first main assault will be to our backside. Roubertus and Hamon, I need you to take four infantry and two archer divisions to protect our artillery. If they take our backside, we will lose all hope."

Roubertus replies, "That gives me sixty thousand infantry and ten thousand archers. I also need five hundred heavy and two thousand light cavalry to ensure success, sir."

Atlandreous says, "No—the artillery will be your best defense. You will have eighty percent of our giant crossbows and catapults for your defense. You will have enough firepower to keep our enemy at bay. This battle is going to be all or nothing. When this conflict starts, I need you to hold our rear defenses for four hours. After that, I will put enough confusion into the Tarentum ranks to turn the tide. Tess, I need you close to Roubertus and Hamon to protect our left flank. I am giving you command of ten thousand light cavalry to protect our left and rear flank and ten thousand archers. You said you want a challenge; you just got it. In between our backside and left flank, you will have our best infantry divisions."

Tess replies, "You will not be disappointed."

Orion asks, "What can I contribute to our cause?"

Atlandreous says, "I need you to take thirty thousand archers and protect our main army with Nieander. I am hoping our giant sloths can do what I think they can do. This will be the first time to use them in combat. If I'm right, the enemy will not know what to do once their heavy cavalry starts to punch through our ranks. You will be the bait and Cainin's down fall. Take the ten thousand archers with the molless bow and make sure your firing solution is adjusted to maximize the destruction on the battlefield with our regular bow. You will have over three hundred thousand warriors to hold our main fortification. You will also have seven hundred heavy cavalry to be used for defense and fifteen percent of our artillery. I also need three hundred heavy cavalry as a backup and to be used in our offensive when the time is right. A hundred thousand of our best infantry will hold our rear and left flank. It is very difficult to take our right flank because of natural obstacles."

Baudan asks, "Where are the other hundred thousand warriors going to stand?"

Atlandreous responds, "Tarasios, Halamik, and Erasmus, you're with me. Tarasios and Erasmus, bring your best cavalry and infantry. We are leaving and going around so we can attack our enemy by surprise. Halamik, you will be the spearhead into this attack. Kassandra and Anastasia, you will get your chance in battle. Baudan, you are in command of our main defenses in Floortatum. Every time we have come into contact, you say you can beat me on the battlefield. Well, you just got the hardest task. The conversation at Castin valley will never be brought up again after this battle. Baudan, you will know when to start your offensive. When you think it is right, hit our enemy with everything you have."

Baudan says, "Wait, I said those things to bring conversation. It was not my intent to be arrogant."

Atlandreous says, "I see confidence, not arrogance. This is why you are in command. The Tarentum artillery will not be able to get up the rocky hills to effectively attack us, and we have the high ground. You will not need much artillery. Because of the terrain, you will be on equal terms with our enemy."

That same night, Cainin gets his other two major generals together. Cainin sends in scouts, but Atlandreous' patrols are stopping anything that gets close to his perimeter. There is no information coming back to the Tarentum military of what is beyond their camp. The Tarentum Supreme Commander is very angry about not knowing what is ahead of him, but he has the confidence in his army to take Floortatum. Cainin thinks he is only fighting the Halotropolis Army at this point. To Cainin, the possibility of Floortatum being a trap is real, but it will take another two days to go around Floortatum and go towards Halotropolis. Because of time and supplies, Tarentum has no choice but to go through Atlandreous' trap. Plus, it will be more difficult for Cainin to go around with his artillery because of the terrain. Floortatum will be tedious and time consuming to travel through, but it is the best way to achieve his first military objective after taking Alnitak.

A Tantalum scout rides quickly to Cainin and says, "We have lost over three hundred scouts trying to find out what is in Floortatum. From the inhabitants, we have gathered that the peninsula's army is located inside that rocky formation. We don't know if it was out of fear that they gave the information or what. What we have gathered from our sources is there are over four hundred thousand warriors hidden in those rocks. I was there interrogating the civilians, and my gut instinct tells me they are telling the truth. To the best of our knowledge, the peninsula is giving everything they have only four to five miles from our location."

Cainin says, "I see. Good. I was about to send in our artillery. That would have been a disaster waiting to happen. We can take out the defense of the peninsula right here. We do not have to destroy the walls of each city-state. Spenser, I want you to take the rear of the peninsula's defense. Berith, I want you to take three hundred thousand warriors and beasts to find the weaknesses of their fortification and take it out. It will be easy after this battle to take the rest of the peninsula. I am hoping to keep all city-states intact."

In the meantime, in the cover of darkness, Atlandreous takes his warriors and cavalry and goes away from the Cainin's army. He goes through his heaviest patrolled areas to conceal his tactics. He takes the long way so he is not detected. It takes him all night. Not one of Atlandreous' forces gets any sleep. The adrenaline of the Peninsula Supreme Commander's army is the only thing holding the byland's counter offensive together.

At early morning of the eighty-fifth day after the earthquake, Atlandreous' army arrives seven miles away from Floortatum. The rocky terrain is keeping his army and cavalry hidden from Tarentum scouts. The enemy scouts they find have been killed or taken captive by the peninsula's patrols. Each prisoner they find says the same thing about the strength and who is leading the fight against Atlandreous.

Three hours after sunrise, the Tarentum military gets into position at Floortatum. Cainin sends in Spenser and Berith to move forward. The Tarentum military, led by Spenser, get into his location ready to attack the rear of the peninsula's defenses. After patrolling with great numbers, the Tarentum general sees their adversary. Berith takes his position to the peninsula's left flank with his heavy cavalry to be used on the front lines to attack. Cainin gets prepared with one hundred thousand archers, eight hundred thousand infantry, and eight thousand heavy cavalry. His forces are in position dead center of the peninsula's defenses.

Baudan looks at the situation and knows he has to order his men to their death and defend the perimeter until Atlandreous goes on the offensive. Baudan thinks every move he makes will depend on what he knows instinctively. At the moment, he does not want the job he has been given, but he has no choice.

Baudan sees Berith's army coming to his left flank. He orders ten thousand archers to reinforce where Tess is located. Even though Tess is royalty, he is not allowing himself to think of the protection of Cetrono's daughter. He is thinking of the peninsula as a whole, and the respect he has for Atlandreous. With such dire circumstances, and the possibility of total annihilation, Baudan is for once timorous of what is about to transpire. The byland defenders are in place to take the beating.

At the peninsula's rear defense, the Tantalum military starts their attack. Roubertus and Hamon have four hundred giant crossbows made from the molless tree and three hundred catapults which can shoot hundred pound boulders one hundred yards towards their enemy. Roubertus and Hamon take command of two different artillery divisions so they correlate their firepower.

General Spenser sends in his heavy cavalry first to attack the byland's artillery. The Tarentum general holds back his light cavalry which numbers over ten thousand. Over three thousand elephants, mammoths, and giant rhinos move up the gradient hill in three different waves and directions. Roubertus and Hamon wait until the Tarentum's heavy cavalry get into range. Spenser's heavy cavalry can only go half the speed because of the rocky terrain.

Hamon looks at the battlefield and at the last possible moment yells, "Fire!"

Four seconds later Roubertus yells, "Fire!"

Hundreds of giant arrows and one hundred pound boulders fly through the sky. Hamon's and Roubertus' two artillery divisions fire half of their weaponry and thirty seconds later fire the second half. In doing so, it keeps a constant bombardment on the battlefield. Right in the middle of the artillery firing, ten thousand byland archers fire at the Tarentum cavalry. Roubertus and Hamon's artillery and archers hit their targets and hundreds of Tarentum beasts hit the ground. Some of Spenser's cavalry stumble over their own dead. Hamon and Roubertus get their artillery reloaded. Because the giant crossbows are more powerful and use the molless tree as its main tension, it is able to shoot further than their catapults. The byland's artillery kills their enemy at greater distances giving them more time to reload. Hamon and Roubertus only have time for one more reload before the second wave of Tarentum cavalry gets into range. Right when Hamon and Roubertus are ready to shoot again, Spenser orders a retreat. Almost four hundred Tarentum heavy cavalry are dead, and four hundred wounded. The byland's backside is too heavily defended for a slow speed offensive by the Tarentum military.

Spenser looks at the battlefield and orders his light horse cavalry to charge. The order is given, and Spenser's light cavalry goes at a slow gallop. The rocky hills are keeping Spenser's horse cavalry from going at full speed. Hamon and Roubertus see it coming and they order their artillery to fire. Hamon's and Roubertus' archers move forward to take on the Tarentum cavalry that makes it through their firing solution.

At the same time, Tess sees what is coming towards the peninsula's backside. Hamon and Roubertus are in trouble from behind. Tess orders three thousand light cavalry to compensate the void. It still leaves her seven thousand to protect the left flank of Baudan's fortification. Atlandreous was right about the tactics that are being used to hit the protectors of the byland. He looks at a distance waiting for the moment to attack. He is anxious to start his counter offensive.

Hamon and Roubertus fire their giant crossbows and catapults and destroy the first and second wave of Tarentum's cavalry, but some Tarentum cavalry make it through. Hamon's and Roubertus' archers fire and send in their infantry. There is not enough cover fire to take on ten thousand Tarentum cavalry. The three thousand cavalry Tess ordered to help the rear makes it in time to take on Spenser's light cavalry right when the bylands start to lose ground.

Spenser sends in his infantry and Hamon takes command of his infantry and takes position on the front line. The Tarentum military wait to send in their heavy cavalry to compensate. The battle goes back and forth. Each army is determined to break the other.

Right when the conflict is heated the most at the byland rear defenses, Berith is ordered to take on Baudan's left flank. Tess has less cavalry to hold her position. The three thousand she sent to Hamon and Roubertus are in deadlock with their enemy. Baudan compensates and sends in Orion with five thousand archers. Orion and his division run to Tess to hold their left flank. Both left and rear of the bylands perimeter are under a full scale attack.

Berith uses his infantry and light cavalry first to attack. Orion's archers make it in time to hold off Berith's army. Thousands of Tarentum's infantry make it through, but Tess' infantry fights them back.

Both of the rear and left flank of the peninsula is at a stalemate for the moment. Cainin looks at the battlefield. He is deciding when to attack. He is waiting for more confusion before he sends in his main assault. The Tarentum Supreme Commander is waiting for his enemy to weaken before he goes in himself.

Atlandreous knows there are thousands of his men dying at his main defense. He has friends and colleges holding their positions waiting for some kind of reprisal. It is really starting to look desperate at the byland's perimeter.

Cainin looks at the battlefield and notices less arrows firing towards his men at the rear and left flank of the byland's stronghold. The Tarentum Supreme Commander sees his men penetrating into Roubertus and Hamon's defense. More of Baudan's infantry are sent in to reinforce Hamon and Roubertus.

Cainin yells, "Let this battle become the stepping stone to a new world. Now take our enemy!"

Cainin's main army and beasts go forward to take on the byland's main army. Nieander and Baudan are ordering their infantry and archers to compensate where they think the enemy will strike. With Baudan only having a little over a hundred heavy artillery pieces to hold off the main assault, Cainin thinks it is time to attack. Over a million men attack Baudan. At the byland's main stronghold, Baudan has a quarter of a million men against one million. Cainin feels confident about the conflict and sends in his light and heavy cavalry to weaken Baudan's front lines.

Baudan takes his heavy cavalry and giant sloths to compensate for what is about to attack him. Every byland warrior is from a different culture and society. They all look at each other as brothers in war and will die for one another. If the peninsula beats back their enemy, they will not look at each other the same way again. There is passion coming from the warriors of the byland to protect and fight for one another. Before, there were religion and cultural differences which split the peninsula. Now, there is compassion, respect, and cultural understanding coming from the determined faces of each person under Baudan's command.

Cainin sends in his main force of seven thousand heavy cavalry to attack. The Tarentum heavy cavalry can go a little faster than the strikes against the left and rear flank of the byland's defenses because the terrain is not as rocky.

Right before the Tarentum heavy cavalry gets into position to attack, Baudan's heavy cavalry moves forward to take on what is about to attack them. The byland's archers move up as well to take on the seven thousand beasts of the Tarentum cavalry. This is where either the byland warriors will hold or break. Cainin is going in for the kill.

Cainin also orders his archers to move forward to help the Tarentum heavy cavalry. Right when the byland's archers are ordered forward, the main battle begins. Beasts from both sides collide with one another, and the Tarentum archers start to fire at the byland's heavy cavalry. Baudan loses a hundred rhino's, elephants, and mammoths within five minutes, and over a thousand Tarentum heavy cavalry make it through Baudan's first line of defense. The battle is going towards Cainin's favor.

Baudan waits to order his three hundred heavy cavalry and moves up his giant sloths. Even though the giant sloths are slow moving, they have a burst of speed to avoid a collision with an elephant and mammoth. Right when Cainin's heavy cavalry is about to hit the main byland's defense, the peninsula's sloths move into position and get on their hind legs and tear their claws into the Tarentum mammoths and elephants as they come in Baudan's infantry. Within ten minutes the byland archers, heavy cavalry, and sloths start to sway the tide of war. The giant sloths even move towards Cainin's mammoths and are very aware of their adversary's weak spots. For every one sloth destroyed, ten Tarentum mammoths or elephants are killed because of teamwork between the archers, artillery, heavy cavalry, and sloths.

Every sloth of the byland has blood all over their bodies. In nature, the giant sloth looks slow and lazy. On the battlefield, the sloth changes its attitude towards being a true protector. The creature has the mindset of a dog protecting his master from harm, and the peninsula's military is its family. The giant sloths and their riders are becoming the heroes to the byland's defenders. The sloths just keep walking to an area with Tarentum mammoths and elephants and tear them up with their claws. The sloths become so ferocious, they knock off their riders and keep fighting the Tarentum mammoths and elephants without guidance.

Baudan's archers concentrate their attack on the Tarentum rhinos. They are the only creatures having success against the giant sloths. Because of the giant rhino's speed, the peninsula's giant sloths cannot compensate and fall victim to the velocity of the horned creatures.

On top of the hill, looking over the battlefield, Atlandreous' is wondering to himself when to attack and take Cainin by surprise. He sees that his army below is losing and then gaining ground. It goes back and forth. The Peninsula Supreme Commander knows he needs to wait for another thirty minutes. A thousand of his countrymen are wounded or dying every minute. It is very hard on Atlandreous to hold back, but he knows it's necessary to win.

On the left flank where Tess is in command, Berith starts to break the byland's lines. The Tarentum military is starting to overrun the infantry and light cavalry of Tess'. Tess moves closer to the front to take command and to divert her strongest infantry to plug the hole. She fights with her sword, hand to hand with her men. Atlandreous sees the left flank at a distance and knows Tess is in trouble, but he still does not budge. He knows if he goes in now, his countermove to take the Tarentum Army will go in vain.

Roubertus gets news and goes straight to Hamon and says, "We are starting to be compromised at our left flank. They are overpowering us. We are stabilized here. We need to send in our reserves to compensate."

Hamon responds, "I'll take command. We need your leadership to keep our lines here."

Hamon gets his men together and Roubertus starts to push his men harder. If there is a major counter move from Spenser, Roubertus will lose his army, but Roubertus gets his second wind and is able to take control of his objectives in battle. Hamon gets on a horse to help Tess' position. Hamon takes command of three thousand archers and a thousand light cavalry that Tess had sent earlier.

Hamon gets to Tess' location and uses his light cavalry to help. Tess is still fighting on the front lines. Hamon can see her at a distance killing their enemy one by one. Anyone coming close to Tess is killed by her sword. Because of Hamon's cavalry, the Tarentum infantry starts to fall back. In five minutes, Hamon starts to turn the tide in the battle. His archers catch up and get in position to reinforce the peninsula's left flank.

The position is getting secure, and Hamon sees a weak spot in the ranks of the Berith's lines and goes in to capitalize on the Achilles' heel of the Tarentum offensive with his thousand light cavalry. He starts to go forward and take more ground. Berith sees an opportunity to take on the peninsula's major offensive and counter. Within ten minutes, Hamon's cavalry is surrounded and the Tarentum mammoths and giant rhinos tear into Hamon's light cavalry. Tess tries to move forward with her archers to compensate and protect Hamon, but it is too late. Hamon's men die at the hands of Berith's warriors.

Back at the main defense of the peninsula's fortification, Baudan and Nieander are getting ready for the next wave of Tarentum cavalry and infantry to hit. Cainin is doing the same and is about ready to send a full scale attack with over a million men and beasts. On the front line are the Tarentum light cavalry which numbers over twenty thousand and the last three thousand heavy cavalry. Baudan orders all of his light and heavy cavalry to fall back and Nieander orders all of the peninsula's archers to get into position to take on the Cainin's offensive. At this point, the peninsula has no more reserves. Any mistakes, Baudan will be doomed.

Atlandreous looks over the hill and says to Erasmus, Anastasia, Kassandra, Tarasios, and Halamik. "It is time. It will take us thirty minutes at full speed to attack our aggressors. Cainin is going in for the kill. In the meantime, our fellow warriors at our fortification will lose over twenty-five thousand warriors. There will be a quarter of a million byland warriors not going home tonight. It has been the hardest decision to hold back. It is time. Tarasios, you take command of our fifteen hundred heavy cavalry and spearhead dead center of their backside. Halamik, Anastasia, and Kassandra, take our light cavalry and take out their strong defensive perimeter. Erasmus, take our infantry and reinforce our two spearheads. By nightfall, this battle will be over."

Cainin's light and heavy cavalry make it through the first line of defense of Baudan's main army. The giant sloths go on their rampage. They intercept anything going inside the byland's fortification. As they destroy everything in their sight, they bring terror to the Tarentum Army. The Tarentum have killed over a hundred of the giant sloths, but in turn, the peninsula's secret weapon has killed over five hundred Tarentum mammoths and elephants. With their size, claws, agility, and aggressive nature, the sloths dominate the battlefield.

Atlandreous gets off his horse and mounts a giant rhino. His army looks at him. They know he will lead the charge. The Peninsula Supreme Commander goes back and forth forming lines to rush the battlefield. The more Atlandreous runs back and forth through his lines the more his army yells and hit their swords with their shields. Everyone on Atlandreous' offensive is ready to die or become triumphant. The Peninsula Supreme Commander stops his giant rhino and looks at his army.

Atlandreous looks at his men and women he is about to lead into battle and yells, "Everyone in Baudan's command is sacrificing themselves for our freedom and culture. Everyone here is representing a different city-state and society. From this day forward, we will no longer be different. We are here united as one, and we will fight united. Let us take our enemy!"

Everyone starts to cheer. Atlandreous looks at his men and has nothing but pride pumping into his veins. He remembers growing up with his friends and now they are leading men into battle. He thinks of the politics he has encountered to get here. It is all or nothing for the leader of the peninsula. Atlandreous goes forward with his giant rhino towards his enemy. The Peninsula Supreme Commander does not care if anyone is following. Before anyone knows it, they follow their commander and go towards Cainin's army. It will take thirty minutes before they engage their enemy.

Tarasios, Erasmus, and Halamik get into their position with their cavalry and infantry to hit their targets. Atlandreous slows down a little to let his men catch up with him. If not, he will be the first to be hit with an arrow. The Halotropolis and Alnilam cavalry have the molless tree bow except for Halamik's men. Atlandreous fell short of bows to give to the Alnitak warriors.

To Atlandreous, it is the longest thirty minutes of his life as he descends down the hill. He is afraid of the unknown. The fear of dying is in his head. He has a long time to think before he attacks Cainin's men. All of the divisions under the Peninsula Supreme Commander come around the hills and small mountains. The byland scouts have done a good job keeping the Tarentum scouts from finding Atlandreous' offensive. It will be a complete surprise.

In the distance, Cainin's officers see Atlandreous' forces coming with great numbers. The Tarentum's rear has no cavalry to protect against an offensive of that magnitude. All Cainin's cavalry is on the front line attacking Baudan's fortification. Atlandreous' cavalry is going full speed. It will take Cainin thirty minutes to get through their ranks of men to counter Atlandreous. All Tarentum officers order their archers to take on the peninsula's counterattack.

Cainin looks back and sees Atlandreous' offensive coming towards him and orders all of his cavalry to break off their attack against Baudan and to counterattack Atlandreous. Cainin goes frantic about what is about to occur. He orders all of his archers at Baudan's fortification to stabilize the battlefield so he can deal with Atlandreous.

In twenty more minutes, Cainin is about to be surrounded. The only thing the Tarentum has is numbers. The peninsula's defensive has put a good dent into the Tarentum military. Over half of Cainin's cavalry is destroyed with little losses to Baudan's defensive perimeter. Floortatum is ideal for the attack against any aggressor. Atlandreous set the battlefield, and Cainin went along with it.

Right before Atlandreous engages, his cavalry shoots their bows and rip right into the ranks of the Tarentum first line of defense. Atlandreous' forces hit at the same time against the Tarentum military's backside. Over ten thousand of Atlandreous' men and beasts lose their lives to the Tarentum archers in the spearhead within ten minutes of hitting their enemy. Halamik hits the strong side of the Tarentum archers and destroys them within twenty minutes. Anastasia and Kassandra use their men to keep Cainin's infantry from counterattacking Halamik.

Tarasios' heavy cavalry slices through the backside of Cainin's forces. There is nothing holding Tarasios at bay, and he slashes through the Tarentum infantry. Some of his heavy cavalry is compromised in battle, but Tarasios keeps going deeper and deeper into the ranks of the Tarentum Army.

Right when Tarasios decides to link up with the other commanders of Atlandreous' offensive, an arrow hits him while he is charging his enemy. Tarasios is hit directly in his right chest. He breaks the arrow and keeps fighting with his giant rhino. Right behind Tarasios is his infantry which keeps destroying anything in sight. Tarasios looks around and sees his fellow men dying. He orders a full scale run to meet up with Erasmus who is trying to meet up with Halamik. There is confusion coming from the commanders of the peninsula, but their drive and instinct is keeping the spearhead going.

Erasmus sees Tarasios' men coming in the distance and orders all of his manpower to link up with his old teenage friend. Right when Erasmus' men are about to take the area, Tarasios is hit with another arrow and falls off his giant rhino.

Other byland warriors see their commander on his back. The way Tarasios is moving, everyone can tell he is in great pain. Tarasios' cannot get up. As if they are a pack of wolves, Cainin's infantry sees the byland general struck, and they go in for the kill. The people under Tarasios' command fight harder to protect him. The pain is so overwhelming that it is difficult for Tarasios to think about the battle zone. Erasmus sees his friend and orders his men to push harder so he can get to the wounded general.

Erasmus' infantry and archers destroy everything in their sight to secure the area. Every bit of fighting is concentrated to achieve Erasmus' objective. Even if it is not the right tactical move at the moment of battle, they fight to protect Tarasios. Because Atlandreous is fighting his own battles, he has no idea of the situation of his friends from Mintaka.

Erasmus gets to Tarasios and picks him up from the ground. Because of the injury and loss of blood, Tarasios does not know what is happening. Erasmus takes him to the nearest warrior with a horse.

Erasmus says to his warrior, "Get him out of here. He is on the verge of giving the ultimate sacrifice."

The byland warrior takes Tarasios away to get medical attention.

Erasmus yells in the middle of battle, "I am taking command of both armies! All heavy and light cavalry regroup to unite with Halamik. All archers and infantry follow to reinforce our spearhead."

The peninsula's army regroups quickly. At the same time, Cainin's heavy cavalry is about to hit Erasmus and Halamik position.

Because Erasmus and Halamik are starting to get surrounded, Atlandreous backs off his attack from Cainin's backside. The Peninsula Supreme Commander knows he will lose a great deal of men if they get surrounded. He pulls out and he reinforces his generals.

Right when Erasmus and Halamik meet up, Cainin's cavalry counterattacks. At this point in the battle, the peninsula has more cavalry than the Tarentum Army. Cainin's cavalry confuses Erasmus and Halamik for a couple of minutes, but the byland commanders are able to regain the initiative. Atlandreous is in the background with his army fighting the outer layer of the Tarentum Army where his armies are trying to link up. Atlandreous is confusing his enemy as to where to fight.

Baudan looks at the battlefield and yells, "Finish your enemy!"

Baudan pushes forward and starts to take ground at the main battle site. The main fortification of the peninsula is starting to turn the tide of the battle. The Tarentum military gets confused. Tess, Roubertus, and Orion have almost demolished their adversary when Atlandreous attacked. Berith has to retreat and reinforce Cainin.

Atlandreous sees his army winning from his offensive and defensive positions. He goes to a hill with an escort and starts to wave a flag of truce to stop the battle. Because of the confusion on the battlefield, the flag goes unnoticed from both sides. After four long minutes, Atlandreous can see a flag rising and waving from Cainin's location. Over a million warriors start to pull back slowly from each other. The order has been given to stop for a summit between the two leaders of both armies.

Everywhere on the battlefield is death. The Tarentum army has lost over five hundred thousand men and cavalry. Atlandreous forces have only lost a hundred and fifty thousand men. Six hundred and fifty thousand men and animals have lost their lives at this battle.

Atlandreous and Cainin meet up dead center to each other. Because both of them agreed to a ceasefire, there cannot be any hostilities until there is a compromise to either fight or to stop the war.

Atlandreous goes to Cainin and says, "Your men have fought bravely today. You still have close to a million men to continue this fight. I don't want to fight anymore. Let us make a truce right here to stop this bloodshed. We can fight on if that is your choice. No matter what, we will at least deplete your army enough to keep our city-states from being overrun. The ratio is in my favor. Your cavalry is in shambles. Your military objectives cannot be obtained."

Cainin responds, "Don't be so sure of that."

Atlandreous asks to come closer to Cainin, and he agrees and tells every general from both sides to give them a moment.

Everyone gives the two commanders the respect to speak without council.

Atlandreous says, "This has to stop right here. Neither one of our kingdoms can take this economically. Both of us need manpower to succeed. If we continue to fight, the kingdoms I represent, or your empire will be able to survive. We have depleted our armies and now we are weaker in numbers. Other kingdoms will think to try and take our societies. It can be a possibility our societies will not last ten years if we keep fighting here. I understand the political situation which is about to occur when you get back to Tarentum. I propose, outside the peninsula, the first fifty miles will be neutral. No one can claim that land. Both civilizations can go there if they choose. The land Alnitak had under their rule will be a part of your kingdom. I don't think Alnitak needs it anymore. In the near future, we will trade with your empire for resources. It will make your economy grow again. We will continue to seek other resources from lands abroad. It seems our society is strongest at sea. When you get back home, you will look like a hero. Where we are standing, it seems we have a lot to lose if we keep fighting."

Cainin says, "What about Alnitak. They attacked us first, and we had no choice but to attack them. We should be able to keep their city and keep it under our rule."

Atlandreous responds, "It will cost your empire a great deal in manpower and resources to restore Alnitak. It holds no value to your society. As a leader of my people, I cannot let that happen. Our two civilizations need to heal first before we get that close to one another. I will level the city to build a defensive wall and rebuild our other city-states. You can go back home and say you made us do it. This will put you in good standing with your emperor. I do ask that you help us take care of the dead."

Cainin says, "We will stop here. I will accept your proposal. I do not have the full say in this. I will have to go back home and let my emperor decide."

Atlandreous responds, "I will come up there myself and speak with your emperor. General to general, I have to ask you why Florick attacked your massive army if he had no tactical advantage."

Cainin smiles and says, "Maybe they felt they had no choice because of the resources in Girulic. I was ordered by my emperor not to attack. I had nothing to do with their aggression."

Atlandreous replies, "In my absence from Tarentum, do you think this will be a problem with the summit you and I are having right now."

Cainin says, "I agree with your thoughts, and I will speak on your behalf."

The Tarentum Army starts to leave the region except for fifty thousand warriors who stay to help take care of the dead. The Peninsula Supreme Commander was fearful of the outcome of the talks with Cainin. The war is over, and Atlandreous is relieved he did not have to go any further. He knew neither empire could benefit from another conflict.

Two hours later, Cainin is on his way back to his homeland. Atlandreous steps out of his tent. There is confusion still in his army. The reports of casualties are getting back to the generals of the peninsula. The death toll and wounded is more than was expected. Atlandreous is so relieved his army did not have to fight on.

Erasmus runs fast to his commander and says, "Atlandreous, you need to come with me. It is Tarasios. I don't know if he is going to make it."

Atlandreous responds, "Where is he?"

Erasmus says, "He is three miles from here. There are people tending to his wounds, but it not looking to good for our friend."

Erasmus and Atlandreous ride to Tarasios. Atlandreous sees his teenage friend he has not really spoken to for years. Tarasios is there just holding on to life, and he is barely conscious. The Peninsula Supreme Commander does not know what to say, and grabs his old teenage friend's hand. Tarasios squeezes so hard it starts to cut off Atlandreous' circulation.

Atlandreous says, "My friend, what can I do for you?"

Tarasios tries to say something, but it takes a minute to regroup his thoughts because of the pain. He responds, "I'm dead. I need you to finish it. I want to go to God. I want you to be the one who sends me to him. I have waited for you to die."

Atlandreous says, "I have always loved you as a brother. I will do it because of your bravery in battle. As a friend, I cannot see you like this."

Tarasios is crying. He knows his time on earth is seconds away from being over. Tarasios looks at his friend from Mintaka and shakes his head yes, and Atlandreous take his sword and stabs him in the heart. It kills Tarasios instantly.

Atlandreous walks off and looks at Erasmus. The Supreme Commander gets on his horse and goes back to his tent. When he gets back to his quarters, he sees Anastasia, Roubertus, Baudan, Orion, Halamik, Kassandra, and Tess. They are there to greet him and tell him of the battle. Everyone is waiting for orders and what to do next. At Atlandreous' tent, every warrior is chanting "Atlandreous". It is like an echo inside Atlandreous' head.

Atlandreous is still upset with Tarasios death and gets off his horse. He looks at Tess if as he wants to break down inside and asks, "Where is Hamon?"

Tess responds, "He gave up his life to save mine."

Atlandreous says, "I see. Baudan, Roubertus, Orion, and Tess come inside my tent."

The four go inside. No one says a word. Atlandreous paces back and forth slowly. A messenger tries to see the Supreme Commander and is asked to leave by Baudan.

Atlandreous says, "We have won here today. Cainin will not try to come back for a long time. We just kicked the bully in the face. I gave Tarentum everything except fifty miles outside the bylands. If your kings do not agree, it will start another war we cannot afford. As for you all, you are the representatives of your city-states. Take our men home and ask Halamik where he would like to live. He is free. He fought bravely today. I, on the other hand, am leaving for a while. I have been strong long enough for our societies. I don't have anymore life or leadership to give. I need time alone to pray and ask for forgiveness from God. You have your last orders from me. Tess you are a warrior. I see you as a lioness, but in human form."

Tess responds, "Halotropolis needs you. The byland needs heroes. Your presence will help start the rebirth of the peninsula. Not only will my own city-state benefit, but the rest of the peninsula will go forward with your presence. Please come back to my city so we can celebrate in your honor."

Atlandreous replies, "I am not a hero. I am just a man. You are the heroes here. Go back home and start your lives all over. This battle gave us the opportunity for our societies to go forward. I do have one more order to give. Hamon and Thanos are believers of God. I want them to be buried in the mountains where I found my faith. Send a team of architects and make them a simple tomb. When I die, I will ask to be buried close to them."

Orion asks, "It will take a year just to get there. We can mummify their remains, but that is stretching it."

Atlandreous responds, "Just make it happen."

Orion says, "Yes, sir. I know our king will want you at home. I don't think the person who saved our kingdom should just take off to wherever."

Atlandreous responds, "A person who just saved kingdoms has the luxury of asking for time to himself. I will say no more. Please—out of respect for a warrior, I need to deal with everything that has happened in the last four months."

The four inside the tent are shocked at Atlandreous' thoughts. They know something is wrong with their leader, but out of respect, they ask no more questions. Atlandreous grabs a few things and orders his servant to bring his horse. The troubled warrior gets on his horse and rides off without saying anything to anybody. As their Supreme Commander is going through his army, they cheer is name. Atlandreous puts up a façade and rides tall for his army.

CHAPTER XXII
FINDING ONES TRUE SELF

Tess goes home to a heroes' welcome alongside with Baudan. The Halotropolian people are proud to have such heroes. As the warriors come through the streets of Halotropolis, there are thousands of citizens giving praise to their warriors. Tess' father looks as his warriors come through his city and salutes them. Cetrono's scouts tell him the Tarentum army is still retreating back to their homeland. The king of Halotropolis is feeling more at ease.

Halotropolian civilians are looking at the parade to see if their loved ones made it back. There are many wives who do not have husbands anymore. A third of the warriors from Cetrono's city are being brought back to be laid to rest. There are frantic people trying to find out if their friends or family members are still alive. Three hours after the battle of Floortatum, Cetrono's people received word of the death toll, and numbers kept rising.

After the war, the followers of God are becoming more prevalent during the parade. People are shouting their faith, and there is little opposition coming from the ones who believe differently. After the procession, Cetrono has a council meeting with his Senate and proclaims God's word as a true religion. Tess is there and hears what her father is saying, and she feels better about her own religious beliefs. That night, Tess goes to her father and tells him of her faith. Cetrono does not accept Tess' devotion completely, but gives his blessing to believe in what she wants to believe.

After being in Halotropolis for five days, she goes to her father at the palace balcony. She really has said little to her father since she told him of proclaiming herself to God, and Cetrono has been concerned of her shunning him. A messenger is leaving Cetrono as she walks on the balcony.

Tess says, "Hello Father."

Cetrono walks toward his daughter and responds, "I'm glad you're here. I need your assistance. Good news, Cainin is almost back into his own empire."

Tess replies, "Father, I am coming to you as a daughter, not a public servant."

Cetrono says, "Atlandreous is at Mintaka. Go to him. Take your time. In ten days, all kings of the peninsula will be here for a summit. Atlandreous needs to be here. You are the only one he will answer to and you can persuade him to come to Halotropolis."

Tess responds, "I know what is wrong with Atlandreous. It has to do with his best friends dying at Floortatum. He was close to them and is blaming himself for their deaths."

Cetrono says, "I've been there. I have lost a great number of friends in past wars. I sent men and women to their deaths for the greater masses. I know what Atlandreous is going through. A leader has to love the ones he commands. A person needs to understand the true definition of being a leader. It is the whole picture; not just the few individuals. There are so many times I've hated myself for decisions which led to deaths. It is up to you to get him past this. I will say no more. Your heart is shouting, and you are not even saying anything. But no matter what, bring Atlandreous to Halotropolis for the summit. It is very important for him to be here. I am asking you as a servant of our kingdom and my daughter."

Tess responds, "Yes, sir." She gives her father a hug and walks off.

Tess goes to Mintaka. She has never been there. It takes her four days to arrive. Without her escort, Tess goes into the city alone. She is lost as to what to say and what to do at this point. In the streets of the small city, everyone is busy doing their own thing. In the quest to find Atlandreous, Cetrono's daughter does not even know where to start.

Tess goes to an older lady and asks, "May I ask where Atlandreous could be?"

The old lady responds, "People have asked, but we give him the respect of his solitude."

Tess says, "I am Tess. I was one of his captains during the battle of Floortatum. I have a message to give him from King Cetrono."

The old lady responds, "So, you are the one. Atlandreous' father has said good things about you amongst our city. As some say, he thinks of you as a daughter. It is good to meet someone like you. Our city has a great deal of respect for his family, but, Atlandreous needs time to heal his wounds. I will respect him and say nothing"

Tess says, "I am coming to you humble. I am here to support him. If I see him struggling to speak with me, I will leave out of respect for him. I hope you can believe me."

The old lady responds, "He is probably at his place where he spars. What people have told me, he goes up there everyday for hours just sparring alone." She points towards the forest. In the background, Tess can see a hill where trees and shrubs have been cleared, and the old lady says, "It is above the hill, you can't miss it. Please don't let me regret telling you his location."

Tess says, "I respect you and your people. I will never do anything to intentionally hurt Atlandreous."

Tess starts to walk up the hill towards the clearing. She knows Atlandreous may need more time to get things in the right perspective. When he left Floortatum, she could tell he was hurting inside and mentally exhausted. As she goes up the hill, she trembles, and her heart starts to beat quickly. Tess is a little reluctant and starts to walk slower so she can gather her thoughts on what to say.

When she gets closer to the clearing, Tess sees Atlandreous helping a couple young boys learn how to hold a shield and sword. Atlandreous sees her walking towards him and smiles.

Atlandreous looks at the boys and says, "Leave us for a little while." The boys start to run home and Atlandreous says, "Hello lioness. How is your father?"

Tess is a little shaky and replies, "Doing well. The kings would like to speak with you. The whole peninsula needs you and so do I. There will be a meeting in Halotropolis in five days."

Atlandreous sees her trembling and responds, "Since I've been back. I have done some thinking. You have been in my thoughts more than you know. You and I have gone through a great deal together. I know I love you. Tess, you showed me the world of God. I thank you for that. You are the most stubborn woman I know, and I respect your personality. I know I want to spend the rest of my life with you, but you're royalty. Your people will not accept a general from another city-state as your husband. We should stop this. Now, you know how I feel, and let me go back to the world I know. I don't want the pressure of being a leader anymore. I have lost two of my best friends and that is enough for any man's lifetime. I am not going to Halotropolis right now."

Tess responds, "I love you too, and this is reason I am about to say something you might not want to hear. Stay here in Mintaka if that is really what you want. It looks like a nice place. I would live here if it were not for reasonability to make mankind better. You have considerable talents in politics and war. In my perspective, you're wasting your time staying in a small community. I understand and respect your time to heal and regroup, but, the person you are will not be able to live to your highest potential living here. You are greater than that. The kings will be in Halotropolis in five days. It is up to you to go."

Tess starts to leave. She sees herself giving grief to Atlandreous. She will not do it for her people, or even her father. To her, it is easier to leave. She cannot take Atlandreous' pain away. In her mind, it may be better for him. Tess respects him too much and she thinks of what she said to the old woman.

Atlandreous stabs his sword into the ground and says, "Right now, I am very angry with you."

Tess turns around quickly and responds in a harsh tone, "Well, I'm still angry with you leaving me without weapons at the delta. What if something happened?"

Atlandreous asks, "Yes lioness. Are you ever going to let that go?"

Tess laughs and replies, "Quit calling me lioness. Yes, I am your friend no matter what happens to us personally."

Atlandreous says, "Okay, let me finish. Because you're right, my anger tells me you're correct in my own judgment of what is transpiring here. I will hate myself if I don't go to Halotropolis. I am better than that. I will not let emotions govern me. I will leave tomorrow. I don't want any kind of heroes' welcome from Alnilam or Halotropolis. After I meet with the kings, I will come back here to live the rest of my life. Before you go, I want you to meet the person who made me who I am. Eat dinner with me. It has been a long time since I have had a guest inside my father's house other than my people."

Tess replies, "I would love to, and I will leave with you. My camp is outside your city. My escort will be wondering where I am if I don't return at sunset."

Atlandreous says, "I will have you back before nightfall, and I will escort you to your camp and back to Halotropolis."

Tess replies, "This will be a treat for me. I always wanted to meet your family. I have heard a great deal of good things about your father."

Atlandreous and Tess start to walk towards Thanos' home. The two knew they acted as children. They start to talk as if they were back floating the Iteru River. It seemed their friendship never ended. With all of the politics, earthquake, and almost war between their two city-states, it makes no difference right now. The friendship has started up all over again. Atlandreous starts to touch Tess' hand as they walk. Tess grabs his hand, and they walk to the Thanos' estate. It makes no sense to the two of how and why they are acting in this matter between each other. With everything that has happened, they see comfort in being together.

Thanos is working with his horses and training them for battle. Atlandreous' father sees them coming at a distance and rides towards them.

Thanos gets off his horse and says, "The most beautiful women on the peninsula, except for my wife, Ledell. You must be Tess. Atlandreous has told me so much about you."

Tess looks at Atlandreous' father and says, "I see where your son gets his persona." She looks straight at Atlandreous and say, "I hope one day, in your older years, you have the same character."

A couple of hours before sunset, Atlandreous and Tess are about to eat at the table with his family. Out of respect, Tess helps with the setting of the table with Ledell. Thanos and his son are doing other preparations for dinner.

Thanos looks at his son, "I can see you both love each other."

Atlandreous responds, "This is something I don't like speaking to my father about. To answer your question, yes. With everything that has happened to us in the last two years, how could someone not. But it can't work with us. She is royalty of a different city-state. I don't think Icaras will approve. Our city-states will be friendly with one another for a couple more years. After that, greed and religion will hamper our relationship again. I don't want Tess having the thought of choosing what city-state to live in."

Thanos says, "Well, you know I am still connected to the Alnilam's Senate. What I am gathering from the kings is unity. With the battle of Floortatum, it proved we can come together, and the kings want all city-states to become one. Your name is coming from all over the peninsula to make it happen."

Atlandreous responds, "I'm not even in the loop of politics. I don't want it, but to bring God to our peninsula, I will. Religion is the only thing holding the peninsula back from being united."

Thanos says, "Religion will always be an obstacle to mankind. It is up to you to encourage our kings. You have the political know how to persuade the kings that God is the only way to bring the peninsula together. You have it in you, and I know you will make the impossible—possible. Changing a person's way of faith is hard to conquer. Even harder in what you did to take our enemy, but people are changing their beliefs already all over our by-land. With this war, the general populace will want the change."

Atlandreous and Thanos laugh like father and son. They go back to eat. During the dinner everyone is smiling across the table. There is little spoken at the table at first. Ledell knows she just inherited a daughter and will treat her as one.

After dinner, Atlandreous escorts Tess back to her camp. Along the way, they never stop talking. Sometimes, they ramble so much they lose their train of thought of what they were trying to get across. Right before they get to Tess' camp, Atlandreous grabs Tess and hugs here. To Tess, it seems like he wanted to kiss her, but Atlandreous backs off. Atlandreous looks at the sky and notices a bright object. The object is stationary, but very bright. It is ten times brighter than the brightest star. Both of them wonder what to make of it. To them, it makes no difference. It is the moment and nothing can take them away from that.

The next morning, the object is still in the blue sky. Atlandreous and Tess ride back to Halotropolis. When they get there, the city greets Atlandreous as a hero. The whole city goes to the streets and cheers for Atlandreous. This is something he really did not want, but he accepts it. He waves at everyone in sight. To the people who believe in God, the star is a sign of rebirth. Because their enemy is almost home, it is seen as a good omen. The astronomers of the city do not know what to make of it. They have seen other things like it, but have no earthly idea what it can be.

Right before he gets to Cetrono's palace, He sees Orion and Erasmus waiting on their commander. Atlandreous and Tess get off their horse to greet them.

Atlandreous says, "I thought you two would be in Alnilam."

Erasmus replies, "King Icaras gave me a promotion."

Orion says, "I received one as well."

Atlandreous says, "I hope I haven't lost my job."

Orion and Erasmus say at the same time, "No—."

The three friends look at each other as they go inside the palace. Atlandreous is wondering what is going on. He says no more and waits to speak with the kings. Tess follows to see her father. She has no earthly idea why Atlandreous is there.

Atlandreous goes onto the balcony where all the kings of the peninsula are together. A servant announces Atlandreous' arrival.

Atlandreous says, "Hello gentlemen. I am sorry about not wanting to be paraded around. I lost two good friends, and I needed time to regroup and get my composure back."

King Richcampous, of Masaba, looks at Atlandreous and says, "We understand. Everything relied on you. It was a great deal of pressure. We agree with the decision of the boundary of the Tarentum Empire and our kingdoms."

King Cetrono of Halotropolis says, "Atlandreous, we have another problem here. All city-states will have to become one, or we will become extinct in the next ten years. There will be hostilities between the continent and our world. We, as city-states, cannot do it individually. We also have religious problems. After the war, more and more people are going to God. However, this light shining in the sky makes things even worse. Both religions are taking claim to the anomaly. The older generations are outraged with what is happening. As kings, we are at the mercy of our people."

Atlandreous responds, "You want my fame of beating our enemy back to make a political and religious statement. Is this the reason I'm here?"

King Lopatheous, of Vasic, says, "We need you as a figure head. You will be in charge of all of our armies and a mediator of our governments. In internal affairs, you will have no say so. We will continue to be kings. The older generations need our guidance. Without them, we wouldn't have a government."

Atlandreous says, "That is not enough to make our peninsula stronger. I need more. You are right with the older generation. They will not change, but our societies need them because of their stability. If you were a Tarentum general right now, who would you fear? If you want unity, we have to start all over right here and right now as one society."

Lopatheous asks, "What are you thinking Atlandreous?"

Atlandreous responds, "Tess, I have something to ask you."

Tess comes closer and says, "I cannot get into this because of my father. What my father says goes."

Atlandreous says, "Okay, King Cetrono, if Tess says yes can I marry her. I'm really in love with your daughter, and she will be the link to bring our people together."

Cetrono replies, "That is my daughter's decision—not mine. I will bless the marriage if that is what you're asking."

Atlandreous asks, "Tess, will you marry me?"

Tess responds, "Yes, but I don't think this is the right time to ask to marry a future wife."

Atlandreous says, "Okay, a circle has started right here." Then he looks at Tess and says, "By the way, I think it is the perfect time. How many men went to kings to ask for a ladies hand in marriage? Anyone could have objected to the idea." Atlandreous looks at the kings and says, "To better ourselves, we have to come together in every aspect. We just received three thousand Alnitak refuges. They are some of the smartest people on the peninsula. It would not be fair to just utilize them in our kingdom alone. We will start schools and military institutions to become better as a society. We will teach the next generations to fight and work together. Our writing needs to become the same. Except for traditional religions, we will teach the new way of writing in our forthcoming schools. Tess, you will be in charge of our future. I will bring our militaries together and keep our enemies away. In honor of doing so, I am asking for Alnilam to be our center point of politics. To ward off our enemy, I want the city to change its name to Atlantis. I want my name and Tess'. To show the world we have come together, we have to make drastic changes. With the writing of our elders, Tess is translated into Tis. By using some of my name along with my wife to be, we will show the world unity."

Icaras responds, "It is a little intimidating. I will agree to the change of my city's name to bring us closer together, but you cannot have my home. We will all come together and build one."

Atlandreous replies, "Agreed."

Richcampous says, "From now on, you are the emperor and protector of the Empire of Atlantis."

Cetrono asks, "As a community, what do we do first?"

Atlandreous goes to Tess and says, "The first thing I am going to do is marry and go to the next step of evolution for mankind. God will be a part of that change. Are you ready to take the journey with me, Tess?"

Tess almost tears up and says, "Yes, together we will make our peninsula better for the next generations of the Atlanteans."

Within a week, Atlandreous and Tess get ready to marry. Both of them are nervous and wonder, like most, is marring the best decision. They both think of the world before the earthquake, and they both know times have changed. The world is changing. To Atlandreous and Tess, it comes down to friendship and taking on the world together. In their hearts, they both know they have the ambitions to do it together. Each has a weakness and the other one has the other's strength.

In front of thousands of people in Halotropolis, Atlandreous stands there waiting for Tess as she walks down the path with her father to marry the new Emperor of Atlantis. The new emperor wonders if he has what it take to make his empire better. Once Tess walks down the aisle, he knows it is time for change in himself and the people he is about to rule.

Right before Atlandreous and Tess are about to consummate their marriage with a kiss, Duncan, the archeologist from present time, starts to fly like a feather and sees Tess and Atlandreous succeeding and making their society better. Duncan sees Tess accomplishing her goals to bring the peninsula's societies together.

Duncan goes forward in time over a period of months to see Atlandreous working on the walls of the entrance to the peninsula. He takes the stones of Alnitak to build the barrier to the continent. Halamik and the Atlantians tear down Alnitak to help build a new society. In Duncan's journey back to present day, he sees

Atlandreous becoming obsessive to keep the rest of the world out of the peninsula. Year after year seems like seconds to Duncan, He sees the building of the seven walls into the peninsula. All of a sudden, the walls are complete.

Duncan sees Atlandreous only having one son. He is five years old. One night, Atlandreous is holding his son looking at the night sky.

Atlandreous says to his son, "See the stars right there." He points at the constellation of Orion and says, "He died in battle a year ago defending God's word outside our peninsula. Because he defended God's word, he will never be forgotten."

Duncan starts to accelerate in his travels of the past and sees the sphinx in Egypt again, just like he saw in his first travels. This time he sees a woman's face on the sphinx. To Duncan, it is Tess' face on the lion.

Right before Duncan becomes conscious to the world he knows, the archeologist sees a keystone. He sees Solomon's temple and the freemasons in his whirlwind back to the present. All of a sudden it goes dark for the archeologist. He sees a seaport where his descendents put a hall of records about their civilization. Then he descends into deep water to see it is almost impossible to get to without billions of dollars for exploration. To him, the true location is unknown.

Duncan goes back and sees the sphinx in Egypt again and starts to float like a feather and descends into the ground like a soul about to go to heaven. He starts swirling like water in a bath tube in what he is seeing. Right when he feels the connection of his present world and the past, he feels the hand of Kyle shaking him to wake up.

CHAPTER XXIII
FINDING WHO YOU ARE
{PRESENT DAY}

Kyle says, "Wake up, Duncan."

Duncan asks, "How long have I slept."

Kyle responds, "About seven hours. Rachael and I checked on you a couple of times. We knew you were in your dream world and didn't want to wake you."

Duncan says, "I needed only one more minute."

Kyle asks, "Why only one more minute?"

Duncan says, "Never mind."

The archeologists go outside their tents. They see the weather is better. Duncan tells them of his travels in his dream world. He knows he has found the ancient society of Atlantis. They pack up their tents and supplies and go down the mountain. On the way, they receive a call on the global phone.

Duncan grabs the phone and answers, "Hello." Rachael and Kyle run to Duncan.

Duncan puts it on speaker and Mr. Callaway says, "How is everyone? I have some good news. I would like to speak to the Ugandan lieutenant first." Duncan agrees and gives the phone to the lieutenant and takes off the speaker phone.

The lieutenant says, "Hello—Yes—Yes, sir—Nothing will happen—We will stay here—I understand—Yes, sir—Thank you, sir." The lieutenant touches the cancel key on the phone.

Duncan asks, "What is going on?"

The lieutenant says, "A Congo helicopter will be here within thirty minutes to pick up the four of us. They have found something inside their country that they want you to see, Duncan. The Congo and Ugandan governments have agreed to share their finds in these mountains. I will be the first to represent the solidarity of my people. It has to do with the constellation of Orion and somehow they knew it. Inside the Congo border is where the star of Saiph is located. It is the foot of Orion. They have found chambers inside the mountain as well."

Within thirty minutes, the Congo helicopter starts to land near the rocky surface. The pilot waves to them to come inside. All are hesitant, and wait until Duncan makes the first move. The helicopter's propellers are loud as they get closer.

Duncan yells to his crew, "Who in the world does Callaway not know?"

The Ugandan lieutenant yells, "The conversation I had was not only him. My president was on the phone as well."

They fly off and look at the mountain from afar and know exactly where they are going. It is on the Congo side of the border. At a distance, they see men moving around an opening. They land, and everyone gets off the helicopter.

A Congo professor runs up to Duncan and points to the mountain. They are about a hundred yards from the site. Nothing is said because of the helicopter's blades. The only thing the Congo professor does is point and hang on to his hat.

The helicopter takes off. The Congo professor says, "We followed your work. Because your work is global now, our nation decided to follow you. We also concluded where you were going on the mountain was the constellation of Orion. Since a spot of the constellation was in our country, we decided to investigate. What we found is this tomb and what you are about to see belongs to the Republic of Congo. We want to know what you found in Uganda."

Duncan asks the Ugandan lieutenant, "This is too big of a find for just one country. Will the people of Congo have access to your country?"

The Ugandan lieutenant responds, "Yes."

Duncan asks, "Mr. Callaway said everything within a minute to make this happen."

The Ugandan lieutenant says, "Everything was straight forward and my president said to do what ever he said to do."

Duncan and his crew go in the chamber. It is like the other chambers, but different. There is writing all over the wall. The chamber is simple but more detailed. Inside, the archeologists find tablets and tools. It has a little more than the rest of the chambers they found on the Ugandan side. They go inside the tomb. It also has a gold sword and a golden bow.

Duncan picks up the bow and says, "Because of what I saw in my dream, I think this is Orion's chamber. I feel different in here, as if I was back in my dream."

Rachael says, "Come look at this. This will change history."

Where Rachael is putting light on the wall Duncan walks over and replies, "I need to get out of here. I need some air."

Duncan leaves and Kyle and Rachael look at the engraved picture on the wall. They are both shocked. It is the sphinx in Egypt and it has a face of a women. On the other side there is a compass and a bull's head in the middle. The pyramids in Giza are in the background. It is so astonishing. They forget about Duncan leaving. Then it finally hits them. They walk outside the chamber and walk towards Duncan.

Kyle asks, "What is going on with you?"

Duncan responds, "That engraved picture is nowhere else but here, right?"

Rachael says, "I have looked over every wall in Spain and here. It is the first time I have seen this."

Duncan responds, "When I was asleep, I saw this picture in real life. It is the same person. It is Tess. She was the first guardian of Atlantis. She brought knowledge together on the peninsula. The picture of the compass and Bull is shocking and I don't know why. The Egyptians say the pyramids are five thousand years old. I think they are seven thousand years prior to what the Egyptians think. I feel the pyramids have been there since the days of the Atlantians. I sense the ancient Egyptians just put their name on the monuments and reinvented it."

Kyle says, "I believe you. Your dreams correlate with our findings. There is evidence that the sphinx could be thousands of years older than thought."

Duncan responds, "Since my dreams, God has come in my thoughts more than before. I feel relieved, fulfilled, and at peace with myself. I don't understand it. I was not that religious before. Yes, I believe in God, but it is becoming overwhelming."

The Congo professor goes to Duncan and asks, "What do you make of the site?"

Duncan says, "It is not the site. It is the engraving of the sphinx inside and the compass. No one needs to know about the engraving yet. Keep this to yourself. I will investigate this more before it needs to become public."

The Ugandan lieutenant says to the Congo professor, "I agree. Your people are welcome to see what we have found. Nothing should be said until a proper investigation is done at all sites. Since this is a joint effort, we should tell our superiors to do the same."

Rachael asks to go back into the chamber to take pictures. Duncan stays where he is at. It is kind of spooky to the archeologist to go back in. In his heart, he knows what is in there. He feels like the people he saw were his friends, and now they are dead.

Rachael goes in and takes pictures. Duncan can see the flash coming out of the chamber. He wants to attempt to get up and look once more. His curiosity is killing him. Then the global phone rings again.

Duncan answers, "Hello." As he puts it on speaker phone, he can tell its Mr. Callaway.

Mr. Callaway says, "I have someone you might want to speak with. I need you to get on a jet and go to London. Go to the United Grand Lodge of England. Mr. Hudson will be waiting on you."

Duncan asks, "What do the freemasons want with me?"

Right when Mr. Callaway is about to answer, Rachael yells, "Duncan, you need to come in here right now."

To Be Continued